Day of the Dogs

By

Robert L. Conley

Not only this book

But my life

Is

Dedicated

To

Grace

PROLOGUE

Looking back, it was obvious to Bob that the change in his life had started some time ago. But the past few days had been the pinnacle of metamorphosis.

As he crawled out of his old, beat-up Suburban with his three boys scrambling behind, his mind wandered back through the last several days. He kept seeing the little faces of his boys as they tried to comprehend the tragedies, and he was still wondering what was going through their minds. All he knew for sure was that he had to make certain they never learned the truth about their mother, and he hoped his lies wouldn't ever catch up to him.

Deep in thought, he strapped his Magnum on his hip and gave Christopher the camera, then grabbed his 8mm Mauser rifle. He'd glued the broken stock back together, and it seemed to be okay; but he was still pissed as hell that it had been broken. He cradled it in the crook of his arm, trying to keep his mind on what he was here to do now. The dogs were still out there, and the last thing he should do was let his guard down.

The boys were told to walk behind their father. Matt and Christopher seemed to understand the severity of the situation, but David skipped along as if nothing was wrong.

The south place began at the first of three levels; and the hay barn and a small tool shed were all that broke up the terrain here. The rest of the acreage on this tier and the two other levels was for the cattle that used to graze here in peace until yesterday, when two mothers had lost their calves. Their peace had shattered before their very eyes.

He didn't really want to have to see the calves, but the pictures were necessary. Besides needing them for the insurance company, he wanted to have them as a reminder of this tumultuous time in his life. It all seemed so surreal even now; and he figured after a few years, he would start second guessing what really had happened. He would likely even wonder if it hadn't been as bad as he seemed to remember; so the pictures would forever keep it clear for him.

He and the boys were approaching the drop-off to the second tier when Bob saw the dogs. Three Toes, Big Dog and the gang were heading east along the South Creek, right toward the location of the calves. Immediately, he forgot about his exhaustion and the pain that still racked his body. Only his anger was forefront.

He grabbed at the boys and put his finger to his mouth. The kids didn't utter a sound, but their eyes told him they were scared to death. Bob's mind started to race.

This pack had already tasted human flesh, so what was he going to do with the boys now to keep them safe? He didn't dare send them back to the truck. Just the noise they would make getting there would get the dogs' attention, and the fact that their little legs would not carry them to safety quickly enough would insure they would be the next victims. No, they had to stay with him.

Bob could feel an east-south-east wind in his face and knew the dogs wouldn't be able to smell him coming. The boys had never learned how to be quiet in the woods, so all he could do now was try to keep track of where the dogs were, and hope for the chance to take them by surprise. He knew the growls from the alpha dog and the squeals by those that felt the sting of the bites would raise quite a ruckus around the dead calf. Hopefully, that would cover any sounds made by the boys.

Bob had always hunted, but it was never for a kill. Instead, he would hunt just because he loved being in the woods, and because he liked to hone the tracking skills that his Grandfather Heard had taught him: the way a leaf was turned out of character; or the timing of an old track; how fast to track depending on the length of the stride and how it struck the ground; how to move quietly through the woods. And he was good enough these days to touch most of what he tracked. These dogs were different, though. They had ravaged the countryside, leaving a blood trail everywhere they went. Now he would have to be a killer just like them.

The pack was headed east toward the calves. He turned to his boys and quietly said, "These are the bad dogs, and they can kill us. You're going to have to come with me now, but you've got to do what I say as soon as I say it. Got it?"

The intensity in his eyes told his sons that he meant every word. He wanted them to have a healthy fear of the dogs, and the looks on their faces told him they understood. Their heads nodded in acknowledgement. He hated to have them in this situation, but they were here now; and he had to make sure they got out of it, but only after he had killed the dogs. He couldn't let them slip through his fingers again.

As he prepared to move on ahead, Bob whispered to them, "Follow in my footsteps. David, I want you right behind me, then Christopher, then Matt. And Matt, if I tell you to, I want you to get your little brothers up the closest tree; and then I want you to get up there, too. And you must do it fast. Okay?"

Matt nodded.

"Now, there won't be any talking from here on out. All of you have to be as quiet as a church mouse. Can you do that?"

David whispered back, "How quiet is a church mouse, Dad?"

"Really quiet, David; so quiet that no one will even know you're around."

David looked up at his dad with wide eyes, like he was looking at a giant; but Bob knew he wasn't. He knew his kids thought he was the fastest gun in the west, but he knew he wasn't that, either. He knew he was nothing more than average, but he was a hero to his kids.

Bob pulled off his hat and ran his strong, yet gentle hands through his wavy, brown hair to make sure it stayed out of his tanned face, and then pressed the hat back on his head. The blue eyes searched his boys one more time to make sure he was making the right decision.

Bob checked both of his guns to make sure they were loaded. The boys' eyes grew even wider when the 22 Magnum spun back into its holster. It was a beautiful Ruger 22 convertible with two cylinders: one for the regular 22, and then the 22 Magnum, which he almost always used.

His other gun, the Mauser, was a little on the heavy side, but the accuracy made up for it. With this one, he was consistent at 500 yards, and 800 yards wasn't even too much of a stretch. It was a sniper rifle that had been handed down to him from his father, who had taken it off a dead German during World War II. The stock had been changed a little since then, but the firing mechanism was still German-made, and as accurate as ever.

Turning his attention back to the boys, Bob motioned for them to be quiet again, and then he started to walk toward the second tier, all the while watching the land around them. He walked slower than he normally would have. He had to give the boys a little extra time just to keep up.

As they made their way toward the calves, his mind was suddenly flooded by the events that had started this whole thing.

CHAPTER 1

A late phone call broke the usual protocol for a Saturday afternoon. Although he had decided to stay late today to attack the pile of paperwork, everyone knew that Dr. Bob was essentially out of the office by this time. He picked up the phone, wondering who would be calling him for an appointment now. But it wasn't anyone wanting an appointment.

"Hi, Bob! This is Dave Slawson. Got a minute?"

Dave was a neighbor to the east of the Rocking C Ranch, a 300-acre horse and cattle ranch owned by Bob's dad. It was located forty miles west of Kansas City, in the rolling hills of eastern Kansas.

"Yeah, sure, Dave. What's up? My cows get out again?"

"No. It's my boy." Dave's voice cracked. "He was out in the field, just behind the house here and – Bob, those dogs got him."

Bob knew exactly which dogs Dave was talking about. All of the neighbors around the ranch had been talking about the pack, some of them having lost animals to the mongrels. "Sam? They got Sam? Oh, for God's sake, Dave! When did this happen? And how bad is he?"

"He's dead."

Bob listened as the voice on the other end of the line became one that could just as easily have belonged to a wailing woman, and he could hear the phone shaking in rhythm to the man's sobs.

When he was able to continue, Dave said, "It

1

happened just a little while ago. The police are here now. We're waiting for the coroner."

"Jesus, Dave. Can I do anything for you? I can be out there in an hour."

"I don't know. I really don't even know why I called you. But you've got family out here, too, and I just thought maybe I should let you know."

"Sure. I'm glad you did. Listen, I'm getting in my truck right now, so I'll be out in about an hour."

Bob had seen the dogs a couple of weeks ago roaming around his fifty-acre field, but had just dismissed it at the time, thinking all the neighbors' dogs had gotten together for a little play time. It was only a few days later that the stories of the killings began to spread through the countryside.

He quickly turned off the lights, grabbed his keys and locked up the office. Jumping in his old Suburban, he took off out of the parking lot, leaving a spray of gravel in his wake.

The trip to Dave's place seemed shorter than usual; probably because Bob dreaded having to see the face behind the heart-wrenching voice he'd just heard. As he approached the house, he rounded the curve on County Road 27 to be greeted by cars lined up about a hundred feet back down the road. Bringing up the rear, he parked and got out of the truck; and a few minutes later, was turning the corner of the back side of the barn, where it seemed the bulk of the crowd had gathered. A few more yards away, he saw Dave and the coroner standing over the mauled boy, the blankets laid off to the side of the body.

Bob's stomach began rolling when he saw Sam. It looked as though there wasn't any area on the body

2

that hadn't been torn up; but his head and chest, which now lay open, seemed to have gotten the worst of it. He could easily see that some of the joints had been pulled out of their sockets, and bone was visible in many places.

Bob felt as though he was going to vomit, but in spite of himself, his eyes kept going back to the area where the face was supposed to be. He recognized teeth and the nasal cavity, but that was about all he could discern. Suddenly, he had to duck around to the side of the barn to get his stomach under control. After a few deep breaths, he headed back to the scene.

The coroner was making his determinations and pronouncing the child dead, just formalizing what everybody knew. And then, none too soon, the black body bag was finally zipped shut.

As Dave wiped his tear-streaked face with the crook of his arm, he glanced up and noticed Bob. Obviously glad to have an excuse to walk away from the gruesome scene, he headed straight over to him. Without any formalities, his first remark was sharp and to the point. "I want you to find 'em and kill 'em, Bob. You're the tracker around these parts, so go find the sons-a-bitches."

"Okay," Bob said as he put his hand on the man's shoulder and gave it a quick squeeze. "But first we've got to let things settle down a little. Some of these folks need to clear out of here, and the cops have to finish with their business. Then I'll see what I can do."

Sheriff Jacob walked up and reached out to shake Bob's hand. "Dr. Bob," he said with a somber nod.

3

"Hi, Leo! It's been a while. How's that shoulder?"

"Never been better. Thanks. But I don't think I can say the same for you. You're looking pretty green around the gills there."

"Yeah. I just remembered why I became a chiropractor."

"So, can you tell us what happened here with those dogs?"

"Well, I might be able to tell you; but with all these people walking all over the history, it's not going to be very easy. If you could move everybody toward the barn, though, I'll see what I can figure out."

The sheriff nodded again and began moving everyone out of the way as Bob headed away from the barn. When he reached the start of the field, he stopped and squatted down to study the ground around him. Then he started walking toward the area where the dead boy lay. Ten feet from the body, he knelt down and scanned everything again.

He started duck walking inch by inch, looking for paw marks in the ground, trying to decipher which dog was which. But with the many feet that had already trampled the tracks, it was difficult for him to come to any real conclusions. He stood and went about twenty feet back toward the field, where the best tracks were; and after another minute, he walked back to Dave and Leo.

"There were nine dogs, most of them about fifty to sixty pounds. One has only three toes on his left front foot, and I think that one is the alpha dog. It looks like he's probably about ninety pounds. And from what I can tell, it was the alpha dog that took

4

down the boy; and then the others finished the job. I'd say it happened about two hours ago, and it took somewhere between thirty seconds to a minute for the dogs to do their damage."

Bob's eyes drifted to Dave's. The man was devastated. Tears had started flowing down his cheeks again, and Bob was sickened by what he had not told them: that it had actually taken longer, and there had been a lot more pain for the boy before he'd died.

"I'm sorry, Dave."

Sheriff Jacob said, "Can you track 'em down, Dr. Bob? I know you don't like killin' anything; but if you could find 'em, we'll take care of the rest."

"Hell, Leo. After seeing this, I think I just might be able to do it. Kill them, that is. This is likely to happen again if somebody doesn't put a stop to it. You know as well as I do that once an animal has gotten a taste of human flesh they usually just keep the habit; so if I find them, I doubt that I'll have much of a choice."

Sheriff Jacob nodded. "We'll let everybody around here know to be on the lookout for 'em."

"Sounds good to me, Leo. In fact, I've got a little time right now, so I think I'll get started if you don't mind."

"Keep me posted, will you?"

"Sure thing."

Bob walked by Dave and put a hand on his shoulder again. He knew there was nothing he could say that would ease the man's pain.

Sam's mother, Carol, was approaching, and Bob turned and gathered her into his arms. She began sobbing uncontrollably as he held her tight, but after a few moments, when she seemed to be calming back down a little, he loosened his grip on her. She quickly took a step back from him and said, "Kill them. Kill all those dirty bastards."

Bob was surprised, first by the calmness of her words, which belied the expression on her face, and then by the quickly-increasing, venomous words that she spat out in a higher and more demonic voice by the second. "Slice their damned hearts out, and show them to them as they die!"

Dave rushed over to her and maneuvered her toward the ambulance, where the Med-Act people took over, thankful just to have something to do. Bob felt a heaviness in his heart as he recognized the look of despair on the woman's face, the same look that his dad had worn when Bob's mother died.

He would always remember that day. Bob had performed CPR on her all the way to the hospital. Even though he had known in his heart she was dead, he couldn't accept the fact that he was impotent in the face of death. He was a doctor, for Christ's sake. And even when he'd had no choice but to acknowledge the fact that she was gone, he still refused to pronounce her dead. He just couldn't say it out loud.

Bob went back to his truck and changed out of his dress clothes and into his jeans, old cowboy boots, a tattered work shirt and hat. He strapped on his sidearm and toad stabber and returned to the tracks where they led across an open field toward the Nine Mile Creek; and then he started to run.

Dave turned back to Sheriff Jacob and asked, "What the hell is he doing?"

"Well, from what I've heard, he can track on

the run. But damned if anybody knows how he does it."

Bob ran straight to the Nine Mile Creek and saw the tracks on the other side. He waded through the knee-deep water and took off running again until he reached the edge of the woods, where he stopped. Out of habit, he offered his respect and thanks to Mother Nature for sharing her beauty with him; but this time, he also thought of his grandfather, who had taught him his tracking skills. He offered his thanks to him, and then thought of the young boy, and added a prayer for his soul's safe journey. Then he continued on into the woods.

As he carefully picked his way through the thorny bushes and low-hanging limbs of the trees, he kept watch on the ground in front of him. The tracks looked like they were about two hours old, and the chances of him engaging the dogs right away were slim to none. But he stayed alert as he moved as silently as he could.

Crossing the Nine Mile Creek had put him on his own property, and he thought of his cattle grazing about a half mile away. He wondered what was ahead of him, and, hoping he wasn't wearing out his requests, silently offered up another prayer for protection.

Suddenly, he felt as though he was being watched, and he quickly crouched down for cover. He looked around, but there was no one he could see. He wondered briefly if it was the dogs; but since their tracks moved on ahead and were so old, he knew that wasn't the case. Finally deciding he was being paranoid, he continued to move on ahead.

As he kept a steady pace along the trail, though, the feeling never subsided. Someone was there. He couldn't see them. As the feeling grew stronger, Bob found himself becoming spooked and finally stopped again. He sat down at the base of a huge oak and leaned his back against it. Shutting his eyes, he began to pray for protection and clarity, and then for peace and guidance. Soon, he felt his heart slow its pace; and the usual comfort he found in the woods returned.

As he resumed tracking, however, the feeling was still there, as though someone was with him, next to him even; but his fear had been replaced with a feeling of comfort and strength. He wondered if it was his grandfather watching over him, or maybe Mother Nature, or God, or whatever 'it' was called. But he knew for sure there was a battle ahead of him, and he was thankful for whatever this Presence could do to help him out.

He had six shots in his sidearm, but with nine dogs all together, he knew the odds were against him. The tracking was plain and simple, but these dogs acted like they'd hunted together for a long time. And if Three Toes was as good as Bob thought, he wasn't sure whether he should tackle this even with the Presence that kept tagging along. But the memory of Carol's grief-stricken request pushed him onward.

He started to run through the South Creek valley, which flowed from the west and ended at the Nine Mile Creek. Suddenly, he saw tracks of two dogs heading up the hill to the north, and he abruptly stopped. He could *smell* them. He'd thought only minutes ago that his senses had heightened somehow, but he'd figured it was just the results of his adrenaline pumping harder than ever. But now he knew it was more than that, and it was eerie. Not only was he smelling things he'd never noticed before, but it seemed as though he could hear every movement of every leaf and limb as the light breeze moved through them. He feared he was going crazy.

After standing still, sniffing and listening for another minute, he decided to stay on the trail of Three Toes and the gang, who had continued west on through the valley. Bob wondered if the two strays were headed back to their den and thought maybe he should have followed them to see; but Three Toes was the leader, and he thought he should watch him more. He started to run after the pack again; but something about the two, lone dogs bothered him, and he stopped a second time. Instinct told him to go after them.

He went back and picked up their tracks and began to follow them up the hill to the first level. He knew the terrain just ahead would flatten out, rise to a second tier, flatten out again, and then rise to the top tier.

As he approached the edge of the tier, he pulled the leather strap from the hammer of his gun and unsnapped the clasp that held his knife. Slowing his steps, he quietly peered over the top. No dogs.

He saw the tracks again, though, and they were headed west along the edge of the ridge. This made them traveling parallel to Three Toes' trail, although lagging behind a bit. He climbed up to the second tier and quickened his pace, continuing to follow the tracks.

A short distance further, the tracks led him back down to the lowest tier, where he'd just been.

Following slowly, he dropped back down the hill to the South Creek valley and saw the tracks of the rest of the pack being led by Three Toes, and after counting the prints, confirmed that all nine dogs were traveling together again. Slowly, the realization of what had just happened began to take shape in his brain. If he had chosen to stay after Three Toes, the two loners would have come up on his back. And then he remembered one of his grandfather's sayings: *Never underestimate the enemy.*

It had been a long time since Bob had gone after a kill, and he had never gone after vicious killers like these before. Now he understood the need to change his thinking about these dogs, or he would surely end up looking at the inside of a body bag just like the boy.

Bob raised his nose slightly and inhaled deeply, but smelled nothing aside from the foliage around him. Okay, so maybe it was my imagination, he thought, as he took off again. He decided to travel a little slower now, so he could keep an eye on everything in front of him and behind him. If Three Toes knew he was being followed, it would be easy for him to circle back around and come up from behind, just like the loners would have done.

The tracks were fresher here, just about forty-five minutes old, so Bob knew he was closer now. He decided to follow until he found where they lived, and then hopefully come back another time with more ammunition and catch them in an ambush. Or, if he had to wait until they returned, he would at least have enough time to set things up. Even better.

He kept his pace even, still going at a slightly faster pace than the pack. The dogs had slowed down after the two strays from the ridge had rejoined them, so maybe they didn't realize they were being followed. Or maybe they did. Bob wondered if he might be out of his league. Nothing seemed logical. Dogs just weren't that smart, at least none he'd ever known. He shrugged off his thoughts, assuming he was just being paranoid or over-thinking things.

He reached the west end of his property and hopped over the barbed-wire fence. It was going to be dark soon, which wouldn't have bothered him in any other set of circumstances; but the fact that there would be almost no moon tonight put him at a great disadvantage. And after seeing the damage the dogs had already done, the thought of being out after dark was even less appealing. If the dogs didn't stop in the next half hour, he'd head back home.

Suddenly, he caught another whiff of the dogs' scent. There were no cattle in this area of the woods, so the underbrush was considerably thicker. More for the dogs to leave their smells on, but harder for Bob to get through. While he could track silently otherwise, it was impossible in such heavy brush. He decided his best approach would be to cover a short distance quickly without worrying about the noise; and then he'd stop and listen.

His trot-and-stop method took him over a mile past his place to the west, and it was starting to get darker now. There seemed to be nothing to suggest the pack was slowing down; and with his day starting at five this morning, he was beginning to get tired already. Being tired made him susceptible to mistakes. He decided to pull off the trail and start again in the morning.

11

Bob knew his dad would be at the ranch, which wasn't very far away; and the fields he had to cross to get there were open, which gave him the advantage over the dogs. He took off in that direction and watched as the night came in fast, almost as though the darkness was chasing him.

He'd made it to the open field and almost to the road that led on to the house when he heard something behind him. The dimming light made it difficult for him to see, but the smell was unmistakable. Three Toes was close. As he laid his hand on the gun, he heard a low, muffled growl coming from the woods behind him. First one, then two, and then more as the crowd gathered. But the fear that he would have normally had and that he knew he should be feeling now wasn't there. Instead, he felt power and confidence engulf him.

He took a few steps toward his opponents and growled back, hoping to push them, to cause them to make a mistake and come out into the open where he could use his Magnum with more accuracy. Then, suddenly, the woods lit up as if someone had flipped the light switch. He could see the dogs, all nine of them, and he could see them clearly. He looked back toward the setting sun, but it was gone. The Presence was with him. Turning back toward the woods, he whispered, "Thank you."

Bob stood still and waited for Three Toes to charge, but the dog merely stood and stared at him, refusing to move. He thought he could feel the dog's heartbeat; and, then, as he looked into the dog's unflinching eyes, he realized that his enemy was every bit as good as he'd feared earlier. For the first time since he'd headed back toward the ranch, he was truly terrified. He continued to hear the dogs in the brush as they kept pace with him along the road leading to the house, and figured they were waiting for him to make a mistake.

As he walked along, Bob began to feel that Three Toes had turned the tables on him. Instead of being the hunter now, he was the hunted. And he wondered if the dog was following him to see where he lived, just like he, himself, had done with the dogs a short while ago.

Never underestimate your enemy.

As he made his way along the road toward the ranch, Bob's grandfather's words continued to echo through his mind. Okay, he finally thought to himself, so let's assume the dogs really are following me home so they can create havoc there. How can I get them off my trail?

Bob felt confident in his abilities with the gun, and he had the knife to use once the ammunition was gone. But he only had to remind himself that there were nine dogs against him, and he decided he shouldn't tempt fate by going back into the woods now. He was grateful to the Presence for its help, but he didn't want to push his luck too far. No, Three Toes owned the woods for now, and Bob figured it was best to concede this time.

Mike and Sherry's house was coming up on his left and was the last one he would pass before reaching his own. When he topped the hill, he could see the lights shining through their kitchen window. As much as he hated to bother them now, he thought it would be a good idea to stop in. He'd warn them about the dogs if they hadn't already heard, and it would give the pack a little time to get bored and wander away. And if they didn't do that, he thought he'd figured out a way to get rid of them.

He made his way to the front door and knocked. As he waited for an answer, he looked around the yard. The place seemed like it had really grown up since the last time he'd been here. A floodlight allowed him to see the intermingling of grass and weeds that hadn't been mowed in a while; and it looked like a storm had taken down a limb from a huge walnut tree that stood at the edge of the yard.

Bob was surprised to see things so neglected with Mike always claiming to be so busy around the place. But, then, Bob never knew what to make of him anymore. They'd been best friends all through middle and high school, but then college and work had taken them in different directions for several years. Eventually, they had finally landed back at their old home places, but Mike had just never been the same. Bob found himself reminiscing and longing for the good old days when Sherry interrupted his reverie by throwing open the door.

"Bob," she said in a surprised voice. "How in the world are you? My, it's been a while! But what in the world are you doing roaming the countryside with all those awful dogs on the loose? Oh, yes, I heard you went out chasing them after they'd killed that poor Slawson boy. Why, everybody's hearts are just broken in two for Dave and Carol. And what in the world are we all going to do with this terrible pack of hounds running around the countryside killing and maiming everything and everybody in sight?"

Bob suddenly remembered why it had been so long since he'd visited with his friend. Sherry's constant chattering was about more than anyone could bear.

"Oh, my word, Bob! Why in the world haven't I asked you to come in and sit a spell? Get on in here and rest those weary bones. I just bet you're worn to a frazzle."

As he stepped inside, he opened his mouth to speak; but before he could get a word out, Sherry continued. "What in the world is wrong with me? Can I get you something to drink? Good gracious, I'm just not the right hostess these days. Of course, out here I don't get many visitors, but I must say I do have my share of friends. So you go on now and sit down anywhere you like. I'm going to get you a cup of coffee. You're looking a little worn out there."

Bob finally took the plunge and butted into her incessant rattling. "Sherry, I wish I had the time to stay for coffee, but I don't. I really need to get back out there, but I could use some pepper if you've got some to spare. I promise I'll get it back to you as quickly as I can."

"Pepper? What in the world do you need pepper for? Are you fixing up something for dinner? That is what you said, isn't it? Pepper?" Sherry disappeared into the kitchen.

"Yeah, pepper. And it's for the dogs," Bob quickly interjected.

Sherry stepped back into the living room with the pepper shaker in her hand and a look of confusion on her face that quickly turned into horror. "What in the world do the dogs need pepper for? Oh, my word, you've killed them, and now you're going to *eat* them?"

There was finally a pause in Sherry's chatter, as she stood in shock at the thought of eating the dogs.

"No, Sherry," Bob said with a laugh. "I need to put some pepper down to keep them from following me on home."

"Oh, thank the Lord!" she said as she melodramatically put her hand to her chest as though to stop a heart attack. "I was worried there for a minute. I mean, I know things have been tough for everybody lately, but *eating dogs*? Oh, mercy!"

Sherry began to laugh, almost hysterically, and Bob knew he needed to grab the chance for retreat while she was catching her breath.

Holding the pepper up toward her, he said, "Thanks a lot. I've got to get moving on along now. The dogs are still out there, so it's best if you stay inside this evening. And you might call Mike to let him know not to lollygag when he's coming in after work."

A genuine look of fear crossed her face, but Bob didn't dare delay his departure. As he walked on out through the ragged lawn, he could hear the incessant talking start up again. The noise was muffled against the screen door, but he still caught bits and pieces of the babbling.

"Oh, my Lord! Those dogs…And our chickens, and the cats…"

Bob kept walking.

"…Oh, sweet baby Jesus!" she proclaimed just seconds before closing the door.

Sherry was great at making a hurricane out of a

drizzle, and Bob really didn't want to hang around to see her melt-down. But more than that, he really was worn out, and wanted to get back to the ranch as soon as he could.

Within seconds of stepping out of the porch light, he could feel the dogs watching him again; and he heard them as they continued on through the woods, always close to him. They obviously had no intentions of staying behind to give Sherry any trouble.

As he took off across the field, the lights went on in the woods again, and, this time, Bob actually felt the muscles relax as his eyes dilated. Although the increasing changes in him were somewhat disquieting, he could see deep into the woods. Again and again, he gave thanks. He could freak out later.

"Oh, sweet baby Jesus," he muttered quietly to himself as he watched them pace back and forth alongside him. They wouldn't cross the open prairie until they saw him disappear into the woods. To wander out before then would put them at too much risk of getting shot. About three-fourths of the way across the field, Bob glanced back over his shoulder and saw, much to his surprise, that he had been wrong in his assumption. The pack was standing in full view just outside the woods, alert and ready to take off. Bob quickened his pace.

He reached the edge of the woods, and as he crossed the threshold, he tipped his hand and began to spread the pepper across his trail and on out, about five feet on each side. One last look back let him know the dogs were still keeping their distance and waiting for him to disappear. But he knew it was only a matter of seconds now before they took off after him.

After spreading another two strips of the pepper, each about ten feet apart, he took off in a run. Then, after another hundred feet, he stopped and spread some more. He could hear them coming now and wondered, briefly, if he should climb a tree, or just wait and try to take them out from where he was; but then he reminded himself of how unprepared he was with just the Ruger and the knife; and he decided to keep on moving. He turned and ran about twenty more yards; and then he heard the sneezing start, and laughed under his breath as he pictured the scene in his mind.

He wished he could have given Dave and Carol some good news tonight: that he'd been able to take out at least part of the pack; but he just couldn't make himself commit to something he felt so unsure of.

His pace slowed to a trot as he continued on toward the ranch; but he changed directions often, while continuing to spread the pepper from time to time. He figured Three Toes might cross through a couple of the strips, but likely not a third or fourth.

When he finally felt it was safe, he slowed down to a walk. The dew was beginning to settle; and he could feel the dampness on his clothes, which caused him to shudder in the cooler night air. But the walk was nice, and he gave thanks to his Guardian, whoever it was, and, then, his mind began to wander. He thought of Sammy and his grieving family, and his heart ached as he thought of the pain Dave and Carol must be going through now. To lose a parent was tough enough; but to lose a child was something that he couldn't comprehend, and prayed he would never have to.

As he neared the house and his thoughts returned to the terrain around him, Bob became aware of a sense of vulnerability where there was comfort before. He wondered if the dogs were close by, but when he stopped and listened, he heard nothing. He sniffed, but smelled nothing. And the darkness of the night didn't allow him to see anything in the woods now.

He was relieved when he finally reached the house. Neil was still up, sitting in his old recliner next to the living room window with his newspaper in his hands. Bob could just make out the tufts of snow-white hair sticking up behind the paper. The old coot was usually in bed by now; and Bob knew he'd been waiting for him to get home; and he braced himself for the onslaught.

Not looking up, Neil asked, "Where the hell have you been?"

Bob resented his dad's constant criticism and demands. He'd always been this way, at least for as long as he could remember; and he'd been able to get used to it.

"Here we go again," Bob mumbled to himself.

Neil slammed the paper down on his lap. "What's that, you say?"

"I said I was just out having a nice stroll in the woods. Why?"

"Just wondering. Heard you were out in these parts and thought you might be showing up. Just didn't think it'd be this late."

Bob knew his father wouldn't press for any details tonight; but he figured it was safe to assume that the old guy would eventually start asking

19

questions.

"I take it you heard about the Slawson boy," Bob said as he laid his gun and knife on the kitchen table, and wearily sat down to take off his boots.

"Yup. And I heard you took out after the dogs that got him. You know, there were things around here that needed done if you were feeling that energetic."

Neil could out-work anybody Bob knew, and he always expected everyone else to be just like him. If there was an ounce of energy left in a body, it was wasted if it wasn't used to get things done. And there were always things to get done.

As he began pulling things out of the refrigerator to make himself a sandwich, Bob said, "Dad, there'll be work to do around here long after we're both dead and gone. But I thought I needed to see if I could track down the dogs for Dave's and Carol's sake."

"Well? So did you?"

"Yes, I did. I just wasn't able to take any of them. I'm not really sure I'm going to, either. The alpha dog is smarter than any dog I've ever known."

"Huh," Neil said in a mocking voice. "And here I thought you were supposed to be the best at that tracking stuff of yours. But now there's a dog out there that's smarter than you. Imagine that."

"Yeah, it's a kick in the ass, ain't it? But you'd better keep in mind that the dogs outsmarted me; so you'd better start carrying a gun on you when you're out around these parts for a while."

"Oh, for Christ's sake, Bob. They're a pack of dogs, not a bunch of terrorists."

Bob's patience, along with his energy, was

20

running low. "Okay, fine. Just remember, they've already killed one person; and I doubt they'll bow down to you just because you tell them to."

Bob had always been respectful of his father, but, lately, the old man had been pushing things a little too much. He just hated losing his patience with him.

"Three Toes, the leader, turned the tables on me enough tonight that, before I knew it, I was the one being hunted instead of the other way around. So just do with that what you want."

Neil had always ruled over his family with an iron hand; and he'd likely try to do the same with the dogs; but Bob hoped he wouldn't end up paying for his stubbornness with his life.

"And just so you know, I'll be heading back out early in the morning to track them again; and I don't know when I'll get back."

Bob busied himself in the kitchen as he tried to ignore Neil's piercing gaze. And then, much to his surprise, he said, "Just don't get hurt."

Bob took his sandwich and headed out to the rock patio. Like most every other farm or ranch in the area, they had a floodlight in their yard; but they chose to leave it off unless they really needed it for some reason. Bob loved sitting outside in the dark watching the stars. And tonight was an extra good night for it since the moon was almost nonexistent.

He settled into the old, metal chair; and the dogs immediately began to haunt his thoughts. He stared into the darkness around him and pictured them out there waiting for him. Bob loved the times he spent at the ranch, and hated that it had become contaminated by the pack of killers. It seemed like everything in life was contaminated with something, though.

The ranch itself was a trigger for both Barb and Neil; and Bob was always caught in the middle. If he went to the ranch for a day, Barb was mad. If he didn't go to the ranch for a day, Neil was mad. Either way, someone always lost, and it was always him. He found it ironic that the very things that caused Barb and Neil to hate each other were the things they had in common. They were both selfish and controlling.

When he was at the ranch, he'd always try not to think about what was waiting for him when he got back home. Barb was known as the Ice Lady to everyone, even to her so-called friends; but to those people she didn't like, she was cold and usually down-right cruel. Regardless of whether they were friend or foe, though, Barb was always conniving. More times than he could remember, Barb had been caught trying to put the moves on her friends' husbands; and, then, that would usually be the end of that. Some of them stuck around; but those were the ones who had no shame or dignity at all, and were doing the same thing to someone else's husband.

But he did have the boys, the only thing that made it worth going back to the city for. And there was also his practice.

Where Bob found great fulfillment and satisfaction in his patients, it was his boys who he considered his greatest achievements. He loved them more than he'd ever loved anyone before. Barb, on the other hand, talked to them like she did him, with a cutting tongue. Bob had tried to calm it down many times; but all it got him and the boys, was more of the same. He'd finally given up and had just learned to ignore it for the most part, while the boys dealt with it by spending a lot of time with their friends.

He would have liked for the kids to spend some time at the ranch with him, but Barb wouldn't even consider it. He knew for a fact that it wasn't because she wanted them near her. It was just that she didn't want them near him. Or Neil. She had hated him even before he had ever had the chance to piss her off. And she did anything she could to lash out at him. In this case, she'd taken away his grandkids.

Not long into their marriage, Barb began to lash out at Neil; but she quickly learned that he was just as good, if not better, at doling it out. The venom would spew between them so hot and heavy that Bob would wonder if it was going to end in a fistfight. But Barb would always back off eventually, and then there would be peace for a while. He thought now that he probably should have taken a cue from his dad on how to handle the situation with her; but that kind of lifestyle seemed just as bad to him as the one he had. He didn't want to live a life that was just about waiting to squelch the next upheaval. So he just ignored her.

He thought about the day she thought he'd taken too long moving cattle with his dad; and she had badgered him for hours after he'd gotten home. He had ignored her that time, too; but, finally, as a last-ditch low blow, she'd shouted at him, "Are you a man or a mouse?" As much as he had wanted to hit her right then, he continued to ignore her just so she wouldn't know she had gotten to him. But she had hurt him deeper with that comment than anything else she'd ever said to him before. He decided that day that he hated her.

23

He had wished so many times he could just take the boys and walk away; but he'd made a promise for better or worse, although this was worse than he'd ever thought possible. If only he had known before he'd sunk his own ship. Leaning back in the chair now, he wondered what he'd done to deserve this.

Bob's foot scraped the rocks; and his jangled nerves tensed, bringing him back to the present. He could hear howls to the north, but it wasn't the dogs. It was coyotes, probably talking about their hunting spree and calling all their friends and families in for the feast. He didn't mind this kind of killing, because it was the plan put in motion by Mother Nature herself: survival of the fittest, the natural food chain, the order of the animal kingdom and all that.

Bob's grandfather had taught him all about the laws of the wilderness, and that the way to stay alive out there was to honor them. But his grandpa didn't know these dogs. They didn't live by the rules, and Bob knew he would have to meet them on different terms – their terms. Just like he had to meet Barb on her terms.

Bob sighed heavily and leaned forward in his chair, elbows resting on his knees. The night had settled in deeper; and, suddenly, he just wanted to crawl into bed and sleep. But before he could move to get up, he saw movement off to his right. Moving only his eyes, he watched as a raccoon waddled toward him, seemingly unafraid. When it was in front of him, it stopped and stood tall on its hind legs as it examined him with its beady, little eyes. Neither human nor animal moved. After another twenty seconds or so, the ball of fur returned to all fours, wiggled its butt, and

24

scurried on its way.

Bob's grandfather had taught him all about animal totems, too, and had urged him to do his best to observe what the animal was there to teach. Raccoons were about adaptability, exploring new realms, who we are, and who we want to be. And they were also about self-defense.

As he dragged himself back into the house, Bob wondered if the raccoon was there on behalf of the hunt of the dogs, or his life with Barb. Or maybe both.

Neil had finally gone to bed; and, so, Bob made his way through the dark to the other bedroom, where he shed his clothes and crawled under the covers. He loved sleeping out here at the ranch with the sounds of the owls, and whippoorwills and frogs. He even loved listening to the train in the far-off distance. In the city, he only heard the traffic and sirens. He couldn't figure out what appealed to Barb about living there; but there wasn't much he could figure out where she was concerned.

CHAPTER 2

Sunday morning came early. He wanted to be out just before daylight, so he'd set his alarm for 4:30; and, now, he quietly dressed and made himself some instant coffee. He didn't want to wake his dad and have to justify his actions again this morning. He went to the gun cabinet and reverently pulled out the old, German Mauser sniper rifle, and then headed out into the cool morning.

He walked cross-country towards the Slawson's to get his truck, and by the time he'd hit the Nine Mile valley, the sun was coming up over the first set of hills in front of him. He found the truck right where he'd left it and crawled inside. As the 454 engine roared to life, he hoped it didn't wake up Dave and Carol. They needed all the rest they could get right now.

It took him about ten minutes to get back to where he'd last seen the dogs and spot their tracks. He grabbed his guns and took off following them. Right away, he saw where they had turned and backtracked once they'd broken away from him. They had headed back toward Mike and Sherry's.

His footsteps quickened, although he knew what he was going to find when he got there. In the yard on the far side of the house, every chicken on the place lay lifeless, and two pigs lay in puddles of their own blood. Bob stood still as he looked at the massacre around him, angry at himself for not believing this was going to happen.

Mike suddenly stepped out onto the porch and said, "What the hell's going on?"

Bob reluctantly walked up the steps to him, wishing the visit with his old friend didn't have to start with this bit of breaking news.

"Hell, Mike. I hate to tell you this, but those damned dogs did a number on your chickens and pigs. Worse than that, though, I think it might be my fault that it happened."

"Everything's your fault, you dumb shit. But believe me, I already knew about the dogs. Want a cup of coffee?"

As the two men turned to go into the house, Bob said, "Last time you offered me coffee, it had enough whiskey in it that I had a headache for three days."

"Yeah, well, you were being a dumb shit then, too."

"I know. That's why I'm worried now."

They walked in, and Bob sat down at the kitchen table while Mike pulled two mugs out of the cabinet. Bob had really missed hanging out with him; but since Barb had gotten a bee in her bonnet about not liking him, he'd just never pushed it. He watched as Mike poured two cups of stout-looking coffee and sat down across the small table from him. Mike scooted one of the cups toward him, hot coffee sloshing over the rim of the cup.

"Where's Sherry?"

"Sleeping. She had a long night last night. We woke up a little after midnight with that God-forsaken racket out there. I grabbed my gun and tried to shoot the bastards, but I don't think I hit any of 'em."

"Shit, Mike. Everybody knows you couldn't hit the broad side of a barn, let alone a dog in the dark."

"Maybe. But I don't think those dogs knew that. I scared the hell out of 'em. At least, I guess I did. But now I want to hear how it was your fault."

"I started tracking them last night; but the next thing I knew, they were tracking me. And since I was headed in this general direction, I thought I'd veer off a little, stop by here, and get some pepper. I really didn't think they'd even take notice of this place, 'cause they were so intent on following me; but now it looks like I shouldn't have been thinking that."

"I thought you were out to kill 'em, not fix 'em supper," Mike said with a deadpan expression.

Bob shook his head and said, "Now who's the dumb shit? Those damned dogs were aiming to make *me* their supper, so I wanted the pepper to spread across my trail."

Mike's face became somber, the laughter now gone. "Okay, Bob, tell me the truth. What's up with these dogs? I've never known you to run from an animal, much less a pack of dogs."

"It's simple. They're evil, and I underestimated them. I took off after them with only my twenty-two and a knife, and then realized there were too many for me to take like that."

Mike looked incredulous, so Bob quickly continued. "Seriously, Mike, these dogs are a lot better than I gave them credit for in the beginning. Three Toes – he's the leader – has a big following and seems to have trained them well. It's kind of scary if you ask me."

Mike sat silently, staring into his coffee. Finally, he said, "You need my help?"

"Nah. You've got enough to do just cleaning up

29

that mess out there, but I appreciate the offer. Besides, I'd be as scared of you with a loaded gun as I am of the damned dogs."

Bob still couldn't read Mike's expression. "Really, though, I'm loaded for bear today, so I'll be fine. A machine gun would have been nice to have; but, since I don't have one, I'll just rely on my old Mauser."

He swigged the rest of the coffee and then stood up to leave.

"Anyway, I'd better get going. Thanks for the coffee. And thanks for not loading it with whiskey this time."

"Sure. And hey, be careful out there."

Bob walked back to the barn and said a prayer over the dead bodies, and he envisioned them in the perfect world as he did. A smile came to his face as he pictured them strolling along in a heavenly farm, all playing together.

Mike watched from the porch. He knew Bob had a good heart; and he knew Grandpa Heard had taught him many of his beliefs along with his tracking skills. He wished he'd spent more time with the two of them when he was still alive; but just like most teenagers, he always had other things to do, the importance of it all eluding him until now. He turned to go back into the house as Bob picked up on the tracks and followed them out of sight.

Bob was back in the woods running last night's tracks within minutes. He had already decided if he saw where they split again, he would stay with Three Toes this time and just watch his back for the loners. It wasn't long before they did it, but this time, there were

30

two off to the right, two off to the left, and Three Toes and the rest moving straight ahead.

Bob followed the tracks all day without ever coming close to seeing any of the pack; but he did get to see a part of the countryside he hadn't seen before. He knew the Nine Mile valley well; but rarely had he traveled west up here, and certainly never this far.

It was six in the evening by the time he headed back to the truck. The tracks had led him all over the countryside with no apparent pattern at all; and he was ready to call it a day, even though he had thoroughly enjoyed the walk.

He thought about how much he loved it out here, even with the dogs shattering the peace that he'd always reveled in. It was only out here that he could let go of the anger and frustration from home.

Bob had tried time and time again to change that part of his life, but nothing he ever did or said was enough. It was obviously a hopeless situation; and he figured he knew what the end result was going to be, in spite of the fact that he didn't believe his boys would be better off without their parents together. But what else was left for him to do?

Back at the truck, he slipped the Mauser through the back window and was reaching to lay his 22 next to it when the odor flitted past his nose; and the hair stood up on the back of his neck. He swung around with the pistol still in his hand, but already the smell was gone. His eyes searched the field and the tree line. But while the smell did not linger, the uneasy feeling that had come over him did. He tried again to catch a whiff as his eyes darted in every direction, but there was nothing. He knew they were out there hiding, watching, sizing him up; and the silence bothered him as he waited for something to happen. Then there was another tiny hint of the odor; and this time, he caught the direction and quickly turned to his right. He still couldn't see anything, but he knew they were there.

Monday was spent at the office seeing his patients, but he had a hard time keeping his mind off the dogs. Each time the phone rang, he held his breath, waiting for the next shoe to drop. But the day was uneventful; and once he had closed up the office for the day, he headed straight back to the ranch.

A prayer of thanks had always been a precursor to entering the woods; but now the prayer also included a petition for protection. Bob was never quite sure what was happening with him when his feet would suddenly begin to run a little faster, the smells became more poignant, or his vision grew uncannily acute; but he was beginning to like it. It didn't scare him any longer, although it wasn't something he felt he should be telling anyone else. But even with the gifts, there was still Three Toes out there; and he had a well-trained pack of followers.

The night was as uneventful as the day had been. There had only been old tracks, no dogs, and no gifts. And after an hour of feeling as though he was chasing ghosts, he headed back home.

The Tuesday afternoon schedule was lighter than usual, with a few patients shortly after noon, and no walk-ins at all. So when Sheriff Jacob called at four to tell him that Mr. Alverson's colt had been taken down, he immediately jumped back in his truck and headed out. As he drove, his frustration grew. The

32

damned dogs never killed while he was nearby; but, instead, they waited until he was back in the city. Was that their plan? To hit while he wasn't available? He didn't put it past them to be that calculating any more.

When he pulled up at Mr. Alverson's place, Sheriff Jacob and a deputy were waiting. Mr. Alverson stood quietly on the porch, stooped over and looking thinner and more haggard than ever before; and Bob wondered if the poor man was going to start crying. He remembered how important these horses were to the old man – how he relied on the income from them just to get by. Now he was one down; and he wondered if this might have been the stud that actually would have put him over the top. As he looked at the defeated expression on the man's face, he wanted to cry with the guy; and his anger swelled. The dogs weren't just causing grief for the families and friends of the dead; they were also trashing these country folks' livelihoods.

Jacob looked at Bob and then eyeballed the guns he carried. "You sure those guns work?"

Bob twirled toward him and said, "Jacob, is that all you're concerned about?"

"Uh, I was just worried that. . .uh, I just wanted to make sure. . .?"

As Bob's eyes scanned the ground, he said, "The guns are fine." and then he took off running.

Alverson stepped up even with Jacob. "I've heard he's staying in the woods tracking the dogs most all night long. That right, Sheriff?"

"That's what Mike Curtis says. Says he takes catnaps in the trees."

Alverson shook his head. "Those dogs are

33

gonna make him nuts if he's not already."

The wind was coming from the west straight into Bob's face; and he could smell Three Toes as if he was right in front of him. He suspected it was going to be another interesting evening; and all his grandfather's teachings were about to pay off.

As he made his way deeper into the woods, Bob thought back to all the times they had spent together just talking and hunting. It was the year he had graduated from high school that Grandpa had died; and Bob had always felt as though their bond transcended life. They each resided in the other's heart; and separation of body could never take that away from them. But he still missed conversing with him.

Suddenly, he recalled something his grandfather had told him once – something about the way he always felt when he entered the woods. Bob couldn't remember it all exactly; but he did remember it had something to do with a 'strange feeling'; and he wondered now if the strange feelings his grandfather had were the same kinds he was having? Had he felt the Presence, too? Had he been bestowed with extrasensory abilities? It wasn't rational, he knew; but then, neither were the things that were happening to him these days.

The scents of the dogs were strong, and Bob's nose led him more than the tracks did. Stopping every once in a while, he would take another whiff, get his bearings, and then take off again, always keeping the tracks in sight.

It wasn't long before he noticed two of the dogs had split off again. An old trick now, he thought, as he headed toward the main pack, but kept an eye out behind him.

After moving on about another 100 feet, he sat down on a fallen log, took off his boots, and, after tying a small piece of leather through the pull loops, slung them around his neck before taking off again. He wanted as much silence as he could get.

The smell grew stronger within the first quarter of a mile, and he began to slow down. Already, his feet were sore from the hackberry limbs, thistles and occasional rocks he stumbled over; and when he glanced down, he noticed they had started to bleed slightly. He thought of the Indians' moccasins and wished he had some about now.

The main pack had stayed together so far with none of them splitting off; and they were straight ahead of him, about two hundred yards. Bob decided getting between the pair and the main pack could possibly give him a better chance of getting the two loners, even if he didn't get any of the rest of them. The thought of being caught in the middle of them made him a little wiggy; but he figured if he could take any of them down, even one of them, the rest might run.

Bob needed to maneuver quickly to get himself in place, and so he began to move again. He was still aware of the pain in his feet; but the adrenaline racing through him seemed to be taking it down a notch. The scent of Three Toes grew stronger as he moved ahead; and he stopped to catch his breath, and waited for the silence to settle back in around him. He had never gotten this close to the dogs before.

Seconds passed, and the scent began to wane. Slower now, he moved along just fast enough to keep track of them. He knew the two that had split off would meet up with Three Toes somewhere soon if they followed the pattern from before; but he wasn't sure when or where it would happen; so he wanted to stay close. As he chose his footing carefully and crept along at a snail's pace, he suddenly caught a whiff of Three Toes again and wondered if he was walking into a trap. He looked around to find a tree to shimmy up if they attacked; and then he sat down and quickly put his boots back on. Not comfortable, but tolerable. Then he continued down the trail.

After covering about ten more feet, he stopped at the tree he had spotted that had branches low enough to access easily; and then he waited. Within seconds, he began to hear the rustle of feet as the two strays squirmed their way through the woods toward him from behind.

Bob checked the straps of his pistol and knife, and made sure the safety was off the Mauser. With his finger on the trigger, he held the rifle to his shoulder and braced himself against the tree.

Again, he heard the two coming in closer; and praying that Three Toes stayed back, he turned to meet the pair. He saw the first dog about thirty yards away, a good easy shot even in the dark; but the second hadn't come out into the open yet. If he was to have a chance at taking out both of them, he knew he had to wait for the one behind to show itself before he started firing.

The first dog drew closer, and Bob could see that he was old and mangy. Seasoned, he thought. While Bob kept his eye on him and watched for the second dog, he also tried to listen for the rest of the pack to come barreling toward him. Old Dog was within ten yards of him when Bob finally caught a glimpse of his comrade about forty yards back. He looked mangy, too, but he was smaller and probably younger than Old Dog.

Bob stood still, waiting for the chance to get them both; but Old Dog was getting closer by the second; and he was beginning to wonder if he was going to have the chance to get them both. Finally, when Old Dog was within ten feet of him, he saw Young Dog race through the small clearing; and he let loose with the first shot, taking Old Dog down. Then he threw the bolt and fired the second shot, but only clipped Young Dog in the hip. Just then, as Young Dog yelped and limped away, Bob heard the rest of the pack begin running toward him.

He bolted another bullet as he spun around and moved forward into the trail of Three Toes. Not making a sound, not even daring to breath, he waited. And wished he'd had the time to reload. He wanted to go head-to-head with the dogs instead of having to retreat up the tree; but to do that he would need to take at least three of the seven coming toward him. The toughest would likely be in the lead, so he hoped he could knock them down at the very least. But none came.

The woods became still; but he could smell them; and his eyes darted in all directions while he tried to keep the gun sighted in at all times. Then he heard the stampede coming toward him again; and he braced himself for the assault.

They approached from his front, but then spread out around and behind him, leading Bob to think his best tactic would be to take them in order of distance. He kept spinning back and forth, watching for the first one to rush him; and then he saw him. The dog came weaving back and forth through the trees with the speed of a demon, face gnarled, with teeth showing and froth flying. As the dog ran through a clearing about ten feet in front of him, Bob fired; and the dog's skull shattered.

Before he could even throw the bolt again, another dog hit him high on his legs; and Bob grabbed for his knife as he fell. With just enough time to twist around to meet his attacker face on, he sunk the blade deep into the dog's chest just as it latched on to his arm, teeth sinking deep into the muscle. Grabbing up the rifle and holding it tight, he smashed the butt of it into the jaw of the dog, causing it to fall away from him with a whimper.

Bob pulled the knife from the lifeless body and stuck it in the ground next to him. Then he quickly ejected and bolted another shell. His arm was mangled, but he was happy to see that the hand still worked as he drew his Magnum.

The next dog was already air-born over his legs; and the pistol landed the shot in the dog's gut; but as the dog went down, his bared teeth caught Bob's chest even as he was cocking the gun for the next round. And then silence settled upon the woods again.

Bob's head began to spin like an owl's as he watched for the insurgence to come again. The dog nearest him began to stir; and Bob swiftly grabbed the knife from the ground and slit its throat.

When he finally felt certain that the dogs were really gone, he looked at the blood that was spreading across his arm, chest and leg. Still holding the rifle, he waited a few more minutes to make sure the dogs weren't going to attack again; and then he began to scoot backwards to the tree he had planned to use as his escape. It was slow going as he tried to protect his wounds while trying to keep his weapons near him at the same time.

Once he reached the base of the tree, he loaded three more 8mm shells from his belt into the rifle, and laid the gun down next to his mangled leg. Then he grabbed the pistol, spun the chamber to the ejector slide, pushed out the empty and loaded another, spun the chamber again, and cocked it. Looking upwards, he knew he would have a hard time climbing the tree now; but since there was no more movement around him, maybe he was home free. Still, he couldn't really believe they were gone.

Laying the pistol next to his leg, he grabbed a bandana from his back pocket and began tearing it into strips. The heaviest bleeding was coming from his arm, so he wrapped it first. As he worked to tighten the cloth as much as he could, Bob thought about how far he was from the closest house, and figured it to be about two miles. He knew he had to stop the bleeding just to get back to civilization.

He took off his belt, wadded up the last piece of the bandana and stuffed it into the tear in his chest. He slipped the belt underneath his right arm and around the left side of his neck, with the buckle positioned over the wound; and with a grunt, he cinched it down as tight as his strength would allow. Then he turned his attention to his leg. Even though it wasn't bleeding as much as the other wounds, he could see that flesh was missing there, too. He struggled to take off his boots and then his socks, which he tied together to make a tourniquet; and he tied it around his thigh.

He was finally able to lean back and catch his breath for a few minutes; and he thought he should go after the wounded dog that had limped away. But he was so tired. He shut his eyes and let his chin fall forward on his aching chest.

When he finally felt as though he could get up and start moving again, he gathered the knife and guns and stood up. The ground tilted underneath him, and he figured he should have waited a little longer. It had been a long time since he'd felt this wobbly without anything to drink; and he wished he had a few swigs of his grandpa's whiskey now just to dull the pain. He had to conserve as much energy as he could just to get home; so he decided to leave the wounded dog for later and find a place to get some rest instead. That meant he had to be out of reach of the dogs. He looked back at the tree that he had intended to use for his escape and figured it was as good a place as any. It wouldn't be easy, but there wasn't much other choice that he could see.

He groaned as he slung the rifle up into a crook in the branches and then struggled to get himself up to the lowest limb. The pain was excruciating as he hauled himself up; and he could feel the bandages becoming soggier by the minute. But, finally, he had managed to settle himself on the lowest limb, propped the rifle against two limbs in front of him, and quickly began to fade away. He would be in a lot better shape with a few hours of sleep, and should then be ready for the trek back home. Assuming he didn't fall out of the tree in the meantime.

Suddenly, he awoke with a start, wincing in pain as instinct caused him to grab for the rifle. He listened intently for the sound that woke him, and then realized it had just been his own snoring. He shook his head and started to smile, but decided it hurt too much. He checked the wounds and was glad to see that the bleeding had slowed considerably; but the pain was proving to be difficult to deal with. He looked at his watch and saw that it was just past midnight. He'd been asleep for a little over two hours. Settling back into the niche of the branches again, he closed his eyes and focused on letting his body relax. Then he remembered the dream that had been playing out in his head just before he'd woke up.

...standing in a beautiful field of tall grass...the sun touching the horizon...a slight breeze across his face...a woman standing in the distance, looking at him...elegant and graceful, with eyes the color of crystal-blue pools of water...the purest love he'd ever felt...the most incredible love beyond all faith or deeds he'd ever experienced...horses running wildly toward him...

As he replayed it in his mind, Bob found himself feeling troubled. Where did this come from? Was it a sign of something to come? And if it was, was it something good or something bad? Or maybe it was just wishful thinking, depending on how you wanted to look at it. Regardless, he figured it didn't matter, since what was going to happen was just going to happen. He had learned long ago that his life wasn't his own. He was just along for the ride. And what a ride it was. A bitch of a wife and three innocent kids who were caught in the cross-fire.

Much to his own surprise, he felt disappointment, and then anger, rise to the surface as he thought of all the times Barb had broken her promises to be faithful and loving. And then there were the times she was just plain hateful, like when she had told him, just a couple of days ago, that she hoped the damn dogs ate him just so she wouldn't have to hear about all his problems. He had tried to convince himself at the time that she was doing nothing more than using words to hurt him again; but he knew in his heart that she really did mean it.

Trying to find some sort of solace, he told himself that she *had* become more agreeable lately when it came time for him to go on the hunts; but as he thought about it a little more, he decided there had to be an ulterior motive. She was never nice to anyone, especially him, unless there was something in it for herself.

The dream of the woman was fading now, just like all his dreams he'd ever had; but he didn't have time to think about it anymore. He still had to go after the wounded dog; then he had to get back to the ranch, where he knew his father was waiting; and most of all, he also needed more rest. Suddenly, the idea of his nice, comfortable bed was enough to spur him on to greater efforts.

"Screw the dog, and screw the tree," he said to himself as he slipped out of the tree.

Moving carefully and as quietly as possible, he listened for any movement around him; but all was quiet. The night was warm, not at all like last fall when snow had fallen early; and the cold, northerly wind had settled like a shroud. It had seemed like a long time before the sun had come back out to stay for more than a few minutes at a time; but then spring arrived a little earlier than usual; and summer seemed to have lasted longer.

Bob wasn't especially fond of the cold, dreary days. At forty-five, he had reached the age now where the biting wind seemed to always sink right down into his bones; and the cold bothered his aging joints. He liked to think he was tougher than that, but he couldn't deny the obvious. Age was definitely creeping in around the edges. At least in the warm weather he could pretend it wasn't.

As he trudged along, Bob knew he wasn't functioning at full speed. The pain in his body seemed to engulf even the parts of him that weren't damaged; and the blood loss had left him weak. Nonetheless, he enjoyed the walk through the woods and fields.

CHAPTER 3

It was about two in the morning when he finally got back to the ranch and stumbled into the house. He was surprised to find his father's head in the refrigerator, searching for something to appease his taste buds. As Bob headed straight for the bedroom, Neil pulled his head out, took one look at him, and bellered like a mad cow.

"Hey! Wait just a minute there. What in hell happened to you?"

Bob turned to see the stunned look on his father's face. Nothing ever seemed to shake up the man; so from the look on his face now, he figured he must look pretty bad.

Neil continued to look him over, mouth agape, until he could finally speak. "I thought this whole thing was some sort of joke. What the hell happened to you? For Christ's sake! You look like you've been half eaten alive!"

"There are three dead, and one wounded."

"To hell you say! Somebody else in their wrong mind is going to take care of the problem now!"

The old man's fervor began to unnerve Bob, but he wasn't going to back down now.

"And just who do you have in mind, Dad?"

Without a word, Neil began looking closer at the wounds. After a moment, he said, "Take your shirt and pants off, and I'll get the alcohol."

"Geez, Dad! Do you have to use alcohol? Can't you use hydrogen peroxide or something? Alcohol just hurts so damn bad!" Bob replied, feeling and sounding like he was six years old again.

"No, those wounds need alcohol. And soap and hot water. Then we'll see if you need to go to the hospital."

Conceding to his father's demands, Bob removed the make-shift bandages and his clothes, and was sitting in only his underwear when Neil walked back in. Without further ado, the gruff old man began silently cleaning the wound on Bob's arm. When he moved to his chest, he finally spoke.

"What in the hell were you thinking, Bob? I thought your grandfather taught you better than to let anything get this close. Didn't you learn anything from him at all?"

Bob looked at him in amazement, but knew it was his father's fear, rather than his anger, that was responsible for the tongue-lashing.

Quietly, Bob said, "He's smart, Dad, and there were nine of them, and it was pitch black in the woods."

"Of course it was dark! You were out there in the middle of the damned night! And I'm not buying that cockamamie story that those dogs are good enough to out-smart a person. Shit, Bob!"

"Then explain something to me. You know I'm good out there; so *you* tell *me* what went wrong. And while you're telling me all about it, would you mind easing up a bit there?"

Bob squirmed further down in the chair as alcohol splashed across his chest; and he yelped before he could stop himself. He didn't want his father to think he was weak, but the pain had finally reached a level that he couldn't tolerate. As Neil began to clean

46

the leg wound, Bob began to slide further down in the chair until he had squirmed his way out into the floor.

As he tried to steady himself, he looked at his dad with weary eyes and said, "I don't think I can stand any more of your doctoring now, Dad; so if I pass out before you're done, will you drag me into the bed, where I started to go in the first place?"

Neil started to open his mouth with a reply but saw that his son truly was fading away. With tears threatening to trickle down his cheeks, Neil whispered, "I'll take care of you, my boy. I promise, I'll always watch over you."

The old man's heart broke; and as he sat down and cradled his son's head in his arms, he resolved that someone, or something, was going to pay hell for this.

With as much tenderness as he could show while struggling with Bob's limp body, Neil's strong arms finally managed to pick Bob up off the floor and drag him into bed. Neil was a sturdy man, especially for his age; and the Irish blood that ran through his veins fueled him as much now as it had when he'd first come to America at the age of five. But while Bob wasn't quite as tall as his father, he was just as stocky; and getting him into bed would have been a struggle for anyone.

Once Neil had his son on the bed, he spread the blankets over him and prayed that he'd be all right. He pulled up a chair and settled down next to the bed, wishing the boy's mother was here now. She always seemed to know just what to do and say in any crisis.

He thought of Zelma often, but tried not to dwell on her passing. And he knew Bob longed for her, too. Much to his dismay, the tears began to flow and sobs burst from him, first out of fear for his son, and secondly from his own grief. He had never cried like this when his wife had died, or even after; but now it was as though the floodgates had opened; and he had no idea of how to close them.

When he was finally able to turn his attention back to the tasks at hand, the physician took over. Looking at the wounds a little closer now, he realized the gashes needed more than just a cleaning; but he knew Bob hated hospitals as much as he did; so he began by laying the skin back in place, and then went in search of the smallest curved needle he had, and the catgut that he had on hand for sewing up the cattle. When he had sterilized everything, he began to stitch up the places where the wounds were gaping. It was almost four o'clock in the morning by the time he had finished and stepped back to admire his handiwork. It wasn't a bad job, if he had to say so himself. He was amazed at how much easier it had been to sew up a passed-out human than it ever had been to sew up a cow; and he thought he should file that observation away for future reference.

Neil quietly cleaned up the mess and checked to make sure none of the wounds were bleeding again; and then he laid his blanket back over his boy to keep him warm. As he settled back into his chair, Neil suddenly realized how tired he was; but then it occurred to him that maybe he should call Barb to let her know what had happened. It only took him a few seconds after that thought registered to decide against it.

Neil knew she didn't give two shits about Bob; and he, personally, couldn't stand the woman. She had

48

never been worth the air she breathed; and since Zelma had passed on, he always felt at a loss when it came to approaching the subject with Bob. A boy's mother was better at knowing what to do and say when it came to things like this. All he could do was watch the loneliness and depression settle in deeper.

Zelma had tried to talk to Neil about their suspicions regarding Barb; but he had always felt uncomfortable talking about it, and had brushed her off by saying that he didn't want to hear it; and it wasn't their business anyway. But now he knew it was his business, because Bob was his son; and he was sick of watching him be Barb's punching bag.

He sighed heavily. Zelma had been right all along. Then, hoping she had forgiven him for being so stubborn all those years and was kind enough to look down on him, he made a silent promise to her and to himself that, when the time was right, he would talk to their boy about the situation. He only hoped that when it was all said and done, he wouldn't have alienated this son, too.

A feeling of comfort swept over Neil as the commitment found its way into his heart; and then he began to wonder what else he could do to make things better for Bob. The question hadn't even been completely formed in his mind before the answer was there. He had to ease up on his expectations, and the work load he heaped on him. The man worked hard in the office and just as hard at the ranch, in addition to making as much time as he could for his boys.

As Neil leaned his head back and closed his eyes, he laid his hand on Bob's arm and whispered, "You're a good man."

Sunlight was streaming through the window when Bob began to wake up; and he knew he was going to be late to work. But when he started to sit up, he realized quickly it wasn't a usual morning; and he lay back on the bed with a groan. He felt like he'd been in one hell of a fight the night before and lost. As he tried to get out of bed again, he realized the only way he was going to succeed was to roll over on his good side, which ever side that was, and fall out on the floor.

When he finally managed to get on his feet, he made his way to the opened bedroom door, and saw his father sitting at the kitchen table.

"I thought you were never going to get up."

"Yeah, me, too. Now that I'm up, though, I'm thinking I should've stayed where I was. I don't seem to be moving so well."

"It looks to me like you ought to be thankful that you're moving at all. But while you're up, you should call Barb to let her know where you are."

"I guess. But I need a cup of coffee more than I need to talk to her right now."

Neil pointed to the half-full pot; and Bob grabbed a cup off the drain board and filled it to the brim. He kept waiting for the usual criticism or orders to begin; but instead, Neil asked, "What are you going to do today?"

The question caught Bob by surprise, and it took him a few seconds to think of an answer. As he slowly sat down in the kitchen chair across the table from his father, he said, "I'm not really sure yet, but I imagine it will be something with Three Toes."

"What the hell does that mean?" Neil asked,

and Bob could tell the answer was not to his father's liking.

"I don't know. I guess I'll plan on getting back on his trail again soon. But it's possible he knows where we live now."

"How the hell did that happen?"

"He's smart, Dad."

"Well, hell. Sounds like I better keep an extra eye on the livestock."

"That's not a bad idea. Maybe even keep them locked up close to the house for the next few days."

As Neil rose from the kitchen table to rinse his own coffee cup, he said, "I've got just a little more fence to fix up on the north place; so why don't you call Barb, and then go back to bed and rest for awhile?" He grabbed his hat and gloves and was out the door without another word, leaving Bob stunned. Neil had never suggested spending any daylight hours in bed.

The old man brewed as he strode across the yard toward the barn. He had hoped to hear something other than he was going back out hunting again. He was worried that Bob didn't have a good enough plan to even stay alive out there with those dogs. Halfway to the barn, he turned on his heels and walked back to the house to find him on the phone with Barb.

Bob had already explained the night before to her when Neil walked back in; and he sat back down to wait until the conversation had ended. Bob stood silently while Barb's stinging voice leaked out of the phone and over to Neil. It was always that way with them – always Barb ranting while Bob listened.

It didn't take long for Bob to hang up the phone

51

and turn back toward his father. Before he could say anything, Neil spoke up.

"This is not good, Bob, this crap about you just going back out to track tomorrow. The more I thought about what you said last night about knowing what you're doing out there and realizing how good you are, it's just not adding up at all. I saw what you looked like last night, remember? So tell me now. What are you going to do?"

His steel-blue eyes cut through Bob much like Barb's words had just cut to the quick; and his pain seemed to dig in deeper. The Slawson boy's face flashed through his mind along with the snarling dogs; and it was suddenly all too much. He sat with a thud as the ever-increasing sense of hopelessness engulfed him.

Neil immediately knew he had gone too far – just what he'd decided last night that he wasn't going to do. Scooting his chair around closer to him, he took his son's hand in his own and watched as the tears began to run down Bob's face.

"I'm sorry, son. Dealing with her, and then me blowing back in here with more shit to throw at you, it's too much to have to think about right now."

Bob had never before heard an apology from his father; and he didn't know whether to be thankful or fearful. This just wasn't normal.

Neil continued. "I know your marriage sucks; and I think what I've been expecting from you has just made things worse. You put your heart into all your patients and your boys; and now there's the Slawson boy, and a bunch of dogs after you, too. I think maybe you're spread a little thin. What do you think?"

Bob hesitantly nodded his head in agreement.

Neil continued. "We don't talk much about things, but I think it's time."

The old man took a deep breath as he tried to figure out how he wanted to approach the conversation he was about to have. Bob just sat, head hanging, trying to get his emotions in check for whatever was coming next.

"It's obvious to me you've got too much on your plate, and there isn't much I can do about some of it. But what I can do is get rid of some of the stress you've had out here. I'll hire someone to take care of the work you do here at the ranch for a while and see how it goes. If it works out okay, we'll keep 'em on."

Bob knew he could count on whatever his dad said, come hell or high water; but the shock of hearing this from him was staggering.

"Now, for the next thing I've got to say," Neil said as he took a deeper breath, "What's happened to you over these past few years? The only time I ever see a smile on your face is when there's something to do in the woods. You don't play your guitar, and I never hear you sing anymore. What's happened, Bob?"

Bob didn't know what to say, and didn't have the energy to say it even if he had known.

"In fact, I've started to think the only reason you like going to the woods is just to get away from everybody. Me included. And that's not good. The last thing I want is for you to need to get away from me. So maybe getting this extra help might solve that problem. Am I right?"

Bob nodded in agreement, still waiting for the bomb to go off.

"Okay, now for the tough part. I know you're not going to want to hear this, but it's time to face some real ugly facts, Bob. That woman you're married to is taking more bites out of you than those dogs ever could. At least the wounds from the dogs will heal; but those from that wife of yours aren't going to unless you do something about it before it's too late. Now, I'm not saying I know what it is you should do; but by God, you'd better do something. What do you think?"

Bob raised his head and looked at his father as he tried to comprehend what he was hearing. He'd always known his dad had never liked Barb much; but now it sounded like he thought she should be cut off at the knees. In essence, Bob thought what he was suggesting was a signature on divorce papers, plain and simple. But this wasn't like Neil. They were strict Catholics, and divorce was never an option. No excuses, no exceptions. Bob wondered if he was really hearing things right, or if the trauma from the night before was still taking its toll on him.

"Well?" His father asked, forcing Bob to reply.

"I don't know, Dad. Things just seem to be out of control. I've always hoped things would eventually settle down with her, but I just don't know anymore."

"Well, it's time you stopped hoping and started making something good happen in your life and your kids' lives for a change."

Bob certainly didn't feel like he needed to be reminded of his responsibilities; but he understood what his dad was saying. Barb had spent her life humiliating him and the boys; and no one should have to live under such tyranny. But at the same time, he was reluctant to break up the family unit, regardless of how sick it might be.

Neil spoke again, this time softer. "I know I don't say this to you very often, Bob; but I want you to know that I love you. And I'm worried about you."

Bob saw the sincerity in the old man's eyes; and while the pain from his wounds didn't allow him much movement, he managed to gingerly put his arms around him. How could he ever express how much those words meant to him?

"Thanks, Dad," he choked out. "If you're sure you don't need me for anything for a while, I think I'll go lie down for a little longer before I have to head back home. Barb just informed me we've got some dinner to go to tonight; and I think I could use as much rest as I can get before then."

Neil's gruffness immediately returned. "Good Lord, Bob. The very last thing you need to be doing is going to some damn dinner tonight. What's wrong with you?"

Bob met his dad's fervor with his own.

"Damn it, Dad; I can't fix all the shit today! I'm lucky I can move, let alone justify Barb's stupid shit right now. I appreciate everything you said, but I don't really feel up to dealing with the mess today."

"You've been justifying and excusing her shit ever since your first boy was born, Bob! I'm just telling you that it's time now for you to do something about it!"

Bob looked at him with pleading eyes, and Neil knew he had crossed the line again.

"You're right," Neil said, throwing his hands up in the air as a sign of defeat. "I'm sorry. I guess I'm going to have to get some practice at not heaping my own shit on top of hers. But you're right; now isn't the time. Go ahead, get some more sleep. I'll wake you up when I get back in from fixing the fence. Shouldn't take me more than a couple of hours; and maybe you'll feel a little better by then."

His father stood and hugged him, and then headed back to the door.

"Thanks, Dad," Bob said, and Neil turned back toward him and smiled.

Bob moved slowly to the bed, lay down and shut his eyes. What seemed like only seconds later, his father was shaking him awake.

"It's two o'clock, Bob. I let you sleep as long as I thought I could."

Bob shook the cobwebs out of his head and began moving as fast as he could. If he didn't get home with time to spare, Barb would never let him hear the end of it.

The drive back to the city gave Bob ample time to think back over the conversation with his dad; and he knew he was right. Moving through life on a good day with all odds in his favor was challenging enough; but without any control, or at least the feeling of some control, he felt helpless, depressed and angry. His dad and Barb had the privilege of controlling their lives; but he had never felt that privilege was extended to him. In fact, now that he thought about it, it was those same people who caused him to always believe that the less control he tried to have, the more he'd get out of it in the end.

And there was his grandfather, too, who had always taught him that there was a predestined plan for everyone, that it was best left to the One who

56

understood what was really going on instead of someone who couldn't see the whole picture, that the person wishing for true happiness must first understand the concept. Bob figured he'd really missed the mark since true happiness had always seemed to elude him so completely thus far. Hell, it had never even been close, and it seemed to just keep getting farther away.

He remembered his own mother often saying, "It's not for us to question why; it's just for us to do and die." She must have known the same thing Grandpa knew. So what was up with his dad telling him to take control now?

The drive ended without any conclusions coming to mind, at least none that felt right to him. But then maybe it was just the pain he felt every time he moved that kept him from being able to reason it all out. He was having enough trouble just staying focused on driving, much less coming up with the answers for all his life's problems.

As Bob walked into the house, he found Barb waiting for him, alternately glaring at him and then looking at her watch.

"You idiot! Where the hell have you been? I told you about these plans hours ago; and now here you are, wandering in with barely time to get cleaned up, and acting like nothing's wrong."

The last thing Bob felt like doing right now was tangling with her; and he wished his dad was there to take control. Instead, he calmly replied, "It's only three, and the dinner isn't until six. It won't take more than half an hour for me to get ready to go. You don't need to worry about anything. We're going to have a nice evening with friends. Okay?"

"Half an hour? Look at you! More like half a day to clean up that mess!"

As she stormed out of the room, Bob started making his way upstairs. He dreaded standing under the water from the shower; but he couldn't wait to get his filthy clothes off. He'd only gotten as far as getting his shirt off when the boys bounded into the house; and, having seen his truck outside, headed straight toward his room. As soon as they were in sight of him, they all three stopped where they were and stared at him, shocked at the sight of the bandages. David, the youngest, looked as though he would burst into tears at any second.

Bob sat down on the edge of the bed and motioned for them to come to him. David reached him first and began to crawl up on his lap. Bob quickly stopped him and asked him to sit next to him. In the meantime, the other two boys had sat down on the floor; and immediately, the questions began. Bob patiently told them what had happened, but gave them the Cliff-Notes version so as not to invoke Barb's wrath on him any further.

When he had finished the story, Matt asked, "So, did you kill them all?"

"No. I didn't get all of them. I just got three, and I think there are six left. But the most important one that I've got to get is Three Toes. He's the leader of the whole bunch."

David's eyes were as big as quarters as he asked, "How do you know his name is Three Toes?"

Bob laughed. "I just named him that, David. Because he has only three toes on one of his paws."

"So why don't you call me Five Toes then?" the little boy asked as he started to giggle.

Matt piped up. "That's stupid!"

"Hey! That's not nice, Matt. Don't call your brother names. You wouldn't like it if he did that to you," Bob interjected.

"But he *does* do that to me!"

Bob couldn't stand to see the boys argue, and tried to do anything he could to teach them differently.

"Do you want to hear the rest of the story, or do you want to argue and then go to your room?"

The boys hushed and turned their attention back to him.

"When I first started tracking this pack, I noticed that the leader of the bunch was also the biggest one of all. And the leader is called the alpha dog."

Matt piped up again. "And he's the leader, because he's the biggest and the meanest, right Dad?"

Bob immediately saw where this was headed in Matt's mind.

"Not really, Matt. Usually the leader is the smartest one. And Three Toes is definitely the smartest."

Christopher said, "Dad! We can go with you next time and help you. You'll have to shoot 'em, cause we're too little; but we can help you find 'em!"

The other two boys nodded in enthusiastic agreement, and Bob grinned at them. He loved his boys so much and was so proud of them.

"Hey, take a look at what those dogs did to me; and if they can do that to me, what do you think they could do to one of you? And you know I can't let anything happen to you guys. Then who'd be my best buddies?"

Christopher suddenly looked sad. "Dad, do you really have to go out there again?"

"Now what would you think of your old dad if he turned tail and ran? I have to be brave, just like you boys are brave. That's what we're supposed to do – fix the things that are wrong in the world, at least those things that we *can* fix. And besides, I'm going to be more careful than ever from now on."

Just then, Barb walked in with her usual nasty expression and ordered the boys out of the room. They reluctantly got up and left, obviously unhappy at having their men time interrupted.

Bob saw his wife looking at the bandages; but even then, there was no comment and no change of attitude from her. He wondered if she still thought he was a mouse; and, suddenly, he was surprised to realize that he didn't even care any more.

As he showered, Bob thought back to the boys and the conversation they'd just had. He felt like a hypocrite by telling them they must fix the things that were wrong in the world, when he wasn't even fixing the things that were wrong in his own house. So he had to question whether he really meant what he'd told them or not. The more he thought about it, the more he knew he meant it. Maybe he was more like his dad than he'd thought. After all, wasn't that what he was saying, too? To fix the things that were wrong?

After his shower, Bob cleaned the wounds again and got dressed in record time. He still had a lot of pain; so he grabbed the aspirin bottle and swallowed four of them dry. He had to be socially correct tonight;

and he didn't think he'd be up to it if he wasn't even able to talk without wincing.

He was ready to go an hour and a half early, and decided he should call Dr. Klyne to verify the time. The phone was answered on the second ring by a woman.

"Hello?"

"Hi! This is Dr. Bob. And you are...?"

"Hi, Bob! This is Grace."

He detected a hint of a southern drawl and said, "Hello, Grace! I must say, you've got a beautiful voice."

"Thank you," Grace added with a laugh.

"Actually, I just called to make sure what time we're supposed to be there, and ask if there was anything you needed us to bring."

"Well, dinner should be ready by six-thirty; and if you want to, you could bring a bottle of wine."

Bob loved listening to her voice, and didn't want to end the conversation this quickly.

"Okay. So what are we having for dinner? You know, so I can bring the right wine."

"Oh, boy! Are you a connoisseur of wine or something?"

"No, I'm technically a beer drinker, but that makes me do stupid things. So we'd better stick with the wine."

"Well, I don't know. I could use the entertainment."

Bob could hear the grin in her voice and laughed. "Maybe that should wait until we get to know each other a little better. How about I bring some red wine? It goes with about anything. Does that sound okay to you?"

"How about a Chardonnay? Sutter Home?"

"Oh, so *you* are the connoisseur!"

Grace burst into laughter and said, "Not hardly. It's just the only name I can think of right now; and I thought I'd impress you with all my knowledge."

Bob laughed with her then said, "Okay. I'm impressed. We'll see you at six-ish or so."

"Sounds good. See you soon."

They hung up, and Bob found himself feeling a little better about the dinner. Actually, he surprisingly just felt a lot better, period. He hadn't taken the aspirin more than five minutes ago; so he didn't think it would have taken effect yet. So what did he take?

Going back to the medicine cabinet, he pulled out the bottle that he'd taken the pills from. Pouring them out in his hand, he examined each one; and every one of them was marked as aspirin. So what was going on with this sudden burst of energy and feeling of well-being? It must have been the shower. Just getting that grime off was enough to make anybody feel better. Or maybe it was just talking with a pleasant person that did it. What a concept.

When it was time to leave, Barb had to do her last minute primping, which put them running late as usual. Bob had gone to the wine cellar, where he kept some nice vintages, and pulled out a California Chardonnay and then grabbed a bottle of Sutter Home. He turned to go back upstairs, but then turned back and pulled a six-pack of beer from the refrigerator.

Barb still wasn't quite ready, although the sitter had already been there for some time. Bob wanted to mimic her previous behavior of glaring at her while looking at his watch; but a fight right now was the last thing he wanted to have to deal with. Instead, he busied himself by cleaning the trash out of the Riviera, the car Barb had just had a fit to have, because it looked like a 'doctor's car'; and he noticed David's car seat was missing, even though he wasn't big enough to be riding without it. She's probably on the prowl, he thought.

As soon as they were finally on their way across town, Barb began her usual prompting; telling him what he should and shouldn't talk about. Most importantly, he was absolutely not to mention anything about the stupid dogs, or the ranch. Basically, he was just to keep his mouth shut all evening. His purpose beyond providing her with money was just to be her chauffer, take her coat and all the while be inconspicuous. He was always in constant training.

CHAPTER 4

They arrived at a beautiful house in Brookside, an old, once-elite part of Kansas City that had aged without kindness until recently, when new blood had begun to restore it to its former elegance.

Klyne's house was a two-story federal style with tall, white columns and a side portico. An old-style, but obviously new, yard lamp stood in the center of the well-manicured lawn. Rows of geraniums lined each side of the walkway from the street to the steps, and giant pots filled with overflowing ferns and petunias sat on each side of the front door.

Bob gently dropped the brass knocker a couple of times, and they quickly heard footsteps approaching. But when the door opened, he suddenly found himself unable to speak. A wave of dizziness hit him, and he leaned against the door frame. He was aware of Barb looking at him and waiting for him to make a move; but he was unable to move anything at all. In the deepest reaches of his brain, he finally heard Barb talking as she pushed him inside. He struggled for composure.

When he finally got his bearings back, he reached his hand out in greeting. "Hi! I'm Bob." He could say nothing more.

"Hi, again, Bob! I'm Grace."

It was the woman from his dream. The very same one. Her dark hair and blue eyes were exactly the same. It was her. He knew it. Then he realized he was staring at her. He quickly glanced down at his feet, but a split second too late. The toe of his shoe caught on

65

the edge of a beautiful oriental rug that spanned the foyer. He flailed as he tried to keep himself upright; and at the same time, he could hear Barb hissing at him. He thought she was saying something about an idiot; but he wasn't listening. His world had just been moved.

He was thankful that he hadn't dropped anything, and he handed a bottle of wine to Grace. She smiled and thanked him, and then headed toward the kitchen with Bob and Barb following.

He could see into the living room as he turned to go. It was long and narrow and looked cozy and elegant. Beautiful artwork adorned the dark, rose-colored walls. Yards of crisp, white fabric draped over the many windows that looked out onto the portico and the small side yard.

He followed Grace and Barb through the family room, which was also quite cozy, though smaller than the living room. And then they were in the kitchen.

The walls were a soft, buttery yellow with dark, hardwood floors. The cabinetry was dark oak with white countertops; and the dining set, also in oak, looked as though it had come from a very-expensive antique store. Windows covered the walls in here, too, and Bob stopped to stare out at the back yard.

A small child's pool sat in the shade of an ancient tree, where a small scotch terrier played. Bob felt as though time stood still.

"Would you like for me to put the beer in the fridge, or would you like to just keep holding it?" Grace asked.

Bob felt like the idiot Barb had been talking about as he handed her the beer, and then the other bottle of wine.

"Sorry. I wasn't thinking, I guess," he said with a sheepish grin.

Grace turned and pointed to a door and said, "Gerald's in the basement loading gun shells, or something. You can go on down if you want. But be careful. He tried to blow up the house yesterday."

Although she had directed her words to Bob, it was Barb who took off toward the door like a bat out of hell. Her obvious eagerness was embarrassing for Bob, and even Grace seemed a little taken aback. But now that he was alone with this beautiful creature, he again found that he couldn't find the breath to speak.

Grace had been in the middle of setting the table when they had arrived; and now she returned to finish the job. He opened his mouth to offer help; but all that came out was unintelligible words.

Grace just looked at him for a moment, and then smiled and said, "I've never heard such an artful language before. What sort of tongue is that?"

After a very awkward pause, he finally managed to say, "It's the sort of tongue that has gotten all twisted up. Sorry. What I meant to say was that I can help with what you're doing, or whatever you need, or...something."

"Thank you, but I'm fine. Just bringing the wine was enough."

"I brought the Sutter Home you wanted," he said, feeling more stupid with each passing minute. "But I also grabbed the other."

"Yes, I noticed. Thank you for the Sutter Home. And the other."

She continued to stand and smile at him as

though he was the best entertainment she'd had for some time.

"I brought some beer, too…for me…or you…or anybody else who might want some. So, what are we having for dinner anyway?"

As she walked over to the stove, Grace said, "Since I didn't know we were having dinner guests until just this afternoon, we're just having plain old spaghetti with garlic bread. It's not much, but it was the best I could do on such short notice."

It was obvious by the change in her tone of voice and the look on her face that she wasn't very happy about the situation; and Bob felt awkward, and sorry for her.

"Well, then, I guess I picked out a decent wine. And, if it makes you feel any better, I probably found out about it around the same time you did."

As she turned back toward him, a towel dropped from her hand; and he immediately rushed to pick it up. He realized too late that he should have moved a little slower; and Grace caught a glimpse of the grimace that flashed across his face.

"You okay? What's wrong?"

Bob put his hand over his chest and replied, "I'm fine, just a little sore from some work I've been doing."

"Yeah? What kind of work?"

"I was fighting evil-doers," he said, trying to sound flippant so she wouldn't press the issue.

"Sure you were. So really, what kind of work?"

"It's true! I was hunting down a bunch of thugs that killed a boy, a neighbor of mine. He was only eight years old. It was really sad. I did manage to kill three of them, but only after they had torn me up first."

Grace's thoughts of him started to change. Maybe he wasn't the goofball she'd thought he was.

"Well, Dr. Bob, for a person who has trouble walking through a door and sometimes speaks in twisted tongues, you seem quite talented after all. Tell me more."

"Ah, it's a long story, and pretty boring, too."

"Try me," she said as she returned to stirring the pot of spaghetti on the stove.

She felt as though something didn't quite fit here. He seemed kind and polite enough, certainly not threatening. But at the same time, he nonchalantly mentioned killing three people. Either he was extremely diverse, or he was a liar.

"Well, I have this ranch...actually, my dad owns this ranch. And there's been a bunch of dogs that have been attacking the neighbors' livestock. I saw them a week or so back, but didn't think much of it, until I saw the boy. His name was...is...Sammy."

Grace laid the spoon down and leaned against the counter as she crossed her arms in front of her.

"You were killing dogs? Not people?"

"Uh, yeah. I thought I was clear about that."

"No, you weren't. But now I'm catching on."

"Crap, if you thought I was out there killing people, I'm surprised you even let me in your house," Bob said in shock.

"I probably wouldn't have if I'd thought that before you were already in the house; but I didn't know until I'd already let you in."

Bob suddenly noticed the spaghetti boiling away, big plops jumping out of the pan and landing on the stove. He knew Grace wasn't aware of it; but he was hungry; and if it was going to be worth eating, something had to be done right away. Grabbing some potholders that were hanging on the wall next to the stove, he quickly pulled the pan off the burner and moved it to the sink.

"Strainer?" he asked.

Grace pulled it out of the cabinet and handed it to him, and then sat down at the table. She was relieved that he'd taken over, and watched as he poured the noodles into the drainer and then began running cold water over them. She'd never seen anybody do that. She wondered if he was some kind of chef as well as a chiropractor, a dog hunter and killer, and a connoisseur of fine wines.

With his story finally told and the noodles just beginning to boil, Bob followed his nose to the oven and opened the door. Meatballs of all shapes and sizes were perched on a cookie sheet; and they were beginning to crust over. All but charred, he pulled them out and sat them on top of the stove.

Not even acknowledging the pathetic meatballs, Grace said, "I want to see the wounds."

"There's nothing to see. They're all bandaged up."

"Let me see the bandages then."

"Why, you don't believe me?"

"No. I believe you. I just want to see."

Thinking she was a bit forward, he hesitated, but finally rolled up the left sleeve of his shirt.

"Let me see the others, too."

Very uncomfortable now, he unbuttoned the top two buttons of his shirt so she could see the top half of

70

the dressing.

"And your leg?"

Bob was stunned. This woman was down-right nuts.

"Grace, I can't pull my pants down and show you!"

"Yes, you can. I want to see it."

"No. I'm not going to do that. If Gerald and Barb walked in while I was doing that, what do you think they'd think?"

Grace laughed as she turned her attention to the strange-looking meatballs.

"Okay, okay. Forget it. I just wanted to…oh, never mind."

Bob pushed her back toward the kitchen chair and continued to prepare the dinner; and Grace was grateful for the help. She hated cooking, had never been good at it; but she was always under constant scrutiny from Gerald every time she tried to fix anything. But that was just the way he was. An asshole.

She had married him, because she loved him; or at least she'd loved the man she thought he was. His charade didn't last much past a week after their marriage; and then his real personality began to show itself. The last five years with him had been spent being humiliated and rejected, and constantly told what a worthless and stupid person she was. But with this being her second marriage, she felt like she had no right to end it, too. If she was so dumb that she couldn't get it right the second time around, she felt like she deserved what she got.

Focusing her attention back on Bob, she said,

"Are you sure you're okay to do all that, I mean, with all you've been through? I can finish, and you should probably be the one sitting down over here."

"I've never felt better," Bob said, smiling at her.

"I just feel guilty having you over for dinner and then you ending up fixing it yourself."

Bob stopped fussing over the food, took a moment to think, then looked at her thoughtfully and said, "Do you believe in divine intervention?"

Grace's eyebrows raised as her shoulders followed suit.

He said quietly, "I do. Now."

She wasn't sure she understood what he was getting at, but decided to let it go. When everything was ready, Grace opened the basement door and called out to Barb and Gerald. She had been so caught up in the conversation with Bob that now she almost wished the goons in the basement would just stay there where they belonged.

Although she'd never met Barb before, and still hadn't really, Grace felt as though she'd gotten a pretty good glimpse of her personality the second she and Bob had walked into the house; and she didn't feel as though there was going to be a friendship developing between them anytime soon. The woman just looked hateful, with snaky, little eyes that sat too far on each side of her face; bucked teeth in a mouth that was as wide as her head; and fat lips that never seemed to stop moving.

"So, tell me about you and your life," Bob said as he sat down at the table across from her.

It was her turn to stammer now. She had never met anyone before who seemed interested in her lackluster life, and for good reason. She'd never done much to talk about.

"There's not really much to tell. I have a beautiful little girl who is at her dad's right now, I have a job, and I have this," she said, swinging her arm outward.

"Did you and Gerald redo this house? It looks really nice."

"Are you kidding? *I* did the house. Everything from repairing and painting walls, to wallpapering, to making the drapes. Gerald did nothing."

Bob was surprised; and he looked out toward the beautiful lawn to ask about it, too.

"Yes, I did that, too. I weeded, fertilized, mowed, planted the flowers, the whole thing. Gerald doesn't care what kind of mess he lives in."

Bob felt the conversation heading somewhere he didn't want to go; so he changed the subject.

"Tell me about your daughter."

"She's perfect. She's beautiful, and smart, and funny. Her name is Melody; she's six years old, but I swear she's an old soul. And she's the greatest joy of my life."

Grace's eyes lit up as she talked about her baby; and Bob loved seeing the pride and the adoration she had for her. He had never seen that look on Barb's face for any of their boys.

Bob laughed at the funny stories she told, and she laughed at him for laughing at her. There was something very comforting that they both felt in the other's company; and their conversation moved fast, as though they had to make the best of it while it lasted.

When she noticed that Bob's wine glass was

low, Grace got up to refill it; and as she returned to the table, she saw that he had slipped off his shoes and was resting his socked feet against the table leg.

"Do your feet hurt?"

"No," Bob replied. "Why?"

"Just wondering."

Bob saw her notice his shoes under the table and said, "Oh, I noticed you were barefooted; and personally, I don't like shoes that much; so I just thought…Do you mind?"

"Not at all. Sometimes I think it would be easier for me to be in jail than to wear shoes."

Bob had noticed the dress that she wore, a white; shapeless; cotton dress that ended just above her ankles, and her complexion was light, almost to the point of being pale. Her black hair had been gathered at the back of her head with a clip. She was beautiful, he thought.

Grace noticed him looking at her and felt her cheeks begin to burn. She turned back toward the kitchen cabinets and began to clean them just to escape his gaze. She knew she looked like a real hillbilly housewife, just like Gerald liked. But she hated the look; and she wasn't at all comfortable with the scrutiny she was getting from Bob.

"So, how much spaghetti would you like?" he asked as he picked up their plates and began to ladle up the noodles.

"Shouldn't we wait for the others?" Grace asked.

"Nah. They were told. So, how much?"

"A tiny bit. And no meatballs. They look a little hard to chew; and I had some oral surgery done just a

74

couple of days ago."

"I noticed your teeth earlier. They look really nice. Very white, perfect."

"Well, they're real, if that's what you're about to ask," Grace quickly interjected.

Now it was Bob's turn to blush. "No. I assumed they were real. But they looked so nice; and I didn't know whether I should say anything before about them; so when you mentioned the surgery, I thought I'd just say it then."

"Okay," Grace said with a laugh.

Bob dished them both up a plate full of food, and added a piece of garlic bread before sitting back down. Grace sat with her hands in her lap, obviously reluctant to start eating.

"Don't worry about them. I'll take care of it."

Hesitantly, she began to eat; and they picked back up on their conversation and laughed as though they had known each other all their lives.

They had just finished their last bites when Gerald and Barb finally came up from the basement. Bob stood up and extended his hand.

"Hi, Gerald! Nice to finally meet you."

"Same here," Gerald said.

As soon as Gerald saw that they had already eaten, he turned to Grace with a reprimand. "What is this? Couldn't you even wait for us to get here?"

Before she could reply, Bob looked at Gerald and poignantly said, "Hot food waits for no one. Dinner was ready when she called about twenty minutes ago; and spaghetti isn't something you can keep warm."

His words seemed to take Gerald by surprise;

and Bob suspected the guy wasn't accustomed to hearing anyone speak up to him. He also figured Barb was about to blow her stack, too; but he was determined not to even give her the satisfaction of looking in her direction.

Grace quietly got up to serve the two of them; but Bob stepped over and gently took the plates from her hands. He seethed as he began dishing the cold food on their plates. Gerald talked to Grace as though she was his lowly servant; and he wished Grace would just rear up and belt him one. Of course, he hadn't been much better with Barb. He waited for a verbal attack from Barb or Gerald; but instead, there was only an eerie silence that had settled over the table.

As he sat their plates in front of them, Bob said, "So, Gerald, have you shot anything lately?"

"Just a little here and there. Mostly at the shooting range, though."

"You may already know this; but if you pack powder too tightly, it has a tendency to blow up in your face."

Bob could see Grace struggle to suppress a smile as she got up to remove Bob's plate along with her own. He moved back to the kitchen and began to wash dishes. Silence settled over the table again, but was cut short when Gerald spoke from one side of his mouth while chewing on the other.

"This is actually edible this time, Grace. Even cold, it's better than most of your meals."

She whirled to face him, ready to deliver a counter-attack; and even though Bob would have loved seeing her tear him up, he thought it would be better for her if he responded on her behalf.

"I thought it was great. Some of the best spaghetti I've ever had," he said.

Grace smiled at him as she slipped more dirty dishes into the sink. Tension filled the air, but Bob was not about to relieve it. In fact, he had meant to create even more; but Gerald had obviously decided not to push things with him. He just hoped Grace didn't end up getting the brunt of it after they had left.

Barb was the one to break the silence this time.

"So, what are you going to hunt?" she asked Gerald.

"I was thinking Bob might let me hunt the dogs with him."

Bob heard the comment, but didn't reply. Barb must have told Gerald about the dogs; and their attempt at a conversation sounded rehearsed. And besides that, he didn't want to talk to either of them if he didn't really have to. He wasn't liking Gerald any, more than he did Barb. But most of all, he no more wanted another person with him on his hunts than he wanted a poke in the eye with a sharp stick.

After another minute of Bob not buying into their manipulation, Gerald finally said, "So what do you think, Bob? I could make it worth your while if you'd let me go hunting with you."

"And just how could you make it worth my while?"

"I could give Barb her sessions for free in exchange for the hunts. I've always wanted to do something like that, hunt something that could hunt me back."

Bob thought for a few moments and then said, "That seems like a pretty staggering payment for a

77

hunt; but if you want to do that, it's okay with me. You're on."

Grace was surprised to hear Bob agree to Gerald's request, and wondered which of them would end up coming home and which would end up dead. This just didn't sound like a good plan to her; but then, what did she know?

Bob and Grace stayed in the kitchen and finished cleaning up while the other two moved into the family room. Grace's mood lightened, and before long, their conversation had them both laughing again, something neither of them had done in a long time.

Suddenly, Barb yelled into the kitchen.

"We're going to watch a movie on TV if you two want to join us."

Grace stuck her head around the corner of the door and said, "We'll be there soon. Just got a few more things to clean up first."

Instead of joining them, though, Bob and Grace sat back down at the table and continued their conversation over a piece of butterscotch pie.

"Did you make this?"

"Yep. Sure did. I can't cook a damned thing unless it's got sugar in it. Then I do okay," Grace said laughingly.

She felt like she should have offered a piece to Barb and Gerald, too, but then figured it would only bring another critique from Gerald. And besides, Barb was trying to lose weight.

It was almost ten when Barb strode into the kitchen and announced it was time to go. Although it was the last thing he wanted to do, Bob knew they needed to relieve the sitter before midnight; and so he reluctantly put his shoes back on while Barb glared at Grace.

As the four of them walked to the door, Bob noticed that Grace was already returning to the same sad person she had been when they had first arrived. But he was feeling a little sad now, too. He had to go home with Barb.

As soon as they were in the car, Barb turned to him and said, "How embarrassing can you be?"

Bob laughed bitterly and said, "*You* were embarrassed by *my* behavior? That's the biggest load of sanctimonious bullshit I've ever heard. Shit, Barb, I wish you could see yourself and your own disgusting behavior. And for your information, I had a good time tonight, which I know just kills you. But from now on, if you don't like it, you know where the front door is."

Barb's mouth just hung open. He had never spoken to her or anyone else in that tone before tonight; and with the snippy remarks toward Gerald, too, she wondered if he had been possessed by the devil. Then she wondered if the devil wore a white dress and had black hair.

She started to wonder if she was losing her hold on the little mouse. Her plans weren't completed yet, so she would have to tread carefully from here on out.

We'll see who goes through the door first, she thought to herself.

Bob felt a little sliver of satisfaction and peace settle over him for the first time in years. There would be no turning back now. He was sick and tired of Barb berating him and the boys; and he was sick of her money-hungry demands. Either he and Barb would have a meeting of the minds and hearts, or there would be a great dividing of the household.

CHAPTER 5

The next morning came much too fast for Bob. It had been another night on the couch; and he felt like he hadn't moved all night. Some major stiffness had settled in around his wounds; and it took him longer than usual just to get up and start moving around.

He went to the kitchen and started making breakfast, something that he loved to do; and the boys seemed to appreciate it, too. Bob knew as soon as the smells of bacon and eggs began to waft up the stairs, they would come bounding down to the kitchen. Christopher was usually the first one to show up, then David; and Matt would stumble in last. It was a fun time for them to spend together; and breakfast was rarely missed.

As Matt was settling in his chair, he said, "Dad, we've been thinking that you need some help with those dogs; and even if we do get hurt, it'll be okay; and maybe you wouldn't get hurt so much; and then maybe..."

Bob cut him off, knowing he would keep rambling on and on if he didn't.

"Matthew!" Matt stopped talking. "That's a very kind offer; and I'm so pleased that you're all worried about me getting hurt again. But there are a few reasons I can't do that. First of all, most people don't move as fast as I do in the woods; and that slows me down. And to get the dogs, I have to move very, very fast. Another thing is that I'd be so worried about the people with me that I wouldn't be able to concentrate on what I was doing; and then I would probably get hurt for sure.

Christopher piped up. "Kinda like me thinking of other things when I'm supposed to be doing math, and then getting it wrong."

"Yes, Christopher. Kind of like that. But besides all that, your mother would hurt me worse than those dogs did if I took you guys out there. She loves you, too; and she would be very upset if anything happened to any of you."

The boys slumped in their chairs, frowns on their faces. But they didn't argue the point any further. Even they knew their mother was a force to be reckoned with.

Bob had been thinking about the situation with the dogs and had finally decided it was time to go to the ranch and stay there until he had gotten all of them. The driving back and forth every day or two was wearing him out as much as hunting the dogs was; and it was precious time wasted.

While the boys were finishing breakfast, he called a fellow chiropractor to cover his patients for a while; and then he threw on some ragged clothes and packed another change to take with him. When he was almost ready to go, the phone rang. It was Gerald Klyne.

"Hi, Bob, how are you this morning?"

"Good, Gerald. What's up?"

"I just thought I'd call and ask when you planned on going back to the woods. Do you know yet?"

"As a matter of fact, I'm heading out right now."

"Really? Do you think I could tag along?

Fridays are days off for me; and all my stuff's already gathered up; so I can just meet you somewhere if it would work out for you."

Bob dreaded thinking about the pasty nerd traipsing along with him all day; but he had told him he could go sometime. He figured he might as well do it now and get it over with. Then he thought of the girl with the blue eyes and decided it might be worth it to tolerate him for a few hours.

"Okay. Why don't we meet up where Highways 24 and 16 meet up in Tonganoxie; and then you can follow me the rest of the way out. What are you driving?"

"It's a small, black Mazda pickup. And, hey, thanks. This'll be fun. See you soon."

"A real barrel of monkeys," Bob mumbled to himself as he hung up the phone.

When he walked back into the kitchen, the boys were finishing their breakfast; and David said in a shaky voice, "When will you be back, Dad?"

Bob knew the little boy was about to cry; and he wondered if it was because he was scared he would be hurt again or because he didn't get to go along.

"I'll be back as soon as I get Three Toes. How's that?"

"Then we probably won't be seeing you for a long time," Christopher said, clearly pouting.

"Don't you worry about that. I'll be back before you know it."

Bob gave each of them a hug and a kiss.

"Be good little men while I'm gone. Study hard in school, be nice to each other, and mind your mother."

He wasn't sure how long it would take him to finish the job; but he thought he should take some supplies just in case. He grabbed extra ammunition, some jerky, flip-topped canned beans and an old army blanket, and threw it into the Suburban along with his backpack. He looked at the clear sky and was glad he'd have a nice, warm day today. Then he jumped in the truck and took off, waving at his three sad boys as he left.

Gerald was waiting for him when he reached their meeting place; and only a few minutes later they were pulling up at the ranch. As they drove down the driveway, Neil walked out with a cup of coffee in his hand and approached Bob's open window. "Here's some coffee." Then, jerking his head toward Gerald, he asked, "Who's that with you?"

"It's Barb's shrink, Dr. Klyne. He wanted to help me out with the dogs; and he seems okay; so I thought I'd give him a try."

"Got a call from Stevenson about a half hour ago. Lost three calves sometime last night. I've got a little bit left on that north fence to do; and I'm going to do it today, just in case you need me."

He said, "Okay, Dad. Thanks."

Bob motioned for Gerald to park his pickup and join him in the Suburban.

When Gerald finally got himself and his guns into the Suburban, Bob took off toward the Stevenson's house.

As they pulled up, Mitch came out of the front door. Bob felt as though the whole countryside must have monitoring devices to let them know when he was going to show up. He stuck his head out the window and yelled, "Get in and show me where the dead calves are."

The man trotted across the yard, and, as he climbed in, said, "How the hell did you get here so fast? I just called yer dad about fifteen minutes ago."

"I have ESP," Bob said with a smile. "So where are we going?"

"I thought you had E-S-P!" Mitch said with a hoot. Then he added, "Just go on back down through that pasture yonder. You'll see 'em."

"Mitch, this is Dr. Klyne. He's going to hunt with me today."

They shook hands and Mitch asked him, "You in good shape, Doc?"

"Good enough to hunt a few dogs."

"I wasn't worried about you keepin' up with them dogs. I was worried about you keepin' up with Bob."

Gerald didn't reply.

As soon as they had gotten to the far side of the pasture, Bob saw the calves and pulled up next to them. He jumped out of the truck with Mitch right behind.

"I think this just happened sometime in the wee hours of the mornin', Bob, but I'm not sure."

"The blood isn't dry; and the tracks are really fresh; so I don't think it's even been that long."

"I heard they almost got you the other night."

"Yeah, they got pretty up close and personal."

The mothers of the calves hovered over the bodies of their dead babies and eyeballed the men warily. Mitch kept a distance; but Bob didn't seem to notice any impending danger from them; and he

85

walked closer to kneel down next to the calves. He studied the tracks, and then touched each one of them as he prayed for them.

During the ritual, the cows approached him one by one until they were all finally gathered around, their heads hung low. Bob touched them, too, and asked God to comfort them.

Gerald walked up to Mitch and said, "What's he doing?"

"I'm not really sure," the man said as he shook his head, "but I can't believe he just walked into the middle of them cows. They're crazy, that bunch is. I'd sure never do it."

Bob had started to circle the area, and Gerald asked again, "What's he doing now?"

"I think he's lookin' for tracks; and that means you best have yer runnin' shoes on, 'cause this is just about the time he's gonna be takin' off like a rooster in heat."

As if on cue, Bob suddenly stood and yelled back toward Mitch. "Hey, take the truck and go on back home. I'll pick it up there. Gerald, we've got to go."

The tracks headed east-northeast, and Bob took off with Gerald struggling to keep up with him. By the time they stopped at the edge of the woods, Gerald was already about fifty feet behind, but was able to catch up just as Bob started to take off again.

"Is this the way it's going to be all day?" Gerald yelled between gasps.

Bob stopped and looked at him. "What do you mean?"

"I mean, are we going to be running like this the

86

whole time?"

"I don't know. We might have to speed it up a little at some point. But I'll try to keep it at this pace."

Bob knew Gerald was having trouble already; and if he'd been honest, he would have told him that this was the fastest he usually ran; but he wanted to keep Gerald on his toes. Plus, he still didn't like the guy much.

"The tracks are fresh, and there are seven now instead of six. They must have added another to their ranks, and it looks like the new one is bigger than Three Toes.

"So?"

"So those two will be the toughest ones to bring down." Bob was beginning to feel like he might as well have brought his young boys with him.

Gerald seemed to be getting exasperated with the whole situation already. "Bob, I'm afraid I'm going to slow you down today. There's no way I can keep up at this pace; so maybe I should just head back to Mitch's place and take the truck back to the ranch. I'll hunt with you sometime when we're not having to chase them down."

Bob nodded and said, "Okay. Next time then." and took off running through the woods again.

By the time he'd gotten to the Nine Mile Creek, he had noticed that the dogs hadn't followed their usual patterns of splitting off or fanning out. Instead, they had kept the pack together this time. He wondered if this was some kind of new tactic, or if they were heading for something in particular. He said another prayer just to be on the safe side.

As soon as the dogs hit the Nine Mile Creek,

they turned and headed north through the water. The rains hadn't filled the creek too high yet; so the going wasn't too bad, especially for the dogs. They have to know I'm on their trail, Bob thought as he maneuvered the twists and turns of the creek while keeping his eyes constantly scanning the areas around him. There were many good hiding places through here; and he worried about an ambush.

About a mile down the creek, he reached the eastern border of his ranch and was grateful to be on more familiar terrain. He stopped and studied the tracks again and noticed that all seven were still together; but they were moving slower now. He figured he couldn't be any more than ten to fifteen minutes behind them, and was glad to see that he didn't have to worry about them coming up from behind. He pulled the leather from the hammer of his gun and unsnapped the strap from around his knife.

The dogs continued on through the creek until they reached the north end of where they had turned westward. Bob's heart sank as he realized where they were going. He quickly pulled his revolver and fired three times to alert his dad; and then he took off running.

He had spent a lot of energy chasing the gang up the creek; but now he had to go faster than ever. Just what I get for saying that to Gerald, he thought.

His lungs began to burn; but he knew he had to get to his father fast. As he ran, he fired three more shots and prayed Neil was out of the way of the pack.

When he topped the last hill, Bob saw the tractor. It had run into a tree. Then he saw his father about six feet from it, lying on the ground, not moving, and covered with blood. The damned dogs had pulled him off of it. Before he even got close, Bob knew his dad was hurt badly. In fact, from the looks of things, it would be a miracle if he was still even alive.

When he reached him, he first checked for a pulse, and was relieved to find there was one. It was weak, but it was there. And from what Bob could tell, there were also four places that were bleeding heavily and had to be taken care of immediately. If Bob couldn't get the bleeding to stop, Neil would never make it all the way back to the ranch alive.

He ripped a portion of his dad's shirt off and wrapped it tight around his dad's arm. Then he pulled his own shirt off and ripped it in half and started wrapping the two places on his legs where the dogs had latched on. Last of all, he took off his T-shirt and placed it over the stomach wound, and, using his father's belt like he had used his own, cinched it up tight. His father opened his eyes.

"You were right. Those are some mean pooches."

If he hadn't been so worried about getting his dad out of there, Bob would have laughed; but he was glad to see the old man still had a little gusto left in him. Bob gently patted Neil's shoulder, and then ran to the tractor. As soon as he reached it, he saw that the radiator had been mangled; and he knew it wouldn't make it twenty yards before the motor froze up.

He began to look around for a couple of limbs as he headed back toward his dad. He was going to have to drag him home and needed some limbs that would be long enough and strong enough to make into a stretcher. After several minutes, he had found what he needed, and, using his old army blanket, managed to rig up something that he thought would make the trip. Then, using his own belt, he strapped the whole thing to his backpack. Finally, he rolled his father onto the rigging and tried to make him as comfortable as possible. Once he had Neil settled, Bob emptied the spent shells out of the Magnum and reloaded it; and then he gave the Mauser one last check.

"Okay, Dad. You ready to go?" Bob said. His father didn't reply.

Bob began raising the backpack high enough to slip his arms through; and he grunted as he lifted the heavy load. He wondered if he'd be able to carry Neil all the way back without completely giving out. Getting him to the road wouldn't be too bad since it was all down hill; but once he'd reached the road it was all up hill from there to the house.

He took off down the grassy slope and realized right away that going downhill wasn't all it was cracked up to be. With the stretcher being a little higher than Bob's feet, he constantly felt as though he was going to be pushed forward. The bulk of the push was on his neck and shoulders; and in no time at all his muscles had started to burn.

He had almost reached the road when he felt the Presence and heard the dogs in the woods on each side of him. "Thank you," he whispered. He knew every minute was vital for his dad, which meant he couldn't go after Three Toes yet. With the load on his back, Bob knew he was more vulnerable than ever; but there was nothing else he could do. Just walk, he told himself.

He continued on to the road and turned south to

begin the ascent of the first hill. Although the load was heavier and harder to pull now, at least the pressure was off his neck for a while, which was a relief in itself. With one foot in front of the other, he finally reached the top. Then he saw the movement off to his left.

As quickly as the movement had caught his attention, his eyes dilated; and he saw the Three Toes in the safety of the trees, pacing back and forth, eyes glued on him; and he saw the two others just behind the alpha dog. Spinning around to look on the other side of him, he saw Big Dog and the others doing the same.

Bob knew he couldn't raise and aim the gun with any accuracy with the load on his back; so if they charged, he would have to drop Neil to the ground and hope for the best for both of them. With the plan in his mind, he began to climb the next hill.

Getting his dad home was tougher than he had even thought it would be. The muscles in his legs burned; and his shoulders ached where the straps dug into his flesh. Sweat poured down his face; and he could feel his stitches being pulled to their breaking points. By the time he had reached the top of the second hill, he could feel his own wounds oozing.

The next quarter of a mile was flat, which gave Bob a little reprieve. He could still hear the dogs as they paced with him; but they were at least keeping their distance. He could feel their eyes on him, and figured they were waiting for the perfect chance to take advantage of him.

The three dogs to his left were far enough away in the woods that he thought any chance of a first ambush was out of the question. But he knew they would come in to help finish off the job if the dogs on the right were to attack. Bob dreaded reaching the bottom of the next hill. The woods closed in on the road; and he knew if an attack was going to happen, it would be there.

He was tired and hurting more than ever now; and he thought he should stop here to check on his dad and catch his breath in preparation for the last leg of the journey home. Slowly, and painfully, he slid the straps off his shoulders and tried to lower Neil slowly to the ground; but it was more than he could do. When the stretcher hit the ground with a slight thud, his father opened his eyes.

"Where the hell...?"

"Sorry, Dad. I'm trying to get you home, and we're just about there. But the dogs are close."

"Well, thanks for waking me up to let me know."

"Listen, Dad. They're in the woods on both sides of us, and they're just waiting for the chance to take us."

Bob could see fear in his father's eyes.

"We've only got a half a mile to go; and we'll be home; and we *are* going to make it. Then when we get there, I'm going to get you to the hospital. Okay?"

"Shit, Bob. Look at you. You're in no shape to get me even halfway up that hill carrying me like this. So I want you to leave me here with one of those guns; and you get up that hill and get the truck. Then come back down and get me. I'll shoot them all while you're gone."

Bob appreciated his dad's suggestion, especially

the humor he still sported in the face of dire circumstances; and he wondered why the old man hadn't ever shown this side of himself before. But the idea was suicide, and he wasn't about to leave him behind. Even if he left him with a gun, and even if he could shoot well, there were seven dogs and only six shots. He would have to be good enough to hit a dog with each shot; and that would still leave one dog left over. And he didn't think he was that good anyway. No, they would either both make it out together; or they'd not make it out at all.

Bob checked his own wounds and saw that the stitches were still in place; but he could tell the skin had pulled around them. Where there hadn't been a gap at all, now there was a small one; and it would spread further and further until he didn't have the added weight on him. He pulled his revolver from the holster and handed it to his father.

"Okay. Now here's my plan. You're going to take this gun; and if the dogs start to attack, I'm going to drop you; so you'd better be ready for a hard landing. Then you take the ones coming from your right. That would be my left. And I'll take the ones from my right, which would be your left. Got it?"

Neil glared at Bob, not saying a word. Bob had never challenged his dad's orders before; and he figured he'd be in for a good whoopin' when it was all over with. Especially if things went really bad.

He hoisted the straps back onto his shoulders and glanced back over his shoulder. "Ready?" he asked. Then before Neil could answer, he took off running, legs straining, and the wounds pulling open more with each step. Then the dogs began to charge.

Trying to break the fall for him as much as he could, he dropped Neil to the ground and heard a grunt as the stretcher hit the dirt.

Grabbing his Mauser, he sighted in on the first dog and shot. The dog went down. Bob knew he'd gotten lucky that the dog had stayed in the open long enough to get him; but the next dog seemed to know better. As this one weaved in and out of trees, all Bob could do was let one fly on the timing. The second dog went down.

Two shots exploded from the Magnum behind him; but he didn't hear a yelp following them; and he prayed his dad was okay.

The third dog was already coming at him hard and fast from the right; and he raised his gun to take aim. But before he could pull the trigger, he heard a third shot from behind, and then, immediately, the report of another gun from atop the hill. Keeping his eyes on the dog in front of him, he aimed and pulled the trigger. The dog dropped.

Big Dog was all that was left on this side, but he had disappeared when his friends began to drop. Bob whirled around to face the rest of them, but they had taken off, too. As they ran up the hill, Bob aimed at the one closest to him and fired; but it was a miss. The dog stopped and looked back at him as though he was laughing or taunting him. It was Three Toes. As Bob bolted another shell, the dog disappeared.

Movement on the road up ahead caught his attention; and Bob turned quickly, thinking it was likely Big Dog. But instead, it was Gerald; and he was coming toward them. Bob turned back to his father as he began reloading his gun.

"You all right, Dad?"

"Yeah, all except for the knot on my head you gave me when you threw me on the ground. But I've got to ask, why in hell don't you use a 30-30 or something that carries more bullets? There's got to be something out there a little more powerful than this piece of shit."

"What difference would it have made? You didn't hit anything anyway."

"That's beside the point. And did you think that a little bit bigger bullet might have helped me hit something?"

Bob shook his head and started walking toward the dead dogs. When he reached them, he squatted down next to them, and, raising his arms in the air, began to chant. When he had finished, he walked back to his dad, reaching him just as Gerald walked up.

"What in God's green earth were you doing over there?" Neil asked his boy.

"I'd tell you, but you wouldn't understand."

"How's everybody doing down here?" Gerald asked.

"We're okay, thanks in part to you," Bob said. "Looks like you got to do a little hunting after all."

"Look's like it. So is there anything I can do to help here?"

"Yes. If you would, you can stay with Dad while I go get the pickup. Then maybe we can all get home."

"Sure. No problem."

Bob took off running toward the house, and Gerald turned to Neil and asked, "Is that all that guy does? Run?"

"He's a good son. Can't complain."

As he neared the house, Bob thought how lucky he and his dad had been by having Gerald show up when he did. Even though it turned out that things were well in hand, another gun was always welcome, especially when his father was using one of them. He was as bad with a gun as Mike.

He jumped in the truck and drove back toward his dad and Gerald as fast as he could, just in case the dogs decided to return in his absence. When he reached them, he and Gerald loaded Neil in the back seat. Bob could tell that his father was in tremendous pain; but the old coot wouldn't admit it if his life depended on it.

As they started back to the ranch, Neil yelled up to Bob, "You know you're not going to take me to any damned hospital, don't you?"

"Dad, you're a mess," Bob answered as he looked in his rearview mirror at him.

"Look, peckerhead. I didn't take you to the hospital, so I expect you to do the same for me."

"Fine. But on one condition. That you can walk into the house on your own. If you can do that, I'll not take you."

"Fine."

Bob drove up to the house and parked as close to the sidewalk as he could. He knew Neil was stubborn enough to do it even if it killed him.

The old man crawled out of the truck and slowly walked down the sidewalk toward the door, while Bob stood nearby in case he started to fall along the way. By the time he had made it to the kitchen, Neil was as white as a sheet and beginning to stumble.

Bob put his arm around his dad's waist and supported him as they walked the rest of the way to his bedroom.

Once the man was seated on the edge of the bed, Bob helped him take off his clothes and laid him down. Now it was his turn with the soap and water. And alcohol.

By the time he'd gathered up all the supplies, Neil had started to drift off. Bob looked at the old man's face and stroked his soft, white hair back off his forehead. Then he began to gently clean, sew and bandage up the wounds. And when he finished, he turned his attention to his own wounds, which he cleaned and bandaged, deciding to forego any more stitches on himself.

Gerald waited while Bob had worked on Neil; but when he began to treat himself, Gerald announced that he was going to head on back to the city.

"Hey, Bob. Thanks for letting me tag along today. But unless you need something else, I'm going to head home."

"No, I think things are fine here. And thanks for the help today. I really appreciate it."

Gerald took his time leaving as he fiddled around with his backpack at the truck. Bob couldn't imagine what all the guy had stashed in there for only a few hours out in the woods; but then, he *was* a little strange. Finally, he heard the little pickup leave.

Once Bob had finished doctoring himself, he cleaned up the supplies, and was checking on his dad again when the phone rang. There were very few people who knew the number at the ranch; and the ringing startled him. He rushed to grab the receiver quickly so as not to wake Neil.

"Hello?"

"Is this Dr. Bob Conley?"

A smile broke across his face.

"Yes, Grace. How are you? And how in the world did you get this number?"

"Gerald had gotten it from Barb; and he gave it to me this morning in case I needed anything while he was out there. And I'm fine."

"Good. But I should tell you that Gerald's already left and headed back your way."

"Oh, goodie," she said wryly. "But that really wasn't why I was calling. Actually, I need someone to take me to lunch tomorrow; and I thought you might be able to help me out."

"Uh, I'm not sure I understand. Is this like some special luncheon or something?"

"It would be if you took me. What do you think?"

Bob hesitated as he tried to sort this out. He would enjoy seeing her again; but this was all just taking him by surprise.

Grace continued, "If you don't want to, I'll understand. But I'm having to pull a Saturday shift this week; and I can usually take a little longer lunch on the weekends than I can through the week. And I tend to be a little on the impulsive side, too."

There was silence on the phone; and Grace was beginning to feel as though she'd really jumped the gun.

"Anyway, I just had such a good time talking to you last night that I thought it might be a good break in my boring day here; and I thought if you weren't too tied up with the dogs you might be up for it.

That's all."

He still felt a little unsure of what was going on, but Bob decided to take the plunge.

"Well, sure. Why not? What time do you usually go?"

"One o'clock is the time I'm scheduled for; but if that doesn't work, I can see if things can be switched around a little."

"One is fine. But I've got to ask you, are you sure this is okay with Gerald?"

"Nothing's ever okay with him; but if you're asking if he knows, the answer is yes. At least, he will. I planned on telling him if you agreed. So you can just pick me up at the main door at KU, east side of the building."

"Is there anywhere in particular you'd like to go?"

"Surprise me. Bye!"

She had hung up before he could say anything else, and he slowly shook his head as he held the phone to his chest. The only woman he'd ever gone out to lunch with besides Barb was Cindy. And that was only on the rare days when things were slow in the office. More than anything, though, the feelings he had about seeing Grace again were strange and disconcerting to him. He thought of those incredible eyes of hers, and wondered what was hidden behind them. The worst thing of all, he found himself really wanting to know.

The guilt began to set in. It was probably just his Catholic upbringing that made him feel like this. After all, he'd done nothing wrong. Yet, he just had to keep his marriage and his boys in the forefront of his mind, and go into this friendship with Grace as just that. A friendship and nothing more.

The sound of snoring coming from the bedroom caused Bob's thoughts to shift. What was he going to do with his dad? Taking him into the city with him was certainly not an option. If his dad didn't strangle him for it, Barb would. But he knew he couldn't leave him out here by himself. Maybe Sherry could watch him for a few days. He laughed to himself as he thought of the cranky old guy and blabber-mouthed Sherry together. Maybe listening to her would make him get well faster.

Deciding this really wasn't such a bad idea, he picked up the phone again and dialed her number, and after ten minutes of conversation – three of it being on Bob's end – they had agreed she would be over within the half hour. It was only ten minutes later that Sherry pulled into the driveway; and before she even had the front door open, she was talking nonstop again.

"So tell me what in the world happened to your dad, Bob. And where is he? Where is Dr. Conley? You have to tell me how bad he is. You know you should have called me sooner. But then it's just like a man to think he can do everything. Mike is exactly the same way. Sometimes I wonder what goes through your minds!"

Her legs were moving as fast as her lips; and Bob tried to catch her before she was able to burst into Neil's bedroom; but he didn't quite make it in time. As soon as she saw Neil, she began another tirade.

"Oh, Lordy! What in the world has happened to this poor man? This is almost too much for me to even comprehend. I can see right now that I've got my work

100

cut out for me here. First, I have to clean things up, and then I've got to get Dr. Conley some good food to eat. A man can't heal without good food. And I'm sure there's laundry to do, and…"

Bob got through the door just as Neil opened his eyes and looked at Sherry, then at him. The old man's expression spoke volumes; and Bob started to think this wasn't such a good idea after all.

"Sherry, I've got to go now. Dad, you take it easy, and I'll see both of you as soon as I can."

Bob practically ran toward the front door, snatching up his backpack on the way without ever breaking stride. He wanted to get out quick before something really bad happened. As he shut the door behind him, he could still hear Sherry inside rattling on and on.

Once he was out of earshot, Bob stopped just to gather his thoughts. The afternoon sun was warm on his face, and it seemed the beautiful hills were beckoning to him. He still had some good daylight hours left; so he checked his guns to make sure they were loaded, and began walking back to where he'd last seen Three Toes.

It didn't take long to pick up on the tracks, and he began to follow the trail. His mind went back to the attack. There was something about Gerald that niggled at Bob's brain; but he couldn't quite put his finger on anything specific. Maybe he just didn't want to like him because Barb did. And if he was going to be really honest with himself, he had to admit that it was a pretty good thing that he'd been along today, even if he hadn't taken out any of the dogs. And Bob really didn't mind the guy tagging along. He just needed to

101

learn how to keep up.

The tracks led straight south through the pasture where his cattle were grazing; and he sped up his pace, hoping to keep them on the run so they wouldn't have the chance to take any of them down. The woods were quiet; and he wished he could take the time to enjoy them more; but this wasn't the time for dawdling. As he broke into a light run, he thought of tomorrow's lunch with Grace. His heart fluttered and a smile snuck out onto his face.

His mind began to click off all the "what ifs", but after a while, he realized he hadn't been paying any attention to anything around him. He climbed to the top of the ridge and sat down on the edge of a rock the size of his house. He had to get tomorrow out of his mind before the dogs showed up again and left him without a mind at all.

Looking out over the Nine Mile Valley, he wondered where his life was headed. His marriage was a wreck, his wife was cheating on him, he never seemed to be able to make enough money to satisfy her, his self esteem was at an all time low, and these dogs were about to kill him. He felt more overwhelmed than he'd ever felt before.

The words of his grandfather kept coming back to haunt him. *The Plan.* Bob had never understood all this about "the Plan"; but he did know if this was it, he sure as hell didn't like it. And then his father's words rang through his head again. Do something, he had said. So which was it? Was he to do something, or was he to sit around and let this 'Plan' keep leading him down the primrose path? His whole life seemed out of control, none of it being what he'd thought twenty years ago that it would be.

It was almost dark before he knew it. He would have to really step up the pace now. He took off in a run; and when he finally reached the herd was relieved to see they were all still there and alive. The cows began to gather around him; and he decided this might be the best place for him to spend the night.

Finding a turd-free piece of ground big enough to lie down on was a challenge in itself; but once he found a spot, he spread out his blanket and lay down on it, using his backpack for a pillow. The sounds of the creek and the rhythmic breathing of the cattle around him had soon lulled him into a deep sleep.

CHAPTER 6

He awoke in that transitional time between night and day. The sun had not shown itself yet; but the sky was getting lighter as the sun made its way toward the horizon. Bob was alarmed to see how long he had slept; and he quickly cleared his head and looked around for anything awry; but everything was intact, including himself. The cattle were calm, a few still sleeping, but most of them up and already eating. After rolling up his blanket, he checked the guns and slung his backpack on one shoulder, then continued to walk back in the direction he had traveled last night, until he was able to pick up the dogs' trail again.

Two hours later, he had only succeeded in wandering all over half the country; and he was starting to feel as though he was getting nowhere fast. Even with the tracks fairly fresh, he had not seen one hint of the dogs. His frustration grew, and he berated himself for not keeping after them the night before. He decided to just head back to the ranch. He sure wasn't making any headway by playing hide-and-seek with the dogs; and he wanted to see how things had gone with his dad and Sherry. And he had to get ready for lunch.

When he got back to the house, Neil was still sleeping; and Sherry was busy cooking breakfast. After he listened to her drone on and on about everything she could think of, he told her he had a phone call to make and then he had to go out for a while on an errand.

Taking the phone into his bedroom, he dialed

the Klyne's number; and Gerald answered the phone. The two men chatted about the day before, and Gerald asked about Neil. Bob thanked him again for his help and told him he was welcome to come out again anytime he wanted to.

Bob felt awkward about mentioning the lunch with Grace and hoped something might come to him while they were talking; but as it turned out, he didn't need to worry.

"Grace told me she was going to have lunch with you today. You still going to make it?"

Bob was surprised, but relieved that Gerald had brought it up.

"I'm glad you brought it up, Gerald. One of the reasons I called was to ask you about it. Are you okay with this?"

"I don't mind. I'm going to be working today anyway. But just be careful with her. She's not too bright …you know, her wattage is a little low."

Bob was taken aback by the comment and wasn't really sure how to respond. After a few seconds, he said, "I didn't notice that the other night, but I'll be sure to keep an eye on her for you."

Gerald told Bob he would call again once he'd figured out his schedule for the coming week; and then the men hung up. Bob gathered up some clean clothes and jumped into the shower.

As he cleaned up, he kept wondering what was up with Gerald's comment about Grace. Was there something about her he didn't know? What she a little on the daffy side? Or was Gerald just being an arrogant ass? He thought he knew the answer but decided not to assume anything until after lunch.

He pulled up at the east door of the hospital a few minutes 'til one. A flood of people were going in and out, some with flowers and some with luggage. Bob couldn't comprehend this world at all. He had studied in hospitals at one time; but the thought of actually being a patient in one was not a concept he could even begin to imagine.

As he glanced back toward the hospital, he saw an unusually beautiful woman who stood out from the rest of the general public. She was tall and thin, and her hair sparkled in the light. She was wearing a black, satin blouse; and a little, black skirt that ended a flattering distance from her knees. But best of all, she was wearing black, patent-leather spiked heels, his greatest weakness. Suddenly, he realized he was gawking and about to drool, and he was ashamed. What the hell was wrong with him? He'd never acted like this before. But she was just so damned stunning. And he looked again.

She was still there, working her way through the throngs that were coming and going; but she seemed to be doing so without even breaking a sweat. He noticed the small, black purse clutched in her long fingers, and the silver jewelry that she wore so elegantly. Even her posture was perfect. The word *aristocracy* came to mind.

Bob made himself look away again for fear that he'd be arrested for stalking or lascivious behavior; but then the door opened; and he turned back to greet Grace. Much to his surprise, it was the woman in black. As she crawled into the truck, he could only stare at her, not having a clue what to say. Finally, she broke the awkward silence.

"Hi, Bob! You okay?"

"Holy shit, Grace! It's you!"

"Who did you think it was?"

Bob was never known to be at a complete loss for words; but now this was the second time he didn't know what to say to this woman. He sat and looked at her, his heart in his throat and his jaw somewhere on the floorboard. She kept looking at him, obviously confused at his surprised reaction.

"So, where are we going to lunch?"

Bob heard the question, but was still trying to wrap his mind around the fact that this was the same barefooted woman he'd seen a few nights ago.

Finally, he said, "Forgive me, Grace. I'm stunned. The first time I saw you, you were wearing a little, Holly- Hobby sort of dress; and you were barefooted; and you weren't wearing any makeup. Even your hair didn't look anything like it does now. I have never seen such a transformation in my life. You were beautiful before; but Jesus, Mary and Joseph, you look like a goddess today!"

She laughed and said in her southern drawl, "Why, Bob Conley, I do believe you have made me blush. But now why don't you head over to Westport and find us somewhere to eat?"

Bob was surprised he didn't run off the road or plow over anybody as he headed south on State Line. It was all he could do to not just stare at her.

Her eye makeup accented the blue pools of her eyes and made them even more dramatic than he'd remembered. And her fair skin looked like porcelain. Her nails were manicured to perfection, and she smelled like heaven.

Somehow he managed to make it to Westport Road and drove slowly east as he tried his best to look for restaurants instead of looking at her. Finally he said, "How about here?" as he slowed in front of Lucille's, a fifties-style restaurant. "Doesn't seem to look too busy."

"Sure," she said. "I've never been here, so I don't know what it's like, but it looks fun."

Bob parked and raced around the truck to her side, while Grace waited patiently and politely for him. Opening the door, he reached his hand out to her; and she took it as she slid smoothly from the seat.

When they were seated and had been given menus, Grace began to comment on the food selections; and, finally, Bob began to find his voice again. After conversing over the menu, they ordered an appetizer of chicken fingers that they would split between them; and then both of them began to relax.

"So, where did you get that accent?" Bob asked.

"I don't know. I grew up in southern Missouri, in the eastern part of the Ozarks. My family transplanted there from Tennessee; but I seem to be the only one in the family with the accent. Pretty strange, don't you think?"

Bob just wanted to keep listening to her talk.

"Brothers? Sisters?"

"I have four brothers and five sisters, all older than me," she said. "So, just so you know, I can take a punch with the best of them. But if you hit me in the mouth, I'll have to kill you. I've been through too much money and too much pain to let these pearly whites get messed up."

Bob thought her smile could surely brighten the

darkness of hell itself; and as he laughed, she continued. "I was really intrigued by your story about the dogs. You must be pretty good with a gun. Gerald took me to the shooting range once; but I shot him in the leg by accident; so now he won't take me anymore."

Bob laughed until he thought he would cry; and when he finally caught his breath, he asked, "How in the world did you manage to shoot him in the leg?"

"Well, the man who was running the show there, you know, the owner of the place? He had already chewed me out a couple of times for not keeping the gun pointed straight down the little alley thing. I didn't know what the big deal was; but I figured it out after I'd shot Gerald. But aside from that, I turned out to be a pretty good shot."

Bob continued to laugh. "Maybe I should send you out to get those dogs. I'm not too sure I'd want to be there with you; but maybe you'd do better at it than I've been doing."

"I do love being outside, at least as long as I've got plenty of good sunscreen and bug spray. But I just don't think I could kill anything with fur."

The conversation flowed like honey on a warm day; and Bob found himself laughing more than he'd laughed in a long time. Her candor and straightforward-ness kept him wondering what she would say next; and she was so vibrant and full of energy, nothing like she'd been at their previous dinner. He thought back to Gerald's warning that she wasn't very bright. What a fool.

Changing the subject, Bob said, "I have to ask you something. You were so different at dinner the other night than you are now. Why?" he asked.

Her answer was simple and direct. "Gerald. He's stupid. He's always worried that I'll embarrass him with my 'hillbilly ways' as he calls them. He doesn't like for me to talk much when others are around, 'cause he's afraid people will find out that I'm just a hick without a college degree. I actually thought I'd done okay that night you were over; but then he got mad at me after you had left, because I'd taken my shoes off."

Bob could tell she didn't like talking about this, and he thought there might be more to the story than she was saying. He changed the subject again, and they continued to get to know one another. The lunch was over much too quickly for him; but he was happy when she agreed to have lunch with him again soon.

As he walked her back out to the truck, he had a hard time not staring at her legs. They were every man's dream: long-and-slender, beautifully-shaped calves and tiny little ankles. God must have made this woman from my very own dreams, he thought to himself as he opened her door; and she climbed back into the truck.

When they pulled back up in front of the hospital, Grace asked, "So, when do you suggest we have lunch again?"

"I'll call you as soon as I know what my schedule looks like."

"Tuesday sounds good," she said nonchalantly.

"I'll shoot for Tuesday, but I'm not going to be sure until I see what's going on by then."

She looked at him and smiled. "I'll see you Tuesday. Don't be late."

111

She got out of the truck and walked to the glassed doors, where she stopped and turned to look at him. Then with a smile and a slight wiggle of her fingers, she disappeared into the crowd, leaving Bob wondering if he'd just dreamed her up.

Since he was so close to his office, he decided to drop by to make sure everything was going okay there; and then he headed back out to the ranch again. He was anxious to see his dad while he was awake so he could tell how he was feeling; and he figured he needed to check on Sherry just to see if Neil had turned her into a bawling mess already. But, as he headed west out of the city on I-70, his thoughts were filled with beautiful Grace again.

He had the feeling that he could be headed for disaster if he kept up the lunches with her; but at the same time, he told himself that he deserved a friend as much as the next person. Yet, every time he saw those legs in his mind again, he would see the disaster again. And it wasn't just a jarring little bump in the road. It was a train wreck of the very worst kind, and he knew it.

When he arrived back at the ranch, Bob knew right away that his dad was feeling better just by the way he was ordering Sherry around. It looked like he had put her to work doing all the things that had been left undone since Zelma had died. Sherry hummed as she oiled the beveled, tongue-and-groove redwood walls; and Bob was glad to see the old place being taken care of again. And he was happiest of all to see that Sherry was surviving his father's regimen.

Bob had always loved this place. The half-split log cabin was a little on the small side; but the large, open rock fireplace and the vaulted ceilings gave it the feeling of being much larger than it really was. He remembered his mother spending hours on end making this her dream home. And even though she'd been gone for many years now, Bob could still hear her voice echoing through the house every once in a while.

His mother had been a great source of love and support for him; and he missed her terribly. He'd spent many nights grieving and longing to have her back after she'd died; and he would never forget the night she had answered his prayers, the night she visited him. He had been sleeping when something woke him. As he turned over in the bed, he saw her standing at his door and started to convince himself he was just dreaming. Then she had walked over and sat down beside him on the bed. As Bob gazed at her, she began to stroke his arm like she'd always done when he was a child; and then he knew it wasn't a dream. He could feel her. The tears had started, and, not wanting her to see him cry, he had reached up to wipe them away. And in that second, she was gone.

She had come to him several times after that, and her visits were always the same. She would be there near him; and she would touch him; but she never spoke a word to him.

Sherry's chattering interrupted his reverie.

"So how did your errand go, Dr. Bob?"

Before he could answer, she was on to other matters.

"I tell you, your daddy has been keeping me hopping like a frog on a hot stove. He's been telling me all sorts of things that need done around here; and I'm a little worried if I don't get them finished soon he's going to be crawling out of that bed and doing them himself. And you and I both know that's the last thing he needs to be doing. I just can't imagine in my wildest dreams what in the world he was thinking when he went out there without anything to protect himself from those animals. My word! I was just telling him that he needed to start taking better care of himself, or the next time he was gonna end up in the hospital. Or even worse, he'd wind up dead just like that poor Slawson boy."

Sherry kept talking even as Bob went into his father's room and closed the bedroom door behind him. Neil glared at him and said, "So, you came back, 'ey? If you had known how mad I was at you, you would've stayed gone. What were you trying to do to me, Bob? I'd rather be out there being eaten by the damn dogs than stuck here in this bed listening to that woman's mouth."

Bob tried to suppress a grin. "I figured you'd get better a lot faster if you had a day or two with her."

"You're a terrible son to subject me to this kind of torture. Shit! I was just telling Gerald yesterday that you were a good son, but I take it back now. You're rotten to the core."

Bob was happy to see the twinkle in Neil's eyes as they bantered. He pulled the chair closer to the bed and said, "I thought maybe you could use a dose of your own medicine. There are times you get to yacking as much as she does; so I figured the two of you could just yack yourselves out together. But I'm glad she's taking care of things around here. The place needed a little TLC; and it seems she's doing a good job of getting things back in order."

114

"Speaking of getting things done around here, I heard her talking to Mike on the phone a little while ago; and it sounded to me like maybe he'd been laid off from his trucking job. Is that true?"

"Hell, Dad, I don't know. You know how he tends to keep to himself anymore. It's hard to get two words out of him these days. Of course, with Sherry around, I guess that's pretty understandable."

"I sure don't want to ask her to repeat anything; but if it's true, what would you say about him taking over some of the jobs out here?"

"I don't see any reason why not," Bob replied. "He's good with the horses and the cattle, and he knows how to bale hay. He'd probably work out just fine."

"I don't know whether we could pay him what he's used to making; but I'd think a little would be better than nothing. If you can get that woman to shut up long enough, why don't you go out there and ask her?"

Although Bob didn't want to do it any more than Neil did, he was grateful that his dad was making the offer and thought he should jump on it before he changed his mind. He opened the door to find Sherry still cleaning and talking, oblivious to the fact that he hadn't even been in the room. Bob walked over to her and stood quietly, waiting for her to take a breath. When she finally noticed him, he put his index finger to her mouth; and she immediately snapped her lips together; and her eyes grew big.

"Sherry, I'm sorry to interrupt you, but I wanted to know if Mike is working these days. And a simple yes or no answer will do fine."

115

She shook her head no.

"Okay. Dad thought if Mike wanted to, he could make a little money by helping out around here until his job picks back up. Do you think he might be interested?"

She nodded her head yes.

"Okay. When you think it's a good time, why don't you talk to him about it; and then he can let us know."

Sherry threw her arms around his neck and said, "Dr. Bob, this couldn't have come at a better time. I thought Mike was going to lose his mind when he got laid off. If you don't mind, I'm going to go over there right now and tell him; and then we'll be right back. Is that okay?"

Bob nodded and Sherry started to run out the door. Suddenly, she stopped and turned back to him.

"He won't have to hunt those damn dogs will he?"

"No," Bob said. "That's my job."

She was out the door and speeding down the driveway before Bob could get back to Neil's room.

Bob knew Mike was a proud man and if he decided to look at this as a handout he wouldn't take the job. But then he thought that once Neil had explained everything expected of him, the poor guy would probably run the opposite direction anyway.

Bob liked the idea of having Mike around. His work ethic was flawless; and he was a good, honest man and a loving husband to Sherry.

He had fond memories of when they had been just boys and he had tried to teach Mike to shoot in exchange for Mike teaching him how to ride and rope.

Bob had gotten the hang of the roping a little bit back then, but doubted he could do it very well anymore. But poor Mike had never learned how to shoot.

He and Sherry had no children, but not because they didn't want them. Bob remembered the agony they went through each time Sherry had a miscarriage and the joy when their son was finally born. Unfortunately, their joy was cut brutally short when the baby died of SIDS at the tender age of two weeks and three days old.

Bob thought back to the funeral, the saddest thing he'd ever seen. A tiny, little, blue-and-white-gingham casket, no more than two-and-a-half feet long. And inside it was little Lucas, looking like he was just sleeping in a pile of lace and ruffles. He also remembered how Sherry had totally lost it when the choir had broken into "Jesus Loves Me". Mike and her brother had to carry her out, and then she'd ended up in the hospital the next couple of days. She had suffered a deep depression for years after that, and then slowly began to come out of it. But to this day no one ever dared to mention Lucas.

Mike had stood solid by his wife through it all, and she had stood by him through thick and thin. Bob was proud to call them his friends even if Mike didn't want to hang around and take the damned job.

Bob had to get back after the dogs; so he made sure his dad was comfortable; and then he headed out to the stalls. Desperate times call for desperate measures, he thought. He'd decided to take Misty out this afternoon, thinking he would be able to cover more area with her. He was getting tired of the hunt and just wanted to get it over with.

Misty was his favorite horse, the most beautiful buckskin Overa Paint he'd ever laid eyes on. And she had a heart of gold and was great at herding the cattle, too.

Bob hadn't seen much of her or any of the other horses in a while; and he knew she was going to be mad at him when she saw him. He'd not wanted to take her out on the hunts, because the terrain was so rough; and Misty tended to be a little on the klutzy side at times. And he hadn't taken any of the other horses simply because they were all too skittish.

As he entered the barn, Bob grabbed a handful of apple treats and strode on through to her stall. When the horse saw him, she turned her rear to him in defiance; but Bob could see her twisting her ears backwards in order to keep track of him. Holding the treats out to her, Bob clicked his tongue, her signal to come to him; but she only turned her head enough to see him. Suddenly, she got a whiff of the treats and spun back around to gobble them out of his hand.

"So am I forgiven, Misty girl?" Bob said as he rubbed her nose. The horse snorted and sniffed at his shirt pocket for more treats.

As he started to open the stall door, the horse began to whinny and turn in circles, eager for the chance to play. Once the door allowed her room for escape, she ran out and straight toward the saddles, where she came to a sliding halt.

Bob talked quietly to her as he saddled her up. "Okay, girl. There have been some big, old, nasty dogs hurting folks around here; so you and I, we've got to take care of things. We're going to check on the cattle and round them up so we can get them in the corrals

118

for the night. That way we can make sure they stay safe."

The horse looked at him as though she understood every word he said and waited patiently until he swung up into the saddle. Then she raised her front legs slightly and took off. Bob pulled her up short of the front door of the house, where he jumped down to gather his weapons. He threw the reins around her neck and went inside to let Neil know he was leaving.

When Bob had finished strapping on his pistol and knife, he grabbed the rifle and went back outside to find Misty still standing where he had left her, waiting patiently like a soldier ready and waiting for the signal to battle.

They reached the gate of the south pasture quickly; and Misty sidled up to it for Bob to open it without having to get out of the saddle. Then they started a slow trek through the woods, meandering from one side of the South Creek Valley to the other, calling and looking for the cattle. Bob felt the Presence; and in the same second Misty jumped and reared, obviously aware of it, too.

"It's okay, girl," he said as he stroked her neck. But he didn't really know if it was okay or not. He had figured out by now that when the Presence came to him, danger was near. He unhooked the pistol and knife.

With the horse settled back down, Bob dropped the reins and let her walk ahead as he pulled the Mauser from the scabbard and laid it across the saddle. They hadn't gone much further when the cattle came into view and Bob caught the whiff of blood. Misty began to prance; and Bob lightly touched the horse's neck, his order to continue moving forward slowly and calmly.

The cattle stood still in a tight group; and it was only when Misty pushed through them that Bob saw the dead calves, four of them, mangled and torn to pieces. Misty began pawing at the ground. Bob slid out of the saddle and placed his hand on her nose to stay put, and for once, she seemed quite happy to oblige.

All the cows crowded back around as Bob approached the calves and their mothers, who stood over them. He couldn't imagine the horror of seeing one's child torn apart; but he knew these mothers were grieving as much as Carol and Sherry had grieved for their children.

As he struggled to stay calm, he fell to his knees next to the young calves. They had been so young, so small and defenseless; and the sadness in his heart was overwhelming as he began to pray for their souls.

Reaching his hands toward the sky, he began to chant again; and the words seemed to come from someone other than himself. He didn't recognize them as anything he'd ever heard, but he knew their intentions. And as the sun warmed his face, he resolved that there was nowhere the dogs could hide now.

Bob whistled as he whipped his hand around in a circle over his head; and Misty began herding the cattle back toward the barn. Bob lagged behind, searching for the tracks of the pack; and he hadn't gone far when he found them.

The sun was just beginning to dip low; and Bob knew he still had to get the cattle taken care of before he took off after the dogs again; and that meant he would have to wait until tomorrow to begin again. His frustration peaked, and his anger boiled over. Why couldn't he just get the job done? Why was he always just a step behind? It was as though this damned hunt was the epitome of his life in general. Always trying his best to please others and take care of business, but always missing the mark just enough to be considered a failure. Well, it was going to stop now. It was time to get down and dirty.

CHAPTER 7

Bob trotted ahead until he caught up with Misty and jumped back into the saddle. A few feet further, he heard more hooves pounding the ground and turned to see Mike riding across the field toward him.

When he reached him, Mike said somberly, "Looks like you lost a few calves back there."

"Yeah. Four of 'em."

Mike could tell Bob was in no mood for idle chit-chat, and so he rode along silently beside him. When they were close to the corrals on the south end of the ranch, Mike spurred his horse ahead to open the gates; and the cattle rushed inside as though they knew there was safety here. Mike began to fill the troughs while Bob carried hay from the barn. After several more minutes had gone by, Bob suddenly stopped and looked at Mike as if he had just awakened from a deep sleep and realized where he was.

"Hey! I probably should have mentioned this before, but have you talked to Dad yet?"

Without looking up, Mike said, "Sure did. Looks like you guys can use some help; and I'm sure thankful for the offer. But if I find out it came my way out of pity, I'm going to hunt you down and give you a bloody nose."

"Yeah, you managed to do that once, but don't forget about the two black eyes I gave you. Besides, it wasn't out of pity. We've needed somebody for a long time, but Dad was just too stubborn to admit it until now."

"Just remember..."

The mood had lightened for a while. Bob whistled for Misty, and she came running. Mike watched as Bob hung grain buckets on her saddle, which she then carried back to the corral and waited patiently while he dumped the grain into the bins.

"You know, that horse of yours is half human."

"That's what she told me when I bought her."

"Bet she'd be worth a pretty penny."

"Yeah. I had an offer once, one that was pretty hard to turn down. But I couldn't do it. She would've probably just ran back home anyway; and then I would've had to give the money back. Hell, she could probably sell me easier than I could sell her."

"How does she do out hunting?"

"She's good."

The men began to close things up for the night.

"Looked like your dad got chewed up pretty bad."

"Yeah. We've had some good quality time together lately sewing each other up. But I think he's healing up pretty good."

"Bob, I've been thinking that I should go with you when you go back out after those dogs. I'm not the best with a gun, as we both know, but it would be good for you to have somebody else around in case of trouble."

"You've got a real point there, but I promised Sherry I wouldn't let you go out after them. Now, if you want to fight with that woman and get her to side with you, I'll bow to the power. But you'd better get ready for a couple more black eyes."

"She's a pretty sturdy woman, ain't she?" Mike said with a laugh.

"That she is. And to hell with you if you think I'm going to mess with her. I'd rather fight Three Toes bare-handed first."

The men laughed again, and Bob almost felt like the good old days were back. He continued. "But you need to start carrying that hog-leg Colt and your 30-30 with you all the time. You may not be able to hit anything, but at least you can try."

"You're probably right. I'll do that. And if you don't mind, I think I'll stick around here for the night just to keep an eye on things."

Bob whistled for Misty and then turned back to Mike.

"Thanks, buddy. I owe you."

When Bob got back to the ranch, he called Sherry to let her know about Mike's plans to spend the night at the south place and asked her to take him some food and the guns. When he hung up the phone, Bob stuck his head in the door to see about his dad, who immediately began asking about the afternoon. Bob settled into the chair next to him and told him about the calves. Neil began to spit and sputter, every other word a curse word.

"Dad, if you don't calm down, you're gonna bust one of those seams I sewed up."

Neil lowered his voice a notch but continued on his rampage. Bob finally interrupted him and asked about his talk with Mike. Anything to change the subject.

As the two men talked about the ranch and the things that needed done, Neil scribbled notes on the back of an old envelope that had been laying next to him on the nightstand; and when they'd covered

125

everything, he handed the envelope to Bob.

"You can give that to Mike tomorrow."

Bob scanned the list of jobs his dad had jotted down; and then, stuffing it into his pocket, said, "He's going to be on his horse all night looking after the cattle; and the more I think about it, the more I think I should get back down there with him."

"Before you go, how are things at the office?"

"Fine, it seems. Jim's taking care of all the patients, and nobody's complained yet. And I know you would never want to compliment Cindy for anything; but she's been doing a great job keeping things running smoothly."

"What the hell do you mean I won't compliment her? I haven't yelled at her in months!"

Neil was obviously still stirred up over the calves and was ready to fight about anything.

"And that's your philosophy, isn't it?" Bob shot back at him. "The only reason to say something to somebody is when they've done something wrong. Well, Dad, that really doesn't cut it. People need to know that they're worth something."

Bob knew he was speaking for himself more than he was Cindy; but it was all true for her, too. And this was a perfect opportunity to get some things off his chest.

"We're all constantly bombarded by somebody telling us that we're not strong enough or we're not pretty enough or we're not something enough. So to have somebody we respect tell us that we're worthwhile every now and then is really important. There are hundreds of Three Toes out there biting our asses off; and it's nice to have somebody helping us keep them at bay from time to time."

Bob could see the shock on his father's face but didn't dare let up until he was finished.

"You always come off as a hard ass, Dad. Somebody who couldn't care less about anybody else's feelings. It's obvious you don't ever want to be bothered with anybody's emotional crap, because you really just don't give a damn."

Neil's eyes widened and his face began to turn all shades of red. Bob could tell he wanted to yell and swear again, but it took him a minute to find something to say.

"What the hell? You don't really mean that, do you?"

"You know I wouldn't risk my life saying it to you unless I meant it."

Neil kept looking at Bob as though he was looking at an alien.

"Do you think that's why your mom always wanted to leave me?"

Bob was stunned. He couldn't believe his father had actually admitted that there had been problems there; but he was even more shocked that he had asked for his opinion.

"Probably. But she always defended you through all my ranting and telling her she should go."

With an incredulous look on his face, which was now moving into shades of purple, Neil quietly said, "You told her to leave me?"

"Yeah, Dad. I did. I'm sorry; but she deserved someone who loved her and not someone who just wanted to manage her."

Neil's expressions were all over the board; and

Bob felt like he was watching a person with multiple personalities. He sat quietly, waiting to see which personality was going to speak.

"Well, thanks for your honesty, I guess. But I think you need to leave now. I need some rest."

Bob got up, wondering whether he'd actually accomplished anything or had just made things worse. The old man's whole idea of himself had been shattered; and now he was left to either come to grips with this new reality or just blow it off. Bob knew his dad had been tough on his kids, too; but he didn't think anything more needed to be said. He had always assumed he pushed them so hard, because he wanted them to succeed. And they had. But because he had managed them like he'd managed Zelma, he had alienated two of the three along the way.

CHAPTER 8

The night went well with the cattle. Bob joined up with Mike for a while; but when he saw that things were well in hand, he finally went back to the ranch to get a little sleep before going back out early in the morning.

Sunday turned out to be yet another bust. Bob was hot on the trail by dawn and back home by mid afternoon with nothing to show and nothing to report.

He called Cindy at home to let her know he'd be in the office the next morning and asked her to call Jim to let him know. The rest of the day was spent going over chores with Mike and Sherry, and then, opting to stay at the ranch for the night instead of going back into the city, he fell into bed early.

By the time he left for the office on Monday morning, Mike was already in the field letting the cattle out to graze; and Sherry was busy at the house fixing meals and cleaning.

When he got to the office, he was surprised to see Cindy had beaten him there and already had coffee brewing.

"Cindy! It's so good to see you again. How have things been? And thanks for the coffee," he said as he poured a big, steaming mug full of java.

"It's good to see you, too, Dr. Bob. Things have been fine here. Jim did a great job with the patients, and I kept up with the scheduling and billing. And you've got a pretty full day today. So before it starts, take a minute and tell me how things are going with you."

She listened attentively as Bob filled her in on the details of everything that had transpired with the dogs. When he had finished, she said, "That's quite the undertaking. I've got to get back to some paperwork soon; but you still need to tell me about your dinner at the Klyne's."

"Oh, it was okay. Gerald is sort of an enigma; and I haven't really figured him out yet; but his wife, Grace, was very pleasant. In fact, she pretty much saved the evening for me. If I'd only had Gerald and Barb for company, I think I would have died of boredom. Or disgust."

"So that's it?"

"Sort of. At least for that evening. But then Grace called me the next day and asked me to take her out to lunch on Saturday, which I did. It might have been a stupid move on my part; but Gerald knew about it and didn't seem to care; and I was actually glad to have a break from the dogs. Of course, I haven't talked to Barb since I've been out at the ranch; so she doesn't know anything unless Gerald mentioned it to her."

"Wow!" Cindy said. "A man with a secret. I've never known you to pull something like this before. And if I'm not mistaken, I thought I saw a little sparkle in your eyes for just a few brief seconds when you were talking about this Grace."

"Shit, Cindy. Maybe the sparkle was just because I've been able to stay away from Barb for a while. Remember her? My wife? Oh, and did I mention that I have kids, too?"

"Okay, okay. I hear you loud and clear, but…"

She was out the door and on to the next task of the day before Dr. Bob could say anything else.

130

Cindy had always known there was trouble at home even though he never talked about it. And she was certain he knew that she knew, too; but it was one of those things that was never mentioned. She had heard enough of the conversations when Barb called him at the office to know things weren't really smooth there; and she had also personally been the brunt of several tongue lashings from her in the past. But Cindy loved her job with Dr. Bob and would never do anything to jeopardize it over someone like Barb.

The morning was fast and furious, with patients booked back-to-back all day. At three in the afternoon, Dr. Bob was interrupted by a knock on the exam room door. He opened it to find Cindy standing there with the phone in her hand. As she handed it to him, she gave him a knowing look and said, "Just lunch, huh?" and then she disappeared down the hallway.

Somewhat confused by her remark, he put the phone to his ear and said, "Hello? This is Dr. Bob."

"Hello, Dr. Bob! How are you?"

"Hi, Grace! I'm fine. And you?"

"Well, I'm pretty good since your secretary tells me you're free for lunch tomorrow. Does that mean you'll be picking me up at one?"

Dr. Bob walked quickly to his office to continue the conversation.

"Where are we going with this, Grace?"

"Well, I'd like to go back to that same place again. Unless you can think of some place better."

"You know that's not what I meant," Bob said bluntly.

"I know what you meant. But what do you mean by where are we going with this? I thought we were just having a good time getting to know each other."

After a few seconds of hesitation, Bob answered her. "Okay. Let's go to lunch. But I've got to say I'm not sure how comfortable I am with all this. But I'll pick you up at one."

"Don't sound so excited about it," Grace said, sounding dejected.

"Sorry, Grace. I really am excited about it, and that's what bothers me so much."

"Relax. I'll see ya tomorrow."

Bob pushed the button on the phone to end the call as Cindy popped her head around the corner. He threw her the phone and waved her off. His heart started to flutter, and he had to pause for a few deep breaths. It was time to get back to work.

The rest of the day was a flurry of activity, and Bob decided to go back to the ranch for the night. He had told the boys he'd be back when he got the dogs so they wouldn't be expecting him; and he knew Barb didn't care if he was there or not. He slept better out there anyway.

The office was just as busy the next morning as it had been the day before; but Bob found himself watching the clock, anxious for one o'clock to arrive.

He picked Grace up at the same place as before. This time he knew who he was looking for; but he was still stunned by how beautiful she was when he saw her again.

Without any ado, she jumped up into the seat and slammed the door. Turning toward him, she looked at him thoughtfully for a moment, and then leaned over and quickly kissed him on the cheek.

"A simple hello would have been enough," Bob said as he smiled at her. "But that wasn't too bad, though."

"It's nice to see you, too," she said as she flashed her perfect teeth at him.

The lunch flew by again as they talked about their lives, the dogs and their jobs. He asked what kind of work she did; and she told him about her job as a Radiology transcriptionist.

"How do you type with those fingernails?"

"Easy. In fact, I type a hundred-twenty words per minute," she said, and then continued to tell him about her job.

"It's not an easy job, typing for those doctors. They can have such a demeaning attitude toward us some-times; but some of them are nice. I'd just like to see them do their own typing for a day just so they'd know what it was like. Gerald always tells me that it's a good thing I've got a brainless job, but it isn't. It's pretty hard. In fact, I'd like to see him type for a day!"

Bob couldn't believe what he was hearing and silently wished he could just punch the guy out.

More than anything they laughed a lot, and Bob felt as though it was the best therapy he'd ever had. While driving back to the hospital, Bob decided to take the plunge.

"So, lunch tomorrow? Same place, same time?"

"And I thought I was going to have to keep asking. Of course!"

"I never do this sort of thing, you know."

"Do what sort of thing?"

"I don't usually go out to lunch like this, especially with beautiful women."

"So why are you doing it?" Grace asked with a little surprise.

"I'm not really sure. I guess something's telling me to take one day at a time and enjoy the moment."

"Now *that* sounds like a good plan to me," she said. "See ya tomorrow."

Bob watched her until she disappeared into the darkness of the building, and then headed back toward the office. He had no idea what was happening here, but he thought he liked it.

As she walked back into the building, Grace thought about how Bob never talked about Barb; but then, she tried to not talk about Gerald except for when Bob asked her questions pertaining to him. She decided it was probably a good thing he never mentioned her, because she didn't know if she'd be able to come up with anything good to say about her.

Grace felt like she was in a whole different world when she and Bob were together. She had never had anyone interested in knowing about her; but, then, maybe once he knew her better, he might not be too interested, either. But he was fun, and funny; and just the little bit of time she spent in his company was enough to brighten her days. She just wondered when it would end.

By the time Bob had finished with his patients for the day, he was anxious to get back out to the ranch. Although he knew he could just call and check on everything, it wasn't the same as being there and making sure everything was taken care of. And Neil had seemed a little quieter than usual since Bob had spilled his guts to him about his lack of respect and support. He knew the old guy was tough; but everyone

134

has a breaking point; and Bob worried about him.

Before he left the city, he thought he should go by the house to pick up a couple more changes of clothes. As soon as he opened the door, the boys converged upon him, and began to bombard him with questions about the dogs. Bob quickly realized they were thinking he had killed them all and was home to stay now. As soon as he began to explain what the situation really was, their excitement dissipated; and they began to pout.

Barb was gone with no word of where she was or when she'd be back; and the sitter had been called but hadn't shown up yet. Bob decided he'd appease the boys by taking them with him although that meant he would have to come back tonight, which he really wasn't looking forward to. But the boys deserved better from both of their parents than they were getting.

The sitter arrived just minutes later; and Bob immediately dismissed her, then turned to the boys and told them to get ready to go with him to the ranch. They were ecstatic. He left a note for Barb on the table telling her they'd all be back early in the evening; and then they took off.

The trip to the country was fun for all of them. Bob told them stories of the hunts; and they told him stories of school and friends. And then just before they reached the house, Bob told them that their grandpa had met up with the dogs and had been hurt 'a little' but would be fine in a few days.

As soon as they pulled up to the house, all three boys jumped out of the truck and ran inside. Bob trailed behind; and by the time he walked into the room, they had already huddled around Neil and were asking questions about his fight with the dogs.

Not wanting to give any of the gory details to them, Grandpa changed the subject and asked them about school. As they talked, the boys fussed over him, propping him up, fluffing his pillows, and offering to get him something to drink. It was the first time Bob remembered his dad being so warm and friendly towards the boys.

Barb didn't like the boys to visit the ranch. Her reasons were many: There was too much work to do, and Bob's brother and sister never came out to help, so why should her boys; The work was dirty, and they'd come home smelling like cow shit and sweat; It wasn't their ranch yet, and it wasn't the kind of work they should be doing; It didn't hold the fantasy for them that it did for Bob. But he and everybody else knew the real reason for her not wanting them at the ranch was that she wanted to hurt Neil. And she'd do that by keeping them from him.

Bob needed to go to the horse barn and hand out some treats, especially to Misty so she wouldn't be mad at him; and he thought he could sneak out the door while the boys entertained their grandpa. But there was no way that was going to happen. The boys were on him like ugly on an ape; and so he told his dad they'd be right back in and motioned to the boys to follow him.

Misty was always much more gentle with the boys than she was with him. He let her out of the stall, and for fun she proceeded to herd the boys into a corner.

Christopher's voice rose above the melee and

giggles in the corner. "Why does she always do this, Dad?"

"I think she's just making sure she smells each of you so if you ever get lost she could find you."

"Maybe she thinks she's a bloodhound!" Matt said.

"Maybe so, Matt."

After Misty had finished sniffing the boys, she meandered through the rest of the barn to say hello to everyone else.

As Bob watched the antics he felt a sense of relief that none of the neighbors had called about any more attacks in the last twenty-four hours. But it bothered him knowing Three Toes and Big Dog were probably out there choosing and stalking their next prey. And worse yet, he had no idea of where to start looking until something or someone came up dead.

The sound of hooves caused them all to turn in time to see Mike riding in from the south place with a big smile on his face. Mike's horse, Buck, was as easy going as Misty; and Mike was fond of hoisting the boys up on the horse's back. Now the boys were wild with anticipation.

Bob had been only nine years old when his dad had put him to work in the fields, and had learned quickly that work was the purpose of life; and he wanted his boys to have a different outlook on the ranch. And he figured Barb's decision to not allow them to visit very often and his decision to not put them to work as soon as they got there was working to his advantage.

It was soon time to go, and rounding up the boys was a chore in itself. They never wanted to leave when they came out; but this time was more difficult as they clung to their grandfather like they were never going to see him again. Neil was different, too. He held them all tight and began telling stories that Bob had never heard before. It was a great family event, and Bob hated to break it up. Maybe, he thought, something good is going to come out of the dogs.

Bob finally managed to pry the boys away from their grandfather; and they headed back into the city. Barb still wasn't home when they arrived; and since Sherry had fed the boys while they were at the ranch, Bob decided to just put them to bed. He could tell they were tired, as was he, and he hoped they might all be asleep before their mother got home.

The clock showed one in the morning when Barb shook him awake. Bob had been asleep for a little over two hours.

As he groggily raised his head and tried to open his eyes, she said, "Wake up, Bob. I want to talk to you about something."

"What? Is something wrong?"

"No," Barb scoffed. "I want to tell you about seeing Dr. Klyne."

"Does it have to be right now?"

"Now is as good a time as any, isn't it? So, yes, it has to be now."

Bob's anger with her surfaced again.

"Look, Barb. If it's not an emergency, it can wait until morning. I'm tired as hell, and the last thing I need is to listen to your bullshit at one in the morning."

Barb's jaw dropped as she glared at him.

Bob grew madder the more he woke up. "You

138

know, other people have the right to sleep at night, too. But then that wouldn't be a problem for you, because you just sleep all day. So whatever it is you've got to talk about, it's going to wait until morning."

Bob grabbed his pillow and headed toward the couch. He had surprised himself again with his fervor, but felt a great sense of satisfaction in putting his foot down.

Barb could only watch him leave and knew there was no stopping him. This was the second time he'd talked back to her lately; and she wasn't at all happy about it. She deserved better treatment than this; and she would get it if it was the last thing she did. But she would wait until tomorrow; and then she would give him a piece of her mind.

By the time Barb woke up the next morning, the boys had already left for school; and Bob had left for work. She was furious.

Dr. Bob got to the office before Cindy did this time and was gearing up for the day when she arrived. He'd already checked with Sherry; and she assured him that his dad was doing okay; but the dogs kept weighing heavy on his mind; and his uneasiness about them continued to grow throughout the day.

He tried to focus on his mound of paperwork, the only thing he truly hated about his job. But within minutes of sitting down in the front of the pile of folders, he found his thoughts wandering to Grace. He wanted to call her just to chat, but then the guilt set in again. He thought maybe he should stop this silliness and just cancel their lunch; but then he started thinking about her again. Finally, he reached for the phone; but for the third time the guilt stopped him; and he slammed the phone back down on its base.

Bob felt pulled apart and had no idea of which way to turn. There had always been women who had come on to him before, and he had always been repulsed. Just the mere idea of another woman in his life was enough to make him run for the hills. And he always knew if anything ever were to happen to Barb, whether it be divorce or death, he would cherish his freedom, his peace, and even his celibacy. He refused to be caught in another situation like he was in now. At least that was what he used to think. But since meeting Grace, things had been different. He wasn't accustomed to these thoughts and feelings that he had toward this woman; and he had to constantly keep reminding himself that he was married and had his boys to think of. But his rationale never seemed to matter. His thoughts always just returned to her.

The morning was finally over, and he was eager for the lunch with Grace. Screw it all, he thought. This is *my* time. As he hurried to his truck to go pick her up, all thoughts of everything except Grace left his mind.

As she walked out of the door at Kansas University Medical Center and strode toward him, he felt like he was in a television commercial where everything was in slow motion just to capture the moment. He saw her hair as it blew in the soft breeze and how she tossed her head to get it out of her face, the way her arms moved at her sides, her hips as they moved so gracefully. It was all in slow motion, as though he was living in a dream. He looked at the outline of her thighs as they pulled against the fabric of her dress, her calves as the muscles flexed with each step. He noticed the way she placed her feet, one

140

perfectly in front of the other, as she walked. It was a dream for him. A dream come true. As he pulled the truck out into the busy traffic in front of the hospital, he looked at her and said, "Grace, when are we going to have an affair?"

The shock on her face caused Bob to suddenly feel embarrassed. What was he thinking? To even consider the thought in the solitude of his own mind was bad enough; but then to say it to her was nothing short of insane. Her response only served to make him feel all the more like a weasel.

"We're not. As much as I might like to, we're both married."

Bob felt as though he could cry, perhaps from relief that she'd given him no options, but more probably from the disappointment that it wasn't going to happen.

When he finally felt as though he could talk without breaking down, he said, "You may be the best friend I've ever had; and I don't ever want to lose that between us. Thanks for being strong when I'm not."

"Well," Grace quietly said, "you are certainly the best friend I've ever had. But to be *my* best friend you'll have to be just as strong when I'm not."

"I will. I promise."

They pulled up at Lucille's, and the conversation moved comfortably into other subjects. It wasn't long before they were both laughing again; and then, all too soon, it was time for them to get back to work.

The afternoon patient load was lighter than the morning's had been; and Bob casually moved from one person to another. This was the part of his job that

141

he truly loved, spending time with his patients, listening to their problems and helping them to feel better. But the thought of the earlier conversation with Grace kept him feeling on edge. He truly was thankful that she had put her foot down, that beautiful foot in those spiked heels. But depression came in there somewhere, too; and that part just made him mad.

The afternoon lull was suddenly interrupted by Cindy barreling down the hall and yelling for Bob. Sherry was on the phone. The dogs had been spotted; and Mike had gone out after them; and she was hysterical. After Bob calmed her down as much as he could, he told Cindy to do what needed to be done with any other patients who came in; and then he took off back toward the ranch as fast as he could go.

He hadn't thought to ask Sherry if she was at home or at the ranch; so he decided to stop at her house first since it was on the way to his. As he pulled up to the house, Sherry ran out to meet him.

"He headed toward the south place on Buck. I'm scared, Bob. You can't let him get hurt. You promised!"

She looked like she had seen a ghost; and Bob wondered if the loss of her child still haunted her, causing her irrational fear. This time, he thought, it might not be so irrational.

Throwing the Suburban into reverse, Bob spun a circle in the driveway and took off. His mind raced as fast as his engine; and he tried to tell himself that Sherry had just misunderstood; and Mike had just gone down to guard the cattle. But the feeling of dread he'd been struggling with all day told him differently.

When he reached the south place, he grabbed

142

his weapons and took off to find Buck's tracks, which he spotted a few minutes later. He figured they were only a half hour old, so he figured he should be able to catch up to him soon. It was only minutes later that he saw Buck running back to the ranch with tail flying and eyes bulging...and no Mike in the saddle.

His heart sank, and his fear rose. With Mike being so bad with a gun, Bob knew there was no way that the dogs would be the ones killed if they had a run-in. If they hadn't already, they would eat him alive given half a chance.

Assuming Buck had headed straight home, Bob turned and ran in the opposite direction. Once he'd gotten to the top of the south hill, he stopped and pulled his pistol, and shot three times hoping Mike would hear and return fire. Nothing. As he reloaded the gun, he noticed the tracks of the dogs a few feet away, and much to his frustration, noticed there were more tracks than usual. Not only were there tracks of Three Toes, Big Dog and the other two that traveled with them, but there were four additional ones now. The pack was back up to eight. The chances of Mike coming out of this alive were seeming slimmer by the minute; and Bob knew he had to get to Mike before the dogs did. As he took off again, he prayed he wasn't too late.

Forging on ahead, he watched for as many signs as his speed would allow and stopped when he saw where Buck and Mike had separated. Mike had continued on to the south; and the dogs had followed, much too closely for Bob's comfort. Again, Bob fired three shots but heard nothing in return. Visions of his father lying on the ground raced through his mind; and his heart began to pound as he ran even faster across creeks, up hills, and through valleys, all the while keeping his eyes glued to the trail. He had only an hour or so before dusk; and he had to find Mike, dead or alive, before then.

Mike's tracks seemed to abruptly slow to a hunt pace, and Bob figured he must be close. A small rise in front of him gave way to an open area; and Bob quietly made his way toward it. At the edge of the open area, Mike's tracks disappeared.

"What the hell are you doing?"

Bob jumped and had his pistol drawn, cocked, and about to shoot by the time Mike had finished the question.

Bob looked around but didn't see him; and by the time Mike spoke again, Bob was beginning to wonder if he had just been hallucinating.

"Hey, up here!"

Bob looked up. Mike sat on a limb directly above him and was grinning from ear to ear. Before Bob could speak, Mike put his finger to his mouth then pointed to the other side of the opening.

In a whisper, Bob said, "You're a piece of shit, you damned idiot! You just scared the hell out of me!"

"Shut up, Stupid. The dogs in front of us think their buddies have killed me; and they're going to be back soon for dinner. Only thing is, they're going to be really surprised when I shoot their asses off as they move into that opening."

"You couldn't hit a train in that opening even if it wasn't moving! You'd just better thank your lucky stars I got here when I did to save your sorry ass."

"Save my ass? Ha! Who's the one on the

ground crapping in his pants? And who's the one in the tree safe and sound?"

Bob *had* just about crapped his pants; and he had to admit that Mike did have a great advantage up there, while he was standing here in the middle of the dog's path.

He climbed up next to Mike, and the two men settled back down to wait. After fifteen minutes had passed, there had been no sign of the dogs.

"Sure looks like you had them pegged just right, Mighty King of the Dog Hunters."

"They would have been here by now; but with all that noise you made getting here, they probably thought a herd of elephants was after them."

"What the hell do you mean, herd of elephants? You're the one with the elephant tracks."

"I had to make them big so you could follow."

Neither of them took their eyes away from their sights as they bantered and snickered.

After several more minutes passed without any sign of the dogs, Mike whispered again. "Did you get those four dogs I sent back your way with Buck?"

"There weren't any dogs following Buck."

"Well, I heard you shooting up everything, and I thought you'd surely come across some of them," Mike said, continuing the ribbing.

"No, Numb-Skull, those were signal shots that you were supposed to respond to so I would know your ass was still moving."

Mike grinned. "You don't need to worry about me. I ain't like you, getting all chewed up by a few little, old puppies."

"You are a real piece of work, you know that,

Mike? Now, are you watching our backs, or are you just busy flopping your lips?"

"Hell, no, I'm not watching our backs. I'm watching across that clearing, just like I was when you showed up. You're the one who's supposed to be watching our backs."

Bob enjoyed the bantering and kept it going. "You're watching the clearing, but your gun can't shoot that far. And even if it could, you'd need the dog holding the damned barrel of the gun up to his head in order for you to hit him."

"Shut up and turn around," Mike retorted. "You just watch the woods."

Bob shook his head and turned to watch behind them. Another twenty minutes passed without incident; and Bob finally stood up on the limb and dusted himself off. He still wore the clothes he'd worn to the office that morning except for the tie that he'd taken off and left in the truck. Now, as the sun was beginning to set, he just wanted to get back home, get a shower, and let Sherry know she didn't have to worry anymore.

"Come on, King Dog, it's time to head back to the ranch. It'll take us a good hour to get back, and I'm sure Sherry is worried to death about you."

"You just don't want me to shoot Three Toes, do you, Elephant Man?"

"Ha! No worries there. He'd have your knee caps chewed off before you could even get a shot off."

"Yeah, right. And this coming from the guy with fifty stitches."

"It was only forty."

They both dropped from the tree and gave each

other a thump on the back.

As they walked back toward home, Mike told Bob that he had heard a ruckus coming from the stables; and when he went to see what it was all about, he noticed the dogs pacing about fifty yards away.

"I already had Buck saddled up; and so I just jumped on and took off after them; and when I had them on the run, I put the reigns in my mouth, grabbed my guns and started firing. I ran out of bullets in the rifle, so I pulled my six-shooter out and just kept firing. I felt just like John Wayne in *True Grit*. The only thing I needed was a patch over one eye."

Bob just shook his head, and they laughed together.

They were about half way back to the ranch when Bob froze. Mike followed suit a split second later; and immediately, they turned their backs to each other and searched the darkening woods around them. When Mike didn't see or hear anything, he said, "I take it you heard something, Bob?"

Bob hadn't heard anything. Instead, he'd felt the Presence again and knew danger was near. But rather than try to explain the odd situation to Mike, he said nothing as he continued to stare into the woods.

"Okay, Bob, say something, man. You're freaking me out here."

"Let's just cover our backs."

Mike heard the low growl just ahead of Bob, and he turned in that direction.

"They're all around us, Mike. Keep your back to me and make sure you're loaded up.

"My rifle's loaded but not my pistol," Mike said as he spun back around.

"Okay," Bob continued in a low voice. "Hand me your rifle."

"What the hell's going on?" Mike asked as he handed the rifle backward to Bob.

"They were waiting for us. Just like we were waiting on them. I just happened to hear them before they got the jump on us."

"Damn! How in hell did you hear them over me talking?"

"Come to think of it, your mouth's always gotten us in trouble, you know that?"

"My mouth may have gotten us into trouble; but it was no doubt your smelly ass that lead them to us this time. But no joke now. You think they're going to attack?"

"They've followed me home more than once. But I usually just spread the pepper, and that takes care of it."

"Did you bring the pepper with you this time?"

"No, damn it. I had to rush out here to save your ass."

"You haven't saved anybody's ass yet."

"Just start moving and keep that rifle to your shoulder. When they come, if they do, they'll all come at once; so take a deep breath and don't let it out until that 30-30 is empty."

As they shuffled sideways, while keeping their rifles shouldered, Bob readied himself for the onslaught. He knew he'd have to take his dogs out fast and then turn to cover Mike. But the dogs stayed back far enough that Bob could only catch a glimpse of them now and then in spite of being able to see through the woods.

148

He noticed that Three Toes and Big Dog were slowly making their way around to Mike's side. The dogs had recognized the weakest link and seemed to know their best chance to get to the men was on that side. The others stayed on Bob's side.

The pack continued to stand off as the men worked their way through the woods. Finally, when the trees thinned, Bob knew they were home safe. He and Mike dropped their guns and settled into a relaxed walk back toward the house. But a hundred feet more and Bob stopped again.

"They're still back there, Mike. I want you to get back and make sure Sherry knows you're okay; and then go to the corral and make sure everything's okay there. Just be as quiet as you can. I'm going to stay here and build a fire and wait to see what Three Toes is going to do."

"Geez, Bob! Haven't you had enough for one day?"

"Just leave your hog leg and some shells and get going."

Mike knew if he didn't get back to Sherry soon she would go nuts; but he didn't like leaving Bob there by himself.

"You're crazier than I thought. I'll go, but you'd better be alive when I get back here."

"Ah, hell. I can take all of them if they come out of those woods."

"Yeah, we all know how good you are. Just be careful," he said as he handed Bob his pistol and took off running toward the ranch.

Mike knew Bob was good with the guns, really good. And the chances of the dogs getting within fifty feet of him were almost nil; but there was still the chance they might try. He hurried to get to Sherry to let her know he was okay, and then he had to get back to Bob.

Bob collected wood and started a fire, and in a short time had a good one roaring. He rolled a heavy log up close to it and sat down. He still felt the Presence, and he knew Three Toes was close. He silently gave thanks for the protection and his gifts. He just wished he knew who he was thanking.

He could see Three Toes in the darkness, just waiting for his chance. Bob proceeded to make sure all leather straps were undone and pistols were ready to pull out of their holsters clean. Last of all, he checked his knife. Then, laying his Mauser across his lap, he waited.

He wanted Three Toes to know he wasn't scared now and would take him on anywhere and any time. He also wanted to show him that he was willing to die in order to protect those he loved, and that he was a worthy warrior who deserved respect. As the thoughts rolled around in his head, he found himself almost liking Three Toes, and wondered if they would have been friends under a different set of circumstances. Maybe the dog had just been pushed around too much and for too long; and this was the end result. He wondered if he could be headed down the same road.

Bob tried to keep his mind clear and focused as he sat there; but, eventually, he found himself thinking of Grace again. He figured Barb was about to spill her guts about all her affairs; or maybe she was just going to leave him. Either way, he needed to be ready for anything and hoped his Guardian might see fit to be with him when it happened.

An hour hadn't passed when a strong odor wafted through the air to Bob. He immediately recognized it as Sherry's perfume, and he knew Mike was close.

"I'm sure Three Toes knew you were coming ten minutes ago, Mike," Bob bellered to him. "What've you been doing? Smooching all over Sherry? You smell like a damned sissy!"

He heard a muffled "Shit!" from far away.

A few minutes later, Mike walked down to the fire with a grin on his face.

"Do I really smell that much?" he asked as he took a seat next to his friend.

"Well, I can say this much: Three Toes wouldn't have any trouble smelling you coming even if he had sniffed a pound of pepper already."

"I couldn't get her off me," Mike said sheepishly. "You were right. When Buck went racing back to the barn, she thought I was dead, sure enough. Then Misty almost kicked the barn down trying to get out. I guess she was going to come and get us."

"That's one crazy woman," Bob said as he chuckled and shook his head.

"Yes, but you couldn't ask for a better horse."

Bob looked at Mike for a few seconds, and then said, "I was talking about Sherry."

"Oh! Well, I guess *she's* a pretty good horse, too."

Bob thought of all sorts of remarks to that comment, but refrained for fear of insulting Mike.

"Yeah, Sherry's the best," Mike said vaguely.

151

"Oh, and your dad's on his feet again and making sure everything is being taken care of. In fact, he was the one who calmed her down when she started to have her little tizzy."

"That's hard to believe. He's never done anything to soothe a person in his life. And Sherry, of all people. Calming her down couldn't have been that easy."

"That's what he said. He was pretty proud of himself."

"The old man is changing. In fact, I'm starting to think he's really got a heart after all. Makes me wonder what's coming next."

A quiet minute went by, and Mike pulled out a thermos of coffee.

"You really do want those bastards to know exactly where we are, don't you?"

"Sure! Why not? I've got the great game hunter with me, so I don't have anything to worry about."

"You're crazy, Mike."

"Actually, I was thinking. Since I've got all this smelly shit on me, why don't you go out into the woods while I stay here and make them think we're just sitting here waiting for them to sneak in. Then you can take them from behind when they close in on me."

"That might not be such a bad idea, King Dog. Just let me have your knife and Colt; and I'll leave my rifle here with you."

As Mike handed over his knife, Bob grabbed a handful of cooled ashes and smeared them over his face. Then he headed toward the darkness.

"Just make sure you get the damned things before they get me; and make damned sure it's a dog you shoot," Mike said as Bob disappeared without a sound.

Bob was more comfortable in the dark since he'd been given the gift of sight; and he felt as though the playing field was a little more leveled now. He hoped he'd be able to take at least one or two; and again he hoped it would be Three Toes or Big Dog. Losing a leader would definitely put the pack at more of a disadvantage; and maybe they would even just disband if the leader was gone.

After an hour had gone by without incident, Mike started to think the dogs had left with Bob right behind them. He decided he would keep the fire going and wait for him to come back rather than head on toward home by himself. He threw a few more limbs on the fire and sat back to listen for a gun to go off.

Bob could smell the dogs and thought they were about fifty yards in front of him. With the breeze in his face, they would have to see him coming to know he was there; and so he moved slowly and silently as he closed in on them.

It took a while for him to get into position, but then he saw the first dog. It was standing ten feet in from of him, pacing back and forth, its eyes focused on Mike. Bob slid the knives from their sheaths and moved with as much stealth as he could toward the dog. It wasn't Three Toes, but it would do. When he was finally close enough, Bob stood still, not moving a muscle, until the dog moved past him within arms length. The first knife went to its throat, rendering it unable to yelp as the second knife entered its chest. Without a sound, Bob quickly picked it up and moved silently back into the woods.

When he was clear of the area that the rest of the pack was covering, he laid the dog down and said a silent prayer. "Great Spirit, please take this creature and let him be happy and healthy with You." Bob gently touched the dog's head, and then silently returned to the path.

As he entered back into the area of the dogs, he quickly knew that something was wrong. There was no sign of the dogs, and no smell of them, either. There was only the smell of Sherry's perfume. Bob wondered if the pack had realized what had happened to their comrade and had decided to change tactics. And then, as he drew closer to the fire, he saw them on the other side of Mike.

"Mike!" he yelled. "Start shooting!"

Mike was up in a flash, firing in every direction in the woods but keeping his shots low. If he hit Bob, he preferred it be in the leg and not the head. In the meantime, Bob saw the dogs circle around Mike and head straight for him; and he began to claw his way up the nearest tree. But just as he was about to swing his leg over a limb, one of the dogs grabbed at his right heel, teeth sinking into his shoe and piercing his foot. The weight of the dog on him left Bob dangling by his hands; and before he could shake the dog off, a second set of teeth latched onto his left foot. He struggled against the dogs, yelling at them and kicking as best he could as he concentrated on hanging on to the limb. He knew if they managed to pull him down it would be over for him.

The first dog finally let go of his right foot; and Bob tried again to swing it over the branch; but again it was caught in the jaws of a dog, this one bigger and stronger than the last. Although he had managed to keep a decent grip on the limb before, now he began to slip.

He could hear Mike crashing through the woods behind him and shooting up a storm; and he yelled at the top of his lungs, hoping Mike might figure out where he was. Immediately, the dogs let go and rushed off into the darkness. As fast as they had come, they were gone.

Bob dropped to the ground and leaned up against the trunk of the tree just as Mike reached him.

"Reload, Mike! I've got us covered for now," Bob said as he raised his rifle to his shoulder.

"Are you okay?" Mike asked between gulps of air.

"Aside from feeling a little like Gumby after having those dogs pulling on me, I'm doing okay. I think they thought I was a chewy bone, but they're gone now."

"Shit, Bob! Can you walk?"

"I can run if I have to."

"Let's get out of here. If you need help, just hang on to me."

Together, they backed out of the woods as fast as they could and made their way back to the fire, where Bob sank onto the log.

"You've got to get back to the house. It looks like they got you pretty good."

"Not really. I'm not sure where all the blood is coming from. You must have gotten lucky and hit one of them, because I don't think this is all from me."

Not even trying to hide his surprise, Mike said, "Imagine that!" Bob had to laugh.

They stayed next to the fire for another hour until Bob felt the Presence leave, and then, knowing the danger was over for a while, they headed back home, Buck following behind.

The walk back to the house was quiet, both men exhausted. Sherry ran to greet them as they came through the door; and the rest of the evening was spent huddled around the kitchen table. For a short time, none of them noticed their pain, mental or physical. But soon, Bob's reality settled back in; and he knew he had to get back to the city. He wanted to see the kids, and he still had to deal with Barb.

CHAPTER 9

It was pushing eleven o'clock when he got home; and as he came into view of the house, something suddenly didn't feel right. It wasn't like the Presence should be with him, but there was just something awry. A Fiero was parked on the street between Bob's house and the house next door. It could have been anyone visiting any of the neighbors; but something about it was unsettling.

Instead of pulling into the driveway, he drove on past and circled the block. As soon as he was back on his own street and within view of the house, he pulled over and cut the engine and lights. He was tired and just wanted to go to bed; but he decided to give it a little time before he just wrote his feelings off as paranoia.

He had to wait only fifteen minutes. A man appeared from behind the house and looked both ways on the otherwise empty street before he left the safety of the shadow cast by the street lamp. Without his gift of sight, Bob couldn't tell who it was; but he was sure he had come from his house.

Once the car had zoomed away, Bob started the truck and proceeded on to the house. After he had locked up the guns in the gun cabinet in the garage, he went in to find Barb rummaging in the refrigerator. She was dressed in a pink, silk negligee.

"Hi!" she said. "What have you been up to?"

Bob decided playing along for a while would be better than reacting like he wanted to, which would have been to verbally castrate her right then and there.

"Nothing other than the dogs. You?"

"Oh, I had the boys stay over with friends tonight so you and I could have some quiet time together. A little one-on-one private time, if you know what I mean."

Even if it had been true, Bob couldn't stand the thought of what she was insinuating; but he knew she wasn't dressed like that for him.

Barb emerged from the refrigerator with a can of Coors and a block of cheese and then pulled a box of crackers from the cabinet. As she went into the family room, Bob began to clean up the kitchen. Just being in the same room with her was more than he could stand; so the longer he could put it off, the better.

After a few minutes went by, Barb whined through the pass-through window between the kitchen and the family room. "Come on, Bob. Come in here and talk to me."

"What do you want to talk about?" he asked as he finished wiping down the cabinets.

"Nothing special. Just what's been going on at the office and out at the ranch. That's all."

He couldn't wait to see where this was leading as he hung up the towel and joined her by the fireplace.

"Well, as you can see by the checkbook, things are good at the office. And as far as the ranch goes, we lost four calves the other day; and Dad got chewed up; but he's going to be okay. The dogs are still out there, and I'm still trying to get them. That's about it."

"Sounds like a lot. Do you need help with the dogs?"

"Nope. Mike Curtis is out there, and he's been helping me out. Do you remember him? He's married to Sherry, the talker. She's taking care of Dad until he can get back on his feet."

"Yeah, I remember him. An alright guy, kind of quiet, good looking. But I was thinking. Gerald told me how much fun he had going out with you the other day; and I thought if you were willing to take him with you again, we could get a few more free sessions from him. What do you think?"

He would have loved telling her what he thought, but it wouldn't be anything she would want to hear. Plus, it was so late; and he had to get some sleep before going back into the office in the morning.

"Well, his bills are pretty outrageous."

"But it's okay, isn't it? After all, I need those sessions if we're going to make this marriage work. So he can go with you again?"

Bob couldn't believe what he was hearing. She had made it pretty obvious that she never cared about their marriage before; so why would she even start trying to pull it off now? And besides that, she had just had a man sneaking out the back door of the house. Bob didn't know whether to laugh or spew.

"Okay. Why don't you have him call me with his schedule; and we'll work out a time he can go back out with me."

"Oh, that's great! And maybe we could all have dinner out at the ranch some time. That would give me a chance to get to know Grace a little better. And it would be nice to see Mike again after all these years."

Nothing was lost on Bob. Barb obviously didn't give a shit about Grace; and she always made it perfectly clear that she hated the ranch and Neil. So if she wanted everyone to have dinner again, why not do it in the city where she wouldn't have to worry about Neil? The only thing Bob saw that might lead her to such a request, the only thing different out there than here, was Mike. But she hardly knew him; and he couldn't think of any agenda of hers that might involve Mike.

"I bet Sherry would fix dinner since she's already out there with your dad," Barb continued.

There it was. She wanted dinner, and she didn't want to have to fix it.

Barb interrupted his thoughts. "I was wondering when you would be coming to bed. I'm kind of tired, but I get really lonely sometimes."

The thought disgusted him. She just had one man in her bed, and now she was inviting him to follow. There was no way in hell he was crawling back into bed with her. Not now, and maybe never. But he didn't want to get into it. He just wanted some sleep.

"I'll be there as soon as I can."

She seemed put off at his answer; and he wondered if it was because she thought he wouldn't be up, or because she thought he would. As she swilled the rest of her beer, she got up and headed to the stairs.

"Hurry," she said.

When she was out of sight, Bob wearily got up and went into the boy's bathroom. He pulled off his shoes and socks and examined the bites on his feet. They weren't bad, not too deep. But he had to disinfect them or they'd turn into a real mess in no time.

He pulled the alcohol out of the cabinet and held his feet over the tub and began pouring. He gritted his teeth to keep from yelling out; and when he was done, he doctored them up as best he could with the Mickey Mouse Band-Aids that were in the cabinet. When he had finished with that, he made his way back to the couch and turned on the TV just to have something to distract his thoughts. As he began to drift off to sleep, he wondered about the source of his new-found assertiveness, and considered if Grace had something to do with it. She was beautiful. And she was his friend. And those two things together were enough to make any man feel like a man.

Bob felt like he had gotten caught up in a tornado and had no idea where he was going to land, or if he'd be dead or alive when it was all over with. He worried about his kids and would do anything to protect them, even to the point of pretending to love their mother. But he had to be honest with himself. He'd not done a very good job of pretending lately. And if he wasn't any good at pretending that he loved her, would he be any better at pretending he *didn't* love Grace?

"We're not in Kansas anymore, Toto," he said as he drifted off to sleep.

His night was restless, often waking in a cold sweat. The cuts, scrapes and bites on his body, though on their way to being healed, ached and felt fresh each time he woke up; and he had to look at them to make sure they hadn't opened up and started bleeding again.

Nightmares haunted him; but then he couldn't remember what they were about when he would wake up and check the bandages. His nerves were raw; and he constantly had the feeling that the dogs were everywhere, surrounding him.

161

Morning came too soon. He woke with a start and had to stop and think about where he was. The smell of breakfast cooking hung in the air; and he knew Matt must already be up. Dragging himself off the couch, he stumbled into the kitchen and was surprised to see that Barb was standing at the stove.

He glanced at his watch and realized it was late in the morning, but it was still earlier than usual for her. Much earlier. His mind was still foggy with sleep; and as he tried to comprehend what he was seeing, he began to feel threatened by the unexpected change in her routine.

Barb set the food on the table as he sat down. He picked up the fork next to his plate; and just as he was about to dig into the eggs, he hesitated. But, then, he figured she probably wasn't out to kill him, regardless of how mean she was. After all, he was her meal ticket.

"You know, Bob, I haven't been paying enough attention to things around here, or to you and the boys. So I decided I'm going to start getting up every morning and cooking breakfast and getting them off to school and you off to work."

He barely managed to hide the surprise in his voice.

"That's nice. The boys would probably like that a lot, but you know we do okay on our own. In fact, Matt's turning into a pretty good cook. He still tends to break the egg yokes every once in a while, but he's trying. And we're getting pretty used to over-hard eggs."

"That's great. And by the way, I thought we would have Gerald and Grace out to the ranch for dinner soon."

Bob looked at her and said, "You said that last night. Don't you remember?"

"Oh!" she said, grinning sheepishly from ear to ear.

Bob was still trying to decide what to make of Barb's erratic behavior. He decided to err on the side of caution but try to keep an open mind at the same time.

"Why don't you set things up with him and then let me know what you all have worked out?"

Bob finished his breakfast and was relieved when he finally crawled into his old truck and took off for work. Even though he didn't trust Barb at all, at least the morning hadn't involved a fight. He suddenly found himself looking forward to what the day might bring; and then he thought of lunch.

He had to talk to Grace today and really make sure she understood what the situation was with him. He wanted her to know that he would never do anything to cause pain for his boys; and he also wanted her to understand clearly that he was married and planned on staying that way for at least another nine years, until his youngest was out of school.

When he walked into the office, Cindy had the phone in her hand, waiting for him. As she held it out toward him, she made silent kissing gestures in the air.

Cindy worried about how much trouble Bob might be getting into. She wondered if she should talk to him about it, even though he was her boss. He might be smart when it came to his patients, but he was still a man; and she knew all too well of the years of abuse from Barb. Any sane person who had spent time with a

163

witch like her would gravitate toward the first woman who was civil to him. But that was just it. Dr. Bob had always lived by a higher standard than that.

She knew he cherished his kids and valued his patients enough that he would never intentionally do anything that might mar his reputation in their eyes. And at one time, he even seemed to love his wife, although she had seen that wane over the years. So now Cindy worried that he was going to jeopardize everything that he'd always strived for without even realizing it.

"Grace!" Bob said. "I was just thinking about you."

"Well, maybe that was why I was feeling the urge to call you."

"What's going on in your world?"

"Funny you should ask. That's what I was wondering about you," Grace answered with a hint of humor in her voice.

"Well, let's see. Barb decided to invite some friends out to the ranch sometime soon. Other than that, nothing much is going on today; at least not yet."

"Hmm. That's funny. Gerald just called me at the office here; and it seems we've gotten that very same invitation. What a coincidence."

Bob and Grace both laughed, and then Bob said, "I'm sure between those two we'll be finding out all the details soon."

Grace's voice dropped a little lower. "I feel a little funny about this, Bob. Maybe even a little more than a little."

"Why? It's just pay-backs for having us over for dinner; and besides, it will be fun. I can show you the ranch; and you can meet my dad and my friends, Mike and Sherry.

There was a bit of silence, and then he added, "I'd really like it if you'd come."

"You mean it?"

"Of course I mean it."

Excitement began to show in her voice. "Will I get to meet Misty and Mask and Buck and all the rest of your horses? I mean…hell, I don't know what I mean."

She giggled like a giddy little girl. The excitement was contagious; and Bob laughed with her, thinking they were acting like a couple of teenagers going to their first dance.

"I know what you mean. And, yes, you'll get to meet everyone."

"So when are you picking me up for lunch?"

"It'll be the usual time. And, Grace, this time I think we need to really talk, if you know what I mean."

"That sounds serious."

"Well, it's a little on the serious side. But right now I need to get to work so I can get out of here on time."

"Okay. See you in a little bit," she said with a tinge of hesitation.

Bob was nervous for the rest of the morning and found himself having trouble keeping his head into his work. He almost wished something would come up to give him a valid reason to cancel the lunch; but this was important, so he'd face it. But he felt like an ass. Here he was, getting ready to clearly define his boundaries to her just after having invited her to the ranch.

When it came time to leave, Cindy noticed that he was more hesitant than usual in getting out the door.

"What's up with you, Dr. Bob? Why aren't you getting out of here? Isn't Grace waiting for you?"

"Yes. But I'm trying to get a little book work done before I go."

"You know, you're a terrible liar, and I know something's going on with you. What is it? Anything I can help with?"

"No, I'm afraid this is something I have to take care of myself. But thanks for asking."

"Well, you'd better get going then. Maybe we can talk a little when you get back."

He knew she was right; so as she turned and walked out of the office, he picked up his keys and took off. When he got to the hospital, Grace was waiting at the door. As she crawled into the truck, he apologized for being late, which she waved off with a smile. But he couldn't make himself drive on yet.

"Look, I've got to get this out of the way before we go, so if things get screwed up we won't have a long, awkward drive back."

Grace was surprised by his abrupt approach; and after a moment of hesitation, she reached over and took his hand. The warmth of her touch melted the ice that was running through his veins.

Bob closed his eyes and took a deep breath before beginning.

"Since I've met you, I've found that you're on my mind a lot. And that's something new for me. I haven't ever let anything get into my head like you have; and it's wonderful and terrible all at the same time."

166

Grace still sat patiently as he took another deep breath and blew it out.

"I'm married, Grace. And I've got to stay that way. My boys... I can't hurt them; and it's going to be nine more years before they're grown and gone. I don't know what you expect from this relationship; but all there can be is a friendship, regardless of how much we might want more. Now I know that's what you said before, but I also know what I feel. And unless I'm really wrong, I think you probably feel a little bit the same way."

Grace still said nothing, so he continued.

"I guess this is where you have to decide whether or not you want to keep this up...the lunches, the dinners, the phone calls. All that."

When she was sure he was finished, Grace leaned over to cup his face with both hands, and gently touched her lips to his. Bob melted under her touch and felt himself responding to her. When she finally pulled away from him, he continued to sit there with his eyes closed, willing his heart to slow down. And then when he could finally catch his breath, he looked over at her.

Trying to sound gruff, he said, "What in God's green earth did I just get through saying?", but instead, it came out sounding more like a plea.

Grace didn't flinch. Softly she said, "I love you."

He opened his mouth to respond, but nothing would come out. His heart was bursting with joy and breaking in half at the same time. He didn't know what to say.

She continued. "I need to just stay friends, too,

even though I'd prefer it to be different. My first marriage was a disaster except for my daughter, and now I'm on my second. When I married Gerald, I promised myself this one was going to last; and I intend to keep that promise. So let's let it go with this: When you asked when we were going to have an affair, I knew two things. I knew that I wanted to, and I knew that I wouldn't. So don't feel lonely in your emotions. Any of them."

Bob was more astounded than ever, and he knew he should be feeling relief. But instead, he wanted to cry from grief.

"Now, if you still want to go to lunch, we'd better get going."

Without a word, he put the truck in gear and took off. The trip to the restaurant was void of any further conversation; but he still couldn't keep himself from glancing in her direction every once in a while. She would just look back at him and smile.

There probably weren't ten words spoken during the whole lunch; and most of those were to the waitress. The silence wasn't awkward, though. Instead, it seemed to be a time of bonding, their eyes doing the talking and their souls doing the listening. Bob felt as though the world had stopped just for him and was waiting for him to crawl aboard.

Lunch ended, and Bob got back to the office to find a heavy afternoon scheduled. He was relieved that Cindy wouldn't have time to talk. He was just too lost in his turmoil, and he didn't want it spilling out all over the place.

The afternoon was punctuated by another phone call, this one from Neil. Another rancher, Mr. Paulsen, had lost three steers, their throats ripped out. Cindy immediately began making other plans for Dr. Bob's patients.

Bob knew Three Toes was baiting him; and his anger fueled him enough that he arrived at the site in record time. He took off to the west into fairly unknown territory again and wondered if Three Toes had chosen this area for that very reason. He traveled slower than usual as he took in the terrain and wondered if he was giving the dog too much credit.

The tracks appeared to be somewhere between an hour to two hours old; but he continued to take his time while he tried to listen and smell everything around him. The Presence hadn't come to him yet, and he felt very vulnerable.

He continued along the trail the dogs had left while watching for any signs of motion around every bush or tree. The only way Three Toes would get the advantage over him here was if the whole pack was to ambush him at once; and Bob wasn't going to let that happen if he could help it.

The tracks suddenly split off, with some going to the right, Big Dog's and a comrade's to the left, and Three Toes' and an underling's straight ahead. Obviously, Three Toes' mind worked much like his own. So now the only thing he could do would be to outsmart him.

Bob stood quietly as he contemplated his options. Which way did Three Toes assume he would go? Did it really make any difference which way he went or was one choice just as good or bad as the others? Bob finally decided the best tactic would be to go after the weakest of the three trails. Yes, that would be the smartest, to take the weakest first and then go after Three Toes. So he didn't do it.

He followed the trail ahead to where Three Toes should have been; and just as he'd figured, he found the weakest dogs there, yapping in a frenzy not a hundred yards away. They and Three Toes had changed position, which meant Three Toes was now on Bob's right, leaving Big Dog still on his left. There hadn't been too much credit given. Three Toes had known exactly what Bob was going to do before he had even figured it out for himself.

The woods were very thick here, which gave the advantage to Three Toes since Bob wouldn't be able to get a shot off until they were right on top of him. All that was needed was for one dog to get to him; and then the fat lady was going to be singing a whole medley of tunes.

The winds were crossing back and forth, which made it almost impossible for the dogs to know his exact location; but they had to know he was close. Bob worried that the longer he waited the less chance he had of getting out alive. So, after giving it a little more thought, he decided to retreat for now. He'd save this fight for another day.

He backed out as fast as he could without being heard and headed to a clearing that he'd remembered seeing back a little ways. He knew he was safer now but still not home free. Bob knew the dogs would begin retracing their steps when he didn't show up; so he had to reach the open field quickly. He began to run.

Within thirty feet of the clearing, he heard the footsteps approaching from behind. They were still a decent distance from him, but they were gaining fast. He pushed his legs to move faster and finally burst out into the pasture. After running another fifty feet, he wheeled around to face his enemies, his Mauser already shouldered and ready for action. Even though there were eight of them, he knew he'd be able to take them in the open.

He held his breath and his pose as his mind clicked through the plan. He would go for the closest ones to him first unless they were neck and neck. Then he'd go for the biggest one. He didn't have enough ammo in the Mauser for the whole job; so he would finish with his pistol. It would be close, but he knew he could do it.

He waited for what felt like an eternity, but no one came. Then he heard the familiar growl, the one that told him Three Toes was there but just out of reach. Then a second growl joined in. He thought it must have been Big Dog. The hair on the back of his neck rose to attention; and he was sure the hair on his dogs' necks was much the same. They wanted him as badly as he wanted them.

Bob decided to sacrifice distance for time and started backing up to give himself more room. And then he saw him; Three Toes was just inside the wooded area, teeth bared and anger growing by the second.

The dog was waiting for a moment of weakness when he would be able to take advantage of the human; but the open space negated any opportunity for that. The mongrel knew what kind of damage the man could cause; and he didn't want to send his army out just to lose them again. Finding good hunters wasn't easy. So they would wait patiently for the human to make a mistake; and it probably wouldn't take too long.

Bob continued to slowly move backwards. When he heard the rush of feet, he stopped and raised the rifle back to his shoulder. But as soon as he'd taken his stand, he'd realized the footsteps were fading. The dogs were running in the opposite direction. Immediately, he started to run; but just as he reached the edge of the woods, something stopped him. That was what Three Toes wanted, for him to return to the thick brush. And he wasn't going to make that mistake again.

There was only another hour or so of daylight left, so Bob decided the encounters had to be over for the day. He hoped for better luck tomorrow, because he was getting really tired of *almost* getting Three Toes.

The hunt was taking longer than he'd originally thought it would; and he figured it was going to take a lot longer still. He knew the Slawson's had placed a lot of faith in him to get the dogs; and he didn't want to let them down. But more than that, he didn't want to have to call them and tell them he'd been close but not close enough yet. The whole county had changed their way of life just to make sure they and their families were safe. They wouldn't let their kids play outside, and everybody's nerves were on edge. Bob felt the pressure he was under to get this problem taken care of; and he had to do it fast.

Several other teams of men had done their best to find and kill the pack; but Three Toes would elude them to the point that none of them had even seen the dogs. And Bob couldn't help but feel as though Three Toes was taking this thing with him personally.

It was only on the drive back to the city that it occurred to Bob how alone he'd felt in the woods. The Presence hadn't been with him, and now he began to wonder why.

Had he been forsaken by the Giver of Gifts? And if that was the case, why? After some lengthy soul searching, the only thing that came to mind was his relationship with Grace. He rationalized to himself that he'd made it clear at lunch that he wasn't going to take the relationship any further. So what more could he do? As much as he didn't want to acknowledge it, he knew that they probably shouldn't even be having lunch; but he quickly tried to shut that out of his mind.

He'd always worked hard to be in tune with the rights and wrongs in life. Day after day had been spent with Mother Nature, learning her ways and understanding what she required from him; and he knew he was expected to offer nothing less than his honesty, integrity, and above all, his unconditional love to the universe and those other pilgrims walking the same path he was. Sadness, and then bitterness, came over him as he thought about giving up the relationship with Grace; but it was the only thing that made sense.

The babysitter had already left by the time he got home; so he brought the boys up to snuff about the hunts and then tucked them into bed. Grabbing an apple from the kitchen, he flopped down on the couch and stared at nothing while he ate, his mind still twisting around in his head.

He thought about calling Grace to talk to her about the dilemma he had found himself in; but each time he decided to do it, something made him hesitate. Finally, he decided the only thing he could do was to do nothing until he felt more confident in his decisions.

He made his way to bed and felt thankful that he'd be able to fall asleep before Barb came strolling in. He hoped she wouldn't pull another stunt like she had the last time when she came in late and woke him up to talk. The alarm was always set for six-thirty, and now he turned it on and was asleep in minutes.

It was ten minutes 'til six when he woke and glanced at the clock. He was glad to see he had a little more time to snooze. But just as he was closing his eyes again, he heard the garage door closing and knew that was what had wakened him, the garage door opening. He listened as Barb's familiar footsteps made their way into the kitchen; and he heard the clink of her keys hit the counter. She had stayed out all night.

Bob began to seethe, not because she had been gone all night, but because he couldn't find the fairness in it all. Why did the universe deem it acceptable for her to carry on in such a disgraceful way while he couldn't even have lunch with Grace without feeling guilty? His mood began to grow as dark as the morning.

Bob thought back to the many times she had pulled stunts like this and how he always chose to pretend not to see it. Not knowing meant not having to do anything about it; and to confront the situation would mean he and the boys would have to endure her wrath or it would be the end of the marriage. But he couldn't pretend he didn't see what was going on any longer. He wasn't a mouse, and it was time she

174

knew that.

He thought he'd done a pretty decent job of making sure the boys knew he loved their mother; but, lately, it had been difficult trying to teach them by example. He'd always believed that marriage was forever; but his commitment to Barb had been growing weaker and weaker, beginning when he knew for sure that she'd been seeing other men and ending when he met Grace.

Was it his increasingly growing hunger for Grace that had given him the strength to fight for himself? Or maybe it was the Presence that had affected him, not just giving him the ability to see into the darkness of the woods, but also the ability to see into the darkness of Barb's soul. Then, maybe it was just the dogs. Maybe having to face their snarling faces and feel the all-too-real wounds they caused had suddenly made him aware of Barb's snarling face and the internal wounds he and many others suffered because of her.

The questions played and replayed through his mind until he thought he would surely go crazy. Perhaps it didn't matter why he suddenly deemed it necessary to take a harder stance. This was a matter of right and wrong, love and promises, deception and confrontation. And he was just the man to do it.

A large part of him wished for the days when he and Barb had first met and he loved her deeply and looked forward to each new day with her. He had wanted to do anything to take care of her, to shield her from all odds in the world, even to the point of sacrificing his relationship with his parents for her. But from the very beginning, Neil believed she was only after the family money; and Bob had refused to listen to the accusations. Eventually, even he couldn't refute the obvious facts; and it was a very humbling thing to have to admit that his father was right.

He didn't want the day to start with a fight, so Bob chose to stay in bed while she fixed breakfast for the boys. He truly wanted this to be a good day free of worries about his wife and her affairs or the dogs or even Grace. Dad and his wounds were going to have to heal without his help; and Mike and Sherry could run the ranch alone. He realized that his world as he knew it would be collapsing soon; but if he had anything to do with it, it wasn't going to be today. Because today, he was going to be happy.

CHAPTER 10

The alarm was about ready to go off, so Bob turned it off and crawled out of bed. His inner resolve and a hot, steamy shower did wonders for both his mind and his body. By the time he was ready to take off for the office, the boys were downstairs fixing themselves bowls of cereal.

He had been right to be wary of Barb's new leaf. She lay passed out on the couch, the smell of alcohol hanging heavy in the air. Choosing to leave well enough alone, he quickly made a healthy breakfast of scrambled eggs and bacon for the kids.

"Hey, guys! Want me to take you to school this morning or do you just want to catch your usual ride?"

The boys yelled in unison for him to take them. Once breakfast was done and the dishes cleaned up, Bob called their regular ride to let her know not to stop today; and then they all rushed to jump in the Suburban.

Christopher was first to the truck, and he promptly claimed the front seat. This triggered an outburst from Matt, and he started to bully him out of it.

Bob quickly interjected, "Hey there, Boy! There won't be any of that."

The morning was pleasant, and things ran smoothly with his patients. Lunch with Grace was great as usual. They were back to chatting as though the strained talk the day before had never happened. Bob found himself wanting to vent about Barb, about how bad his marriage was, that she didn't understand him, and all the other boo-hoos that were generally part of an affair; but he knew it wasn't appropriate. He didn't want his time with Grace spent on such negative things. And they weren't having an affair anyway.

When lunch was over, they reluctantly made their way back to the Suburban and headed back toward the hospital. It seemed to Bob that it became harder and harder for them to pull themselves out of the little world they had created there at Lucille's and get back to their individual realities. Grace's declaration of love yesterday seemed to make it even more difficult today.

Bob pulled out of the restaurant parking lot and began heading west on Westport. Grace dreaded these trips back to work more than anything. It would be at least twenty-four more hours before she would see him again; and the more she was with him, the more she realized how utterly despicable her relationship with Gerald really was.

When Bob made an unexpected left turn onto Bell Street instead of going on forward toward the hospital, Grace wondered where he was going. Without saying anything, she just looked at him with her eyebrows raised.

"I'm not sure about this, Grace, and I don't want you to turn around; but I think we've got somebody following us. I saw them on the way to Lucille's but didn't think anything about it until now."

Grace kept her eyes straight ahead. "Is it a big, black car?"

"Yeah. How did you know?"

" 'Cause I've been seeing it a lot lately, too. I was a little nervous about it at first; but nobody ever bothered me; so I figured what the hell and just started ignoring them."

"No shit? You think Gerald is having you followed to see what you're up to?"

"I wondered about that right at first; but I've seen them parked near our house and following him when he leaves for work by himself. I never said anything to Gerald about it, because I figured he'd just make some smart-assed remark about me being paranoid or something. But I always thought it was him they were after, at least until now."

Bob continued to drive randomly but stayed at a steady pace. "Can you think of anything at all that they might be looking for?"

"I know the IRS is hot after Gerald. He's been cheating on his taxes since I've known him, and they finally caught on to him. I always file mine individually; and I do it straight up; so I don't think they'd be after me."

"I don't think the IRS has people followed."

"Well, I don't know," Grace said. "The more time I spend around Gerald, the more I'd like to put a hit out on him."

Grace giggled, and Bob couldn't believe she was being so nonchalant about it all. He had never encountered a situation like this before and wasn't sure he was going to be able to accept it as easily as Grace did. He wanted to find out who these guys were; and if he could, he was going to do it right now.

"Fasten your seatbelt," he said to Grace in a quiet but demanding tone of voice.

With an amused look still on her face, she snapped it into place; and then Bob checked to make sure there was no other traffic on the street. Suddenly, he punched the accelerator; and then just before reaching the end of the block, he slammed on his brakes, causing the truck to turn sideways, blocking both lanes.

The black car had stayed a good distance back from him; and as he jumped out of the truck and started running back toward it, it quickly reversed into a driveway and took off in the opposite direction, squealing the tires as it sped away. Just able to get a glance at the license plate, Bob was only able to tell that it wasn't a normal Kansas or Missouri plate; but he couldn't make out exactly what kind it was.

He walked back to the truck to find that Grace had managed to keep her composure and her sense of humor. But her southern drawl seemed more pronounced now. "You sure do know how to show a girl a good time, Dr. Bob."

"I got an A in 'Good Times 101' in college," he managed to banter back although he wasn't sure he was in the mood. "I wonder what the hell they're after. And why wouldn't they just stop and talk to me instead of taking off like that?"

"Maybe they've heard how good you are with a gun, and they're scared of you." Grace grinned at him, and he couldn't help but feel his tension draining away.

"Yeah, right. Somehow I think those guys are as good with a gun as they are at getting away."

He headed the truck back toward the hospital, and they both grew quiet again. As Grace began to crawl out of the truck, she leaned over to kiss him. Bob quickly reached to hold her back and said, "No. Not now."

Grace seemed a little surprised and then put on a contrived pout. "Why?" she said in a childish whine. "It's simple, Gracie. We're meant to be when we're meant to be."

A smile broke out across her face, and Bob reached for her warm, feminine hand and gave it a very slight squeeze. She gave a quick squeeze back, and then she jumped from the truck and headed into the hospital.

As he watched her walk away, he thought to himself how stupid he was and wondered where the crap in his brain even came from. Was this part of "the Plan"? Is that where these split-second thoughts and behaviors came from? Or was he sticking his nose into something he shouldn't have it in and messing up "the Plan"? Maybe it didn't have anything to do with destiny. Maybe it was just his prerogative to make his own choices.

"Ah, hell," he muttered to himself as he pushed it all from his mind and headed back to the office.

He kept watch in his rearview mirror for the black car to show up again; but it didn't. Even so, he couldn't shake the feeling that he hadn't seen the last of it yet. For a fleeting moment, he toyed with the idea of calling the cops; but by the time he reached the office, he'd decided to just blow it off. Right now he had to get his head back into his patients. And besides, if Grace could be that nonchalant about it, maybe he should be, too.

He kept waiting for the call from someone about the dogs, but none came that afternoon. From three-fifteen to three-thirty, he had a short break; so he called Mike just to touch base. Everything was okay, at least until he told him about Barb's big plan for the dinner on Saturday. Mike suddenly grew quiet again, almost as if the last few days had never happened.

"Uh, Bob, I'll be sure to let Sherry know about it; but I've got a bunch of stuff I need to take care of at my place; so if you don't mind, I'll just see you sometime on Sunday."

It was as though a light suddenly went on in Bob's head. All these years of Mike's silence and brooding had something to do with Barb.

"Jesus Christ, Mike! What's up? I mean, really?"

"Just that. Just stuff."

Bob knew he needed to have a talk with him soon, but now obviously wasn't the time. Mike didn't seem too willing to open up, and Bob didn't have much time to listen. But he resolved he would press the matter as soon as possible.

With the walk-ins and the scheduled patients who he already had on the books, the afternoon turned out to be busier than he'd expected. By the time he locked up, it was six-forty-five; and he was tired. He decided to stay in the city for the night. Things were apparently fairly calm at the ranch; and this would give him some extra time to spend with the boys.

Fortunately, Barb had plans for the evening. As he was pulling up into the driveway, she was walking out to her car, dressed to the nines. She merely waved as she pulled out past him; and he heartily waved back, glad to see her go.

The boys were watching TV when he walked in, and their faces lit up when they saw him.

"Hey, it's Dad!" David yelled as he ran over to him and threw his arms around his daddy's hips.

"Hi, Dad!" Matt said. "Are you going back to Grandpa's tonight?"

Bob told them he would be spending the night with them this time; but first he had to call and cancel the sitter again, assuming she had been called at all. He caught her as she was walking out the door to come over; and he apologized for the erratic scheduling of late and promised to make it up to her soon.

The rest of the evening was spent having dinner, going over homework, running a load of wash, and baths for the boys. Then, as their reward for being so cooperative and helpful, they all got to play a game of Operation before heading off to bed. As he tucked them in, Bob wondered how Barb could be so selfish and thoughtless. He could tolerate it more when she was that way with him, but to leave the boys so often was just inconceivable.

Friday came and went, again without incident. It was another long day with everyone trying to get in before the weekend; and Bob was glad to have another evening with the boys. He hoped Barb had other plans for the evening again.

As it turned out, she did. She was just getting ready to call the sitter when Bob walked through the door; and he tried to be cordial so as not to delay her departure.

"Hi! Taking off?"

"Yes, I've got an appointment with Gerald, and then I thought I'd swing by to see Ellen on the way home. You going to be around tonight?"

Bob assured her that he would be there until

morning; but he had cancelled his Saturday patients and would be going early to get back out to the ranch.

"Yes, I'm really looking forward to the day out there. It should be fun."

Bob had no idea what this was about. She had never been eager to go out there, nor had it ever been anything even remotely like fun when she was there. But to save them both an argument, he agreed with her and waved goodbye as she drove away.

Bob rounded up the boys and took them to McDonald's, their favorite place to eat. But more than eating, they played on the toys until they were about to drop.

The plan for Saturday had been worked out between Barb and Gerald. The men would meet at their usual spot and drive on out to the ranch; and then Grace would drive to Barb's later in the day so they could drive out together. Bob felt a little nervous when he thought about the two women spending that much time together and hoped Barb would be civil with Grace. But since the boys would be with them, he figured Barb wouldn't get too crazy. She knew they would tell on her if she was mean.

Saturday dawned a beautiful day, sun shining and birds chirping. And Barb was passed out on the couch.

Bob quietly fixed a pot of coffee, and then, as it was brewing, poured himself a glass of orange juice and sat on the deck to enjoy the morning. When he figured the coffee was done, he went back inside and filled his thermos and then grabbed his keys to load up the truck.

He was to meet Gerald at seven-thirty; and then

184

they'd head on out to the ranch; but he was running a little early so decided to take a few minutes to check the fluids in the truck. As he raised the hood, he noticed the black car sitting halfway up the block, engine idling.

Acting as though he hadn't seen them, he casually pulled the dipstick out and wiped it off, stuck it back in and checked it again. It was perfect, but he shook his head in mock aggravation and then meandered back into the garage. Once he was out of sight of the car, he ran through the kitchen and out the back door, hoping his acting was better than he thought it was.

It didn't take him very long to jump a few fences and work his way up the block through the neighbors' backyards until he was able to situate himself just past the car. Unfortunately, there was a pristine lawn void of trees or bushes that he had to cross in order to reach it. After making sure no one was outside that would notice him and give him away, he silently scurried across the lawn in a crouched position until he reached the rear of the car. Quietly, he fed the dish towel into the tail pipe, and then, still hunkered down, waited for the car to die. As he waited, he noticed the license plate: Government.

After no more than a minute, the car sputtered and then grew still. The driver tried to start the engine again, but it only continued to sputter. Slowly, Bob crept around to the driver's side and up to the opened window.

There were two men inside, both of them desperately trying to read the lights on the dash to see what had happened to their car. Neither of them

185

noticed him until he stood up and put a stiff finger to the driver's head. Immediately, the man behind the wheel threw his hands up in the air as a sign of surrender. His cohort froze in place, his arm extended toward the dash.

"Okay! Who are you guys and what the hell are you doing here?" Bob asked in his most demanding voice.

"Don't shoot!" the driver squeaked out even as sweat began to blister up on his forehead.

"Then you'd better start talking." Bob had to struggle to keep from laughing while keeping his voice hard and clipped. "And no bullshitting me, either. I want to know why you were following me yesterday and why you're sitting here now."

"Okay. We're really not following you. We've been ordered to keep tabs on someone else. That's all."

"And just who is it you've been ordered to keep these tabs on?"

"Uh, that's classified information," the guy said, obviously scared not to tell but just as afraid of the consequences if he did.

"Not anymore it's not. Spill it!"

"Uh, uh, well, okay," the guy said as he decided to err on the side of caution. "It's Dr. and Mrs. Klyne."

Bob decided it was safe now to reveal his "gun"; and when he stuck his hand in front of the men's faces, their expressions immediately changed from fear to anger. Bob let out an amused laugh as the men's expressions grew even more menacing.

"Hey, now don't get pissy or anything. I just had to know. So if you're actually supposed to be following them, what the hell are you doing here watching me?"

The driver puffed up even more as he tried to re-establish his authority. "Dr. Klyne *is* going hunting with you today, isn't he?"

"Yeah. So?"

"So the rest of it isn't any of your business." Both men were obviously embarrassed by getting caught so easily; and the driver continued to try to regain the upper hand. "We've said too much already, so why don't you just get on with your day now."

"Okay. But I've got one more question before I tell you how to get your car started again. Is Grace involved in any of this?"

"As I said, you already know too much."

Bob hesitated for a few more seconds and then moved to the back of the car and yanked the towel out of the tailpipe. As he walked back by the window, he gave the towel a little shake at the men. "Okay. You're good to go."

"Hey!" the driver yelled. Bob stopped and turned back toward him. "You might keep this little conversation to yourself, if you know what I mean." Bob waved them off and continued on back to his truck.

When he reached the meeting spot, Gerald was already there and waiting. With a honk and a wave, they continued on to the ranch.

As Bob drove down the driveway to the house, he immediately noticed how good the place looked. Mike had been busy. The lawn had been mowed; and the scraggly honeysuckle bushes had been trimmed for the first time in their lives. Even the farm equipment had been put in the barn for the day. Bob was impressed.

As Gerald strode toward him, he was already talking about how eager he was to get out in the woods again; and Bob found himself wishing Mike was going out with him instead, even though he couldn't shoot. It would have been a good time to talk to him about whatever it was bugging him about Barb. Bob had a sinking feeling that he knew what the problem was; but he prayed he might be wrong about this one.

He wanted to check on his dad before he took off after the dogs, so he motioned for Gerald to follow. Neil was sitting in a chair at the table with a cup of coffee and a stack of mail in front him. After the perfunctory introductions, Bob asked, "Have you heard anything else from any of the neighbors about the dogs?"

"Yes. Just this morning old man Peterson called about seven o'clock and told me he'd seen the bunch of them just north of his place. But so far, he's not had any trouble from them.

Bob turned to Gerald and asked him to go on out and get his gear in the back of the Suburban. If he brought as much this time as he did last time, it would take him a half hour to get it all situated.

Gerald looked to be in fairly good shape, but the way he ran left some room for doubt. And in spite of his idiosyncrasies, he came off as having a strong will, which made Bob think it wouldn't be too bad having him around when they faced the dogs again.

He also knew Gerald spent a lot of time at an indoor shooting range and figured he was a pretty good shot, at least at close range. Fifty yards was the maximum shot indoors; so he was probably adequate up to one hundred. Bob noticed he carried two 45 semiautomatic pistols in shoulder holsters and another on his leg, and assumed he'd be fairly adequate at the long shot since he also carried a scoped 223. The rifle would be good for about six hundred to eight hundred yards; but Bob didn't know of any expanses like that in the wooded areas where they'd be. But the gun looked impressive. To finish off his stash, Gerald wore a backpack that looked to weigh at least forty pounds; and Bob couldn't even begin to imagine what all was in it.

After Bob had chatted with his dad a few more minutes, he rejoined Gerald; and both men crawled into the Suburban and took off for the Peterson's farm. As the crow flew, it was a little over a mile; but to get there by dirt roads, it was right at four.

"What kind of terrain will we be covering today?" Gerald asked. "And why don't we take the horses?"

"It'll be pretty heavy woods and brush, some pretty steep hills and valleys. And there are a lot of fences we're going to have to deal with. That's why we're not taking the horses. Can't take a chance on getting one of them hurt. You know, they get crippled up, and then they're no good for much of anything after that except for being a pet. And they're pretty expensive pets.

Gerald let out a snide laugh. "The hell I'd keep them as pets. Like you said, that would be expensive. I'd shoot them first."

Bob found Gerald's response appalling and wasn't even sure how to respond appropriately; so he said nothing. He swore to himself that he'd never let him on any of his horses. If he didn't get the horse killed, the horse would undoubtedly kill him with an attitude like that.

When they arrived at the Peterson's place, Bob told Gerald to get ready to take off while he went up to let the family know they were there. Before Bob reached the porch, Mr. Peterson walked out the front door to greet him.

"Hi there, Bob! Good to see ya!"

"Thanks, Pete! Good to see you, too! Thought I'd let you know I was going out to look for the dogs. Where exactly did you see them?"

"Just north and a little east of here, about a mile away maybe. Ya know, just past that old barn up there."

"Yeah, I know where you're talking about. Okay. I brought somebody with me for a little extra help this time, so maybe we'll have better luck getting them today."

Pete slid his hands into the sides of his overalls. "I gotta tell ya, Bob, I called the police as soon as I saw 'em; but they just told me they'd spent too many man hours already and they weren't going to waste any more. Can you believe that? Said they'd leave it up to the property owners to take care of the problem. Shoot fire, I wonder if us 'property owners' get to do the rest of their jobs, too! I swear, I gotta wonder what they get paid for sometimes."

Bob saw the frustration on Mr. Peterson's face and felt bad for the old guy along with the rest of the community. But he also found a little relief in knowing there wouldn't be a lot of other guns out there today.

"It's okay, Pete. I won't give up on it. I may not

190

be the fastest at finding them, but I'll get them sooner or later. Just keep that in mind, and you keep being careful until then."

After calming the old guy down a little, Bob walked back toward the truck feeling the heavy load on him all over again. He had to get those dogs. It was up to just him now. He hoped he could come through.

As he rounded the back end of the Suburban, he saw Gerald waiting for him; and he felt the creases in his forehead smooth out as he struggled not to burst out laughing. He had worn his camouflage pants and jacket, but now he stood there with a painted face to match it. Bob thought he looked like GI Joe with a backpack. And cologne. He turned his back to Gerald quickly and busied himself getting his own gear ready to go. He didn't want Gerald to see the laugh that was trying to escape.

The cologne smelled a lot like Musk; and Bob wondered whether it would bring the dogs in or scare them off. The one thing that was for certain was that they'd be able to smell him a mile away.

It wasn't usual for Bob to bring his bull-barrel twenty-two High Standard Military Model pistol; but this time he shoved it in his shoulder holster just in case.

"You sure do carry some light-weight guns there, Bob. Twenty-twos? I'd think you'd carry forty-four mags."

"Twenty-twos do just fine for me. After all, one shot in the head is all that's needed."

"Yeah, assuming you hit the head."

"I don't assume anything," Bob said as he closed up the back of the truck.

191

Gerald held up his two-twenty-three for Bob to get a good look at it.

"You should carry a flat shooter like this instead of that rifle. The trajectory of yours takes quite an arch from everything I've read."

"I have to aim at the chest when the shot gets long, but I want the stopping power this bullet gives me. That way I don't have to shoot at the same target twice. And the bolt action gives me enough time to find my next target so I'm not wasting shells."

Bob noticed the large, twenty-shell clip coming from Gerald's rifle and then added, "Besides, Gerald, no one shoots back when you're hunting dogs."

Bob grabbed his own backpack and started off across the field. He didn't use the pack very often; but he knew there was a chance they'd be out for a while today; and a little snack along the way might be useful.

He headed in the direction Pete had indicated, and Gerald followed behind. Within about a hundred yards, the tracks became visible. Gerald appeared deep in thought as they headed toward the woods.

Finally, Bob stopped and turned toward Gerald. "Okay, now's the time to speed up a little."

Gerald didn't say anything. They walked in and out of woods for about forty-five minutes, stopping now and then for Bob to get a better look at the tracks. He hoped Three Toes would slow down or stop to rest somewhere along the way so he'd have time to catch up to them.

Bob silently gave thanks for the breeze that hit his face. If the dogs were to get a whiff of Gerald's cologne, they'd have enough time to set another ambush. But with the wind coming in this direction, he didn't think they'd pick up on it. Then he thought maybe the dogs wouldn't want to be close to someone who smelled like that.

Gerald's eyes darted in every direction as they moved ahead; and his expression was one of sheer terror, as though he expected the dogs to jump out at him at any second. Bob knew it wouldn't happen like that but decided not to tell him. Gerald needed to stay alert; and the adrenaline pumping him up right now was at least enough to keep him moving faster.

It was obvious the backpack was getting heavier by the minute. Maybe Gerald wasn't in as good a shape as he thought. He could exercise all he wanted in a gym; but climbing these hills out here was something else; and getting back down them was as bad as getting up. The dogs had an advantage over them just by the fact that they had four legs to maneuver the terrain. And they weren't carrying backpacks.

Another half hour of trotting through the woods, and Bob could see Gerald was getting winded. He wanted to stay tight with Three Toes; but if Gerald pooped out on him, he wouldn't be much help when push came to shove. He decided to stop.

"Maybe we should stop for a bit. Three Toes has slowed down; so this might be our last chance to collect ourselves before we meet up with them."

Gerald immediately sank to his knees and shrugged the backpack off. Bob knew he was relieved for the chance to rest.

"How far before you think we'll see them?" Gerald asked with enthusiasm in spite of having to gasp for air.

"We were an hour and a half behind them when

we started, and I figure we've made up about forty-five minutes. So I'm thinking we're about halfway there if they keep up their same pace."

Smoothing out a soft place to sit, Gerald asked, "How often have you had to do this anyway?"

"I've never *had* to do it before. This is the first time we've had a pack that's turned this vicious. But I usually come out a couple times a month anyway just to be in the woods."

"Man, you should start bringing in some heads. They'd look good in that log cabin."

"I only kill killers. There are enough hunters out there killing things without me doing the same. I just hunt to see how close I can get."

This was obviously a new concept for Gerald.

"You never kill anything at all?"

"Just like I said, I've killed a few of the dogs from this pack we're chasing; and I did kill a few deer and turkeys when I was younger. But I finally figured out that I feel better about myself if I just hunt to observe, not to kill."

"Well, that sounds very morally superior."

"I wouldn't say that. I don't compare myself with anyone else, and I don't like other people doing it either. I'm just me. My decisions are mine, and they're not based on what other people think or do. I just try to do what seems right for me."

"There's got to be a definite right and wrong. So who's right, you or the hunters who kill?"

"I just told you. My decisions are mine, and their decisions are theirs."

"But you've got to have an opinion."

"Yes, I do have an opinion. And I just told you

194

what it is."

"But it's only human nature to compare oneself to others in your own group."

"And what group are you considering here? Hunters? Killers? Men in general? Regardless of how you want to categorize people, to me we're still just all people. And I go back to what I said before; it's an individual thing. If you want to look at it from a legal standpoint, I guess all of us could be grouped together since we're all subject to the law. But morally, we're all left to our own."

Gerald smirked and shook his head. "There's another category, too. Besides legal and moral, there's psychological, too."

"I don't agree, Gerald. I think psychologists go overboard putting people into nice little niches that sometimes, if not most of the time, don't fit."

"And I think you tend to complicate things way too much by giving the human race credit where it isn't due."

"I'm not giving anyone credit for anything. I think each person earns their own credit."

"Well, I'd beg to differ with you; but it's an interesting philosophy, I guess."

Bob knew it was time to get started again. They had already lost too much time with this bantering; and he figured they'd have to stop again along the way for Gerald to rest and probably get something to eat; and he wanted to get as much distance under foot as they could before their next recess.

When Bob stood up and grabbed his pack, Gerald realized the break was over and reluctantly got up and donned his backpack again. Bob tried to move

195

quickly to make up for the lost time; but Gerald continued to move slower and slower as they went. Constantly having to stop and wait for him was frustrating for Bob; but he kept reminding himself of the advantage of having the guy there. And he didn't want to make a scene with him, at least for Grace's benefit.

CHAPTER 11

When Grace arrived at Barb's house, she was surprised and disappointed to learn the kids weren't coming along with them. Barb said it was because they wanted to hang out with their friends; but then she also added that they were too much of a bother, and she preferred they not be around their grandfather anyway.

"That ranch is a bad influence on the boys. When they get back home, after spending any time out there at all, they just aren't right. They're always all sad and mopey, and they just make me so mad."

Grace made Barb mad, too. She was pretty enough, and she had a great figure. But she held her head as though she thought she was better than everyone else; and Barb knew she was nothing more than a dumb hick. Just the way she talked was proof of that; and she didn't know how she was going to be able to tolerate her for a whole day. At least she'd worn shoes today.

Grace wasn't quite sure how to take Barb. She was taken aback by the way she bad-mouthed Bob even though the remarks were supposedly said in jest. She tried to see the woman in a good light, but an underlying harshness kept Grace a little off kilter.

She asked Barb about the dogs and wondered out loud if Gerald would be in any danger out there. Barb seemed indifferent to the situation, and Grace couldn't help but wonder if she even cared.

"Well, I saw how tore up Bob was last weekend; and I have to admit that I've been a little nervous about Gerald going out. Things may not be the best between us right now; but I worry about him and don't want to see anything bad happen to him."

Barb's ears perked up right away.

"So what's the problem between you two?" she asked.

"I don't want to air my dirty laundry, ya know. He's just not very sensitive."

"Not sensitive how?"

"Oh, he likes to tell me how useless I am; and he tells me what to wear and how to act all the time like I'm too stupid to know."

"So does Gerald know how you feel?"

"I don't know. I try to talk to him about things sometimes, but he just never listens. He'll just crawl back down to the basement and load bullets or leave and go to the shooting range."

"Well, if he's that bad, why don't you leave him?"

"When I met him, he seemed very much in love with me; and I figured since he was a psychologist he would have his shit together and be a good husband to me and a good father for my little girl. But it turned out he wasn't much of either. But still, that doesn't negate the fact that I care about him very much."

The two women swapped stories about their men and the kids, and the trip quickly came to an end.

When Grace saw the ranch, she was beside herself. It was beautiful, and so peaceful. How could such a setting be a bad place for the boys? Nestled in the middle of nowhere were hundreds of acres with more trees and flowers than she had ever seen in one spot. And there were also little feathered and furry creatures everywhere she looked. She had grown up on a small farm in southern Missouri, but it wasn't anything as beautiful as this.

When the women walked into the house, Sherry was busy in the kitchen juggling pots and pans as she labored over dinner. With no introductions offered by Barb, Grace smiled at Sherry and introduced herself. Sherry reciprocated the introduction and then told her that Neil was in the bedroom and that she should go on in and meet him.

Softly knocking on the half-opened door, she stepped on through and said, "Excuse me for interrupting; but I wanted to meet the man who owned this beautiful piece of heaven. I'm Grace, Gerald's wife."

Dr. Neil smiled warmly at her, amused by her southern drawl, and said, "Why, thank you, Ma'am, I think this is a pretty special place myself. And it's good to meet you."

Grace immediately sat down and began asking the old man a million questions. She seemed enthralled with the place and with him and spoke with the enthusiasm of a child. She drank in every word he said and then asked for more.

Neil was taken by the girl; and the more he chatted with her, the more enamored he became. After only a few minutes, he had fallen in love with her and wished she had been his little girl instead of the ingrate that he'd had. He had never met anyone who he took such a liking to so quickly; and he was surprised that Grace could make this kind of impression on him. The bond between them grew with each passing minute.

After about twenty minutes, Grace told Neil that she should try to help Sherry with dinner.

"I'm not the best cook in the world. Well, I'm really not much of a cook at all. But I'm pretty good at cleaning up, so I really should go try to do something useful."

Neil smiled at her and waved her on.

When Grace walked back into the great room, she noticed Barb sitting on the couch flipping through the channels on the television, and was surprised that she wasn't helping Sherry, nor were the women even speaking to each other. The only sounds in the room came from the banging and clanging around the stove and the ruckus from the television. Grace volunteered her services; and Sherry politely let her know that things were in hand and there was nothing she needed to do.

Finally, Barb spoke up.

"So, where's Mike?"

Grace saw Sherry stiffen up and hesitate before answering without turning to face Barb.

"He's not going to be here today. He's busy taking care of things at the house."

Grace was beginning to feel uncomfortable with the tension in the room, and so slipped back to Neil's room.

"Excuse me again. I was wondering if it would be alright with you if I took a little walk around the place here? There are just so many things to see, and it's such a nice day. And Sherry won't let me help with anything in the kitchen."

"Sure, go on ahead. Just be careful not to wander too far away, what with those dogs out there and all."

"I promise; I'll stay really close to the house

here. Would you like to go out for a few minutes? I could help you."

"No, little girl. I appreciate the offer, but I think I'd be better off staying right here. Besides, I've already seen everything out there."

Grace excused herself then and headed toward the front door. As she walked by, she asked Barb, "Would you like to go for a little walk? I just wanted to go out and get a little fresh air and enjoy the place a little."

Barb sneered and said, "Hell, no! I've seen enough of this place to last me for the rest of my life."

Grace wandered on out, secretly glad that Barb didn't want to join her. She wandered down the sidewalk that was lined with irises of every color imaginable, and saw further out into the yard where rose bushes were laden down with red and white blooms.

As she rounded the barn, she saw horses in the pasture and squirrels playing tag in the trees. The birds were chirping all around her, and she was amazed at the clarity of their songs.

Moving on around to the back side of the house, she was elated to see the lilac bushes that grew there, her favorite flower of all. She walked to them and buried her nose in the purple clusters, reveling in the scent that she remembered from her childhood.

A screech from above her drew her attention to a hawk that soared on the air currents; and she wished she could fly, too, so she could see even more of this heavenly place. And then she started to sneeze.

It was time to get back inside.

CHAPTER 12

They had been traveling at a good clip when Bob stopped again. The dogs had been turning to the east and traveling into even more territory Bob wasn't familiar with. They didn't seem to realize they were being followed. Three Toes kept a slow but steady pace straight ahead while the rest of the dogs wandered off here and there but always headed back to rejoin their leader.

"How close do you think we are now, Bob?" Gerald asked.

"Close."

The wind was coming from the north, which was to their advantage in that the dogs couldn't smell them; but it was a disadvantage for Bob in that he was just as unable to smell them. He began to pick up his pace. Suddenly, the Presence was strong. He stopped and took the leather straps from his gun and knife and took the safety off his Mauser. He turned to Gerald and motioned for him to be quiet and then pointed toward his safety.

The open area quickly changed to wooded, and then a short ways farther was what appeared to be a huge ravine. Although logic told Bob it must drop down to the Nine Mile Creek, he wasn't sure about these parts and decided to check it out.

He reached the edge of the drop-off and saw that it did, indeed, drop down to the creek; and he was in awe of the depth and width of it; but before he could turn to get back to the trail, he was hit by a heavy force and was immediately plummeting down the rocky cliff. His rifle fell from his hands, and both pistols fell from their holsters. By the time he had finally reached the bottom, he was already covered in blood; and his last thoughts were of the dogs that were headed toward him. Then blessed darkness surrounded him.

"Well, looky there. I didn't even have to shoot the mighty hunter. Old Three Toes is going to get his wish, and I'll get mine," he said with a lewd grin on his face.

Gerald looked over the side one more time to make sure Bob was dead, and from the looks of him knew there wasn't a chance in hell of him making it through that alive.

He was glad to get the backpack off, and quickly went to work pulling out two, large plastic bags of raw meat and spreading it around the edge of the cliff. The last two pieces he tossed into the ravine, where they landed on the rocks close to the body.

"I'd normally hate to waste such good meat; but this time, I think it's well worth the cost."

He stuffed the empty bags back in his pack and then pulled out his GPS, which he put in reverse, and headed back to Peterson's, where Bob's truck was.

He already had his story worked out: Bob had told him when they first took off that if he couldn't keep up and they got separated, he was just to go on back to the ranch and wait for him, which was exactly what had happened. He had thought about going on and trying to find him, but didn't dare with the dogs close by and him not knowing the land very well.

Gerald was pleased with the turn of events. He hadn't been sure how he was going to accomplish his plan of getting rid of Bob; but he had hoped something would present itself. He hadn't wanted to just shoot him, because it would have been too easy to trace it back to him. But this way, no one was going to think to blame him, even if they found the body. The ravine provided the perfect solution to the perfect crime. Now all he had to do was get rid of Grace. He wasn't sure how he would do that, either; but, if worse came to worst, he was sure Barb would come up with some devious plan. Then all he had to do was keep up his ruse long enough to marry the Ice Bitch; and then he'd figure out some way to get rid of her, too.

It wasn't long before Bob began to be aware of the pain searing through his body. There was so much of it that he couldn't even tell for sure what was damaged and what wasn't. As he began to try to move, he quickly discerned that some of his lower ribs were more than likely broken and possibly his left arm, too, although it was hard to know about the arm since he could hardly move it without causing worse pain in his rib cage. When he was finally able to lift his head, he saw the meat on the rocks next to him.

It wasn't a dog that hit me! It was Gerald!

He knew then that he had to get out of this ravine as fast as he could. With his own blood fresh and pungent along with the raw meat, the dogs would be on top of him any minute. But his main driving force now was to catch up with Gerald and beat the shit out of him.

Gerald found his way back to the truck, where he sat for a while as though he was waiting for Bob. When Pete came out, he told his rehearsed story.

"Oh, well. I'm not too surprised," Mr. Peterson said. "He probably got wind of the dogs and took off after them. And I've heard he can run like hell, so I'm not surprised ya had to come back on your own."

"Yes, he can run, that's for sure."

"I don't think the man is all human, if you ask me. I've heard stories. There must be some sort of animal in him the way he hunts and tracks. Why, I've even heard folks say he rides the deer. Now, what kind of man can get close enough to a deer to ride him? But there are some say they've seen him."

Suddenly, Gerald wasn't feeling so sure of his plan. Maybe he should have shot him. Then he reassured himself that even if the fall hadn't killed him, the dogs would. As the scene played out in his mind, he began to regain his confidence. Bob was dead, one way or another.

Bob decided his first plan of action was to figure out what wasn't injured so he could decide how best to get out of this mess. Reaching out with his right hand, he grabbed a piece of meat and tossed it gently away from him. *Well, that arm works.*

He began to try to get up, but the pain stopped him before he'd gotten more than a couple of inches. He lay back to catch his breath, and then, through sheer willpower, forced himself to sit upright. After another minute for the world to stop spinning, he began to try to get the pack off his shoulders.

Sitting was next to impossible, because the pain in his ribs made it difficult to breath; and the added movement as he struggled with the straps over his shoulders just magnified everything. After he'd gotten the pack off, he worked on getting his holster off of his shoulder and then set his attention on taking off his shirt. Once he had it off, he wrapped it around his ribs as tightly as he could and then wedged one of the sleeves between a couple of big rocks off to his left. Using his right hand to pull the other sleeve, he cinched the shirt down hard around his ribs and fought the urge to scream. Any sounds that carried to the dogs would just draw them in to him quicker.

Next, he examined his left arm as much as he could. It was almost impossible to tell if it was broken since he couldn't get much motion from it due to the ribs. The one thing he did know for sure, though, was that it hurt like hell. And then he heard the dogs.

Quickly, he looked around for his rifle, which he spotted further up the ravine, broken to pieces. His twenty-two Magnum was nowhere in sight, which only left him with his High Standard. If he could get himself in a position where they couldn't surround him, he might be able to defend himself with that. But that was only if they came at him head on, *and* if he didn't miss a shot.

With a little help from his right hand, he wedged his left hand into the folds of his shirt and then forced himself to get to his feet. If he was going to survive this, he had to get his mind off the pain and into whatever it took to stay alive.

Once he was up, he moved out into the creek and began to walk downstream; but the water was just deep enough to slow him down a little. He could hear the dogs coming closer and prayed for some sort of protection around the corner. Struggling to stay calm, he kept moving ahead. *One foot in front of the other.* His gun was already getting heavy.

"I'm sure Bob will do fine out there without me, so I think I'll just wait here a while longer. If he doesn't show up soon, I'll take the truck and head on to the ranch; and you can have him give me a call when he gets back."

Mr. Peterson nodded in agreement, but his expression was one of concern.

"It'll be fine," Gerald added. "I'll come back and pick him up as soon as he calls."

"Okay," Pete said. "See ya later then."

After Gerald had waited for another twenty minutes, he started up the truck and took off, unaware of Pete watching him from the door.

When he got back to the ranch, he retold the story and then said, "I stopped and told Pete what had happened; and he was going to go out and see if he needed any help. So I don't think there's anything more we need to do."

Finally, Barb spoke up. "Sherry, when is that food going to be ready? It smells awfully good, and I'm starving."

Sherry didn't answer. Instead, she walked over to Neil and quietly said, "Bob would never leave a person out in the woods. And I can't see Mr. Peterson going out looking for him. He's just not that healthy. Something doesn't seem right."

She could tell by the look on his face that he had already thought the same thing; so she added, "Would you like for me to call Mike and ask him to check on things?"

Neil nodded yes.

Gerald had already joined Barb in front of the television set; so Sherry slipped into the back room to make the call. Grace moved to the sink and began to wash up some pots and pans. She always cleaned when she was worried or scared.

Bob spotted a fallen tree jutting out into the creek where some cattails grew. He laid his gun on the rotting trunk and proceeded to rub some of the murky water from the edge of the creek on it, careful not to get the gun too wet, but enough to mask any smell he might have left on it. Then, leaving it there, he snapped off one of the cattails, stuck the end in his mouth and pulled until the outside shaft pulled off. As quietly as he could, he moved out into deeper water and carefully lowered himself below the surface. With the shaft providing him air, he figured he would be fairly safe until the dogs left. And he had made it just in time.

The yapping of the dogs surrounded him, and from the directions of their sounds, he knew they were on both sides of the creek. One of them sounded as though he was trying to walk out on the fallen tree but then returned to shore. Bob concentrated on breathing through the shaft as he listened to the pack approach from both sides and retreat, only to repeat the action again and again. They were confused.

Finally, the sounds of the dogs began to fade; but Bob waited patiently underwater for several more minutes to make sure they weren't going to return again; and then he began to ease himself out of the water.

He looked around in every direction; and when he didn't see them anywhere in sight, he pulled himself out of the creek and onto shore. Finally, he sat down on the bank and leaned his back against the root end of the tree and closed his eyes.

Mike pulled up at Pete's house and jumped out of his pickup. As he reached back inside to grab his guns, Mr. Peterson stepped out on the porch.

"Hey!" Mike said when he heard the door slam. "I thought you were out looking for Bob."

"No, that there city slicker told me Bob was fine. But I wondered about him. He looked kinda shifty, if ya know what I mean."

Without a reply, Mike took off running into the woods. Over fences, down gullies, across the creek bed, back and forth, all the while moving ahead and watching for Bob or the dogs. He even tried looking for tracks but never seemed to see the things that Bob did out here. *How in the hell does he do it anyway?* In the open fields where he could see farther, he felt more confident and moved faster; but in the woods, he figured he'd have to trip over him in order to find him.

He had traveled a fair distance when he had to stop to catch his breath. As he stood there gulping air and willing the stitch in his side to go away, he thought maybe he should just shoot the idiot when he found him just for putting him through this.

It was taking a lot longer to find him than Mike thought it would; and he didn't feel like he'd gained much by running. Maybe, he thought, he should slow down a little and not be so anxious.

He took off again, this time walking instead of running; and he kept a closer watch on the ground. He had been out for about an hour now, but there was still no sign of his friend. He thought about yelling for him, but didn't want to draw the attention of the dogs in case they were anywhere around. And then he remembered the three shots.

Aiming toward the sky, he pulled the trigger three times in rapid succession and then waited.

210

Nothing. He walked on for about another fifteen minutes and then let off three more shots. Still nothing. Mike was growing more worried but more determined with each step he took. And then he heard it. Shots rang out from the distance, but not just three. There were many.

The ravine created a wind tunnel full of smells. Bob sat and waited for quite a while, listening, watching and smelling for the dogs to return. There were many new scents wafting around him, but he was only interested in one.

It didn't take long for the dogs to give away their location. Hoisting himself up on his knees, he peeked around the end of the old tree just as one of the dogs stuck his nose out from behind a bush about a hundred yards down the creek. He slowly reached for his pistol and pulled it toward him, propped it on the tree and took aim. As he fired, he heard the yelping of the dog and figured he'd made some sort of contact; but he fired a few more rounds just to be on the safe side.

He knew the rest of the pack would show up soon now, but he didn't know from which direction. If they were all to come from the same direction, he'd probably be able to get most of them; but more than likely, they wouldn't.

Figuring the water would slow them down a little, he got to his feet and made his way back to the center of the creek, his gun held solidly in his right hand. Another sharp turn in the ravine was just in front of him; and he could hear at least three of the dogs coming at him from that direction. He heard some above him, too, and then some behind him. He braced the pistol against his thigh and prayed he'd be steady enough with one hand to hit his targets; but with them surrounding him, he knew he wouldn't be able to take them all. He would just have to try to take as many as he could and hoped one of them would be Three Toes. Bob stood ready.

Familiar gunfire suddenly rang out from around the bend; and Bob knew the shots wouldn't hit anything; but he was grateful for the attempt and hoped that the noise would at least divert the dogs' attention. He swung back around to face the ones he'd heard coming up the creek toward him; but they were gone. He yelled to Mike to let him know where he was.

"What the hell are you doing down there with that damned, little pea shooter?" Mike yelled down to him as he peered over the edge of the ravine.

"The same thing you are with that elephant gun. Did you hit any of those dogs?"

"No. You?"

"No," Bob quipped back.

"Then don't get so uppity with me, Yahoo. You look like a mess again. You need to quit while you're still alive. Those dogs are gonna have you for dinner soon."

"Shut up and help me out of here."

"I saved your life once today. Isn't that enough?"

"This pea shooter is going to shoot right up your butt if you don't help me get the hell out of here. I'm going to walk back down the creek and find the rest of my stuff…I've got a rope in my backpack…then you can either start helping me out of here or you can start picking lead out of your ass. It's up to you."

The men walked back down the creek, where Bob gathered up his backpack and the pieces of his gun. Then he positioned himself directly beneath where he'd been pushed.

"Hey, Mike! Don't stomp around up there much. I want to see if there aren't some tracks up there."

"What kind of tracks?"

"Gerald tracks. I have a feeling he pushed me off that ledge."

"Of course he did! He showed up at the ranch telling the story of how you two had gotten separated and then how he walked back to the truck, and how Pete was going out looking for ya."

"Yeah, right."

"When Sherry called to tell me about it, I took off to Peterson's place myself; and, sure enough, there he was, not knowing anything about going out to look for you."

After pulling the rope out of the backpack, Bob slipped the strap of the pack over his right shoulder and looped the rope around his neck. Then he began to climb as far up the side of the hill as he could using just one arm.

"What are you doing? I thought you were going to throw me the rope," Mike said.

"If you hadn't noticed, I'm not in really good shape here; so if you'll just shut up for a minute, I'm going to get as close to you as I can before I start trying to throw it up there."

Bob took it slowly, finding a solid foothold and

a tree or rock that he could rely on to hoist himself up on. About a third of the way up was a spindly tree that jutted out of the side of the cliff; and he thought if he could make it up that far, he might be able to throw the rope up the rest of the way.

It was slow going; but as long as he focused on what he was doing and kept his left arm relaxed while his right one did all the work, it wasn't too bad. The problem was that the backpack swung freely off his right shoulder and was constantly in his way.

He finally made it to the tree and wedged himself between it and the wall of the cliff. He pulled the pack off his shoulder and stuffed it into a fork in the branches, and then positioned himself in such a way that he could get good leverage for the throw.

In the meantime, Mike had managed to lower himself about fifteen feet down the side of the cliff using the same tactics Bob had.

"You ready?" Bob asked.

"Yeah. Let's have it."

Bob wrapped his left leg around the tree trunk as best he could, then swung the rope like a pendulum a couple of times to gain momentum. Then, with a grunt, he swung it hard toward Mike. It landed about five feet to the side of him.

"Good throw, Cowboy."

Bob just glared at him as Mike began to work his way across the side of the cliff toward the rope. Once he had it in hand, Bob said, "Good climbing, Monkey Boy."

Mike slowly made his way back up to the top of the cliff.

"You'd better not take off with that rope and

leave me here or you're going to have hell to pay."

"Shit, you can't give anybody hell with the shape you're in."

Once he was back on more solid ground, Mike made a harness in the end of the rope, looped the other end over the limb of a tree that was perched on the edge of the ravine, and then dropped the harnessed end back down to Bob.

Slipping it down around his hips, Bob slung the backpack on his shoulder, and then wove his right arm around the rope several times.

"Ready," he yelled up. "Just pull and I'll try to walk it as much as I can. And don't drop me."

It wasn't as difficult as either of the men had thought it would be; and soon Bob was back on the ledge at the top.

"Geez, you must weigh a ton and a half!"

"No, you're just a weakling. But thanks for the help."

"Sure thing."

As they headed back to the truck, Mike took the backpack and slung it over his own shoulders. They walked in silence for a short distance, and then Bob spoke.

"I think I'd be stupid if I didn't think Gerald and Barb have a thing going on. I can't prove anything, though. But while I was lying down there waiting for the dogs to come and eat me, I kept trying to think why Gerald would want me dead; and then I remembered that Barb took out an extra insurance policy on me a few months ago. Hell, they've probably been planning this for a long time, and I just played right into their plot."

Mike didn't say anything. After another short distance with neither of them talking, Bob continued.

"Listen, Mike. Things haven't been the same between you and me for some years now; and with everything that's happened here lately and you not wanting to talk to me about it, I'm starting to draw my own conclusions. You don't have to say a word, but I want you to know I'm really sorry for the shit Barb pulls."

Mike just looked at him, still not saying anything but now wearing a pained look on his face.

Bob said, "Don't worry about it. Things were over for me and her a long time ago; and the only thing I'm mad about is that if you'd told me before, I wouldn't have been pushed off that damned cliff today."

The guys grinned at each other, and the bantering continued all the way back to the truck.

It was four in the afternoon by the time they reached Mike's pickup. All Bob wanted to do was to get back to the ranch and clean up and kill Gerald, and not particularly in that order; but when they cleared the woods, he saw the black car that he'd seen earlier in the day; and an audible moan escaped him. The two agents were leaned up against it smoking cigarettes; and they looked like they meant business as they started walking toward him. Pete Peterson joined the crowd from his house.

"Dr. Conley, this is agent McGinnis, and I'm agent Jack Redding from the FBI. I think we met earlier this morning; and by the way, we're sending you a bill for any repairs on the car."

"That's what you drove all the way out here

216

for? To give me a bill for your damned car?" Bob asked incredulously.

Before either of the men could answer, Mike piped up again. "Damn it, Bob! How many times have I told you not to mess with other people's cars? You keep that up, and you're going to turn into the black sheep of the family."

Bob's eyes shot daggers at Mike; and the two agents looked at each other, wondering what was going on.

Finally, Redding said, "No. It's not because of the car that we're here. I need to know where you're headed right now."

"I'm going back to my ranch to shoot a guy, and then I'm going to hand him over to you. After that, I'm going to take a shower and then swallow a whole handful of pain pills; and when all that's done, I'm going to pour myself a tall glass of whiskey. Want to join me?"

"Sorry, Mr. Conley. We can't let you do that."

"It's *Doctor* Conley to you. And why in hell can't you let me do that?"

Actually, *Doctor* Conley, we can't even let you go home. You're dead as far as Gerald knows, and we need to keep it that way for a while."

"Can I shoot him then?"

"No. You won't be able to shoot him then, either."

Mike interjected again. "Shit, Bob! These guys just aren't any fun at all."

"You won't be able to shoot him, because he will hopefully be in our custody by the time you see him again."

217

Bob spoke more seriously now. "Look, guys. This idiot tried to kill me; and you're asking me to just let him go; and *maybe* he'll be in custody at some point down the road? What makes you think he won't be out looking for me as soon as he realizes I'm not dead?"

"Like I said, you're going to stay dead until we get him. And we got him on camera when he pushed you off that cliff, so there won't be any problems proving he's guilty."

Bob was livid. "You were close enough to take his god-damned picture, but you didn't do anything to help me? What's wrong with you two? I've been out here trying to stay alive while a pack of dogs were after me and then dealing with that lunatic…while you're out taking pictures!" Bob looked like he was going to have a stroke as his face turned redder by the second.

"Sorry, Doctor Conley. We didn't see that little move coming; or we would have done something before; but then when he pushed you, we thought you were dead, too."

"Well, thanks a hell of a lot! And, oh, by the way, how did you know where we were to take your little pictures?"

"Let's just say that we've been watching."

Bob was still mad. "Great. So now tell me what's really at the bottom of this. It sure wasn't because you were worried about my well-being; so if you want me to cooperate, spill it."

McGinnis looked at Redding as though he was waiting to see how much he was going to reveal.

"He's got a round-trip flight for two tonight,

going to Vegas. The flight leaves at nine," Redding said a little reluctantly. McGinnis scowled at him, obviously not pleased with his partner.

When he didn't continue, Bob glared at him. "Yeah. Go on."

"He's bringing in a shipment of cocaine. We think he's been doing this for a long time now, years even. But this is the first time we have a shot at catching him and his cohorts in the act."

Bob looked at Mike, and they both knew Gerald wasn't going to be shot tonight.

Finally, Bob relented. "Okay, so what do you want us to do?"

"We want you to go back to the area and keep playing dead. We'll give you a radio so we can alert you if it looks like Gerald is heading back toward you."

Mike said, "Maybe we should have Peterson fix him up a big pot of beans so he can bloat up really good before he heads back."

Bob wasn't amused. "Maybe you'd like for the dogs to take a few chunks out of me, too, just to make it look really good."

"Okay, guys. We don't have to go that far. Just go on back and get back down to where you were when he left you. And if I let you know he's coming, just lie still and try to look dead."

"That won't be too hard for you, Bob. You've already got the smell down."

Bob still wasn't smiling, and the suits didn't seem entertained, either.

"Alright. Enough chit-chat here. Mike, you need to get to Bob's dad and tell him what's going on.

I don't want him to have a heart attack. Just make sure he keeps quiet."

"You know my dad!" Bob asked incredulously.

Redding didn't respond to his outburst. "McGinnis, you go over everything with Mr. Peterson until you think he can answer any questions that Gerald might ask."

"Do you know my damned pant size, too?" Bob interjected.

"Why don't I leave?" Pete said. "I don't mind taking off for a while, and I'd just as soon not have to deal with that joker again."

"Sorry, Mr. Peterson. I wish I could tell you to go on, but I don't think that would be a good idea. I really don't think he'll come back; and even if he does, he probably won't want to talk to you anyway. But you need to go on with McGinnis just in case. He'll walk you through everything you'll need to do."

"So what else do you know about me?"

"And, Mike, I think when you talk to Bob's dad, you should warn him not to trust anybody out there."

"Yeah, and tell him not to trust these idiots! They'll let a person die, if it's up to them!" Bob added.

As Mike started to head on to his pickup, Mr. Peterson and McGinnis headed into the house; and Bob turned to head back to the creek.

Redding said to Bob, "Wait a second. Before you leave, I wanted to ask you where you learned to track like that."

Bob, obviously still pissed, kept walking as he said, "An old Indian taught me. But I'm surprised you didn't already know!"

220

Redding shook his head and said, "Okay. But one last thing, Doctor Conley. Would you like to be there when we get him tomorrow? We could send a car for you."

Finally, Bob stopped walking and turned back around to face Redding. "Wow! I finally get a choice about something!" He stood with his head down for a few more seconds and then said in a lower voice, "I don't know. We'll see. And by the way, the name is Bob."

As he retraced his steps back to the ravine, Bob untied his shirt from around his ribs and put it on like before. He was relieved to find that his left arm was moving a little now.

Sherry and Grace met Mike as he walked up to the door, eager to know about Bob.

"No," Mike said. "I traipsed all over the place out there; and I got lost a few times; but I didn't see him anywhere. I saw his tracks a couple of times, so I think he's probably okay."

As he talked, Mike moved on through the house until he was positioned so he could see Gerald's face. He hated having to lie to Sherry; but he wanted to see what kind of reactions came from Gerald, Barb and Grace.

"I did see those dogs, though. I took a few shots at them, but I think all I did was scare them off. They took off running up the Nine Mile Creek just as fast as they could go."

He watched as Gerald glanced over and exchanged looks with Barb, and hatred welled up inside him.

Luckily, Neil had gone into the bathroom just

221

before Mike had come in; so when Mike saw the old man shuffling back toward the great room, he rushed to him and put a supportive arm around him. As he did, he whispered to him, "Bedroom." Neil looked confused and started to say something; but when he saw the look in Mike's eyes, he just nodded.

"I'm going to help Neil into the bedroom, and then I'll be right back," he announced.

Once they were in the bedroom and Neil had gotten settled on his bed, Mike told him the story as quickly as he could in very low, whispered words. Neil's expression turned from fear to anger.

"Now, Neil. You cannot let any of those people out there know what's really going on. Can you do that? Can you keep a poker face?"

"I don't know," Neil answered. Mike wondered if the old man was going to break down in tears or if he'd just have a heart attack there on the spot. "Maybe you should just tell everybody that I'm not feeling up to eating at the table; and then you can bring me a tray in here."

"Okay. That sounds like a good plan. And I'm sure a little more rest won't hurt you any, either. You're looking a little pale, and I know this isn't easy for you. I'll just go out and tell them, and I'll be back really soon with some food."

Mike pulled his gun from his holster and handed it to him. "In the meantime, keep this somewhere near you but well hidden. Just in case."

Mike walked back into the great room to find Sherry setting the last of the heaping bowls of food on the table. As he began piling a plate full of food, he announced that Neil wasn't feeling well and was going to eat in his room.

"Here you go," he said as he sat the plate on the old man's lap tray. "Now listen. I'm going to take Sherry and get out of here really quick. I don't want her here in the middle of something that could turn ugly. And besides that, I think if I hang around much longer I may end up shooting that bastard myself. So do you think you'll be okay here for a while?"

"Yes, I'll be just fine. Me and my friend here," Neil said as he patted the blanket that hid the gun.

Mike grinned at him and said, "See you in a bit."

He walked back in to the dinner table and started to sit down; and then, as though he'd just remembered, walked over to the phone and dialed his parents' number. After a few minutes on the line, he hung up and told Sherry that his mother was sick.

CHAPTER 13

"Do you think we should go over there?" Mike asked, knowing full well that she'd want to jump and run to the rescue.

"Oh, my! Yes!" she exclaimed. "What in the world is going on here? First Bob, and then Neil all torn up! And now Momma! I do declare, I don't know which end's up these days!"

Mike grabbed his wife's purse and began leading her toward the door. But Sherry wasn't done yet.

"Oh, wait a minute, now. Grace, I think you know where everything is here in the kitchen; but if anybody needs anything, and you're not sure where it is, just look around, and you'll find it. And it was really nice to meet you."

Mike pulled Sherry on out the door.

The three remaining guests sat down and began to eat while Neil listened to their chatter from the other room. The more he listened to them, the madder he got. *How dare them come into my house and eat my food while my boy is out there still in danger.* He put his hand under the covers and grabbed the gun. *I've got half a mind to just go out there and shoot them all right between the eyes.*

When dinner was over, Gerald said, "Grace, I think you should drive my truck back home. I'll ride back to Barb's house and take your car on up to the airport."

Before Grace could respond, Barb added, "And we'll have to leave right now if he's going to get there

225

in time. Sorry I can't help you clean up first."

It wasn't long before Grace poked her head around the corner of his door, and, seeing that he was awake, walked in to get his dishes.

"Sorry to bother you, Dr. Conley, but I thought I'd see if you wanted anything else to eat before I put the food away."

"No. I'm fine, thanks."

Then I'll just take your dishes, if that's okay with you. Are you feeling okay?"

"I've felt better."

"I know you must be worried to death about Bob, but I'm sure he'll be fine."

Neil knew better than to trust anybody at this point, but he wanted to like the girl. He normally didn't meet many people who he liked, and he didn't want to think his judgment of her was wrong. Nevertheless, he had to be cautious. He decided to sit tight, keep his mouth shut, keep the gun close by, and wait to see what transpired next.

When she had finished cleaning up the kitchen, she returned to Neil's bedroom and sat next to him on the bed. She gently took his hand and said, "Thank you for sharing this beautiful place with me today."

Neil melted again and decided that there was no way she could have anything to do with Gerald and Barb's scheme. She had to be just another innocent bystander who was going to get caught in the crosshairs.

"I need to go now; but things are cleaned up in the kitchen; and all the food is in the refrigerator. I hope you feel better soon."

Grace stood to leave as Neil squeezed her hand

goodbye.

The FBI watched as Gerald and Barb left the ranch and approached the turn that would indicate whether they were going into the city or back toward Peterson's place. They headed towards Peterson's. Redding immediately picked up his radio and alerted Bob.

Bob had hoped it wouldn't come to this; but since it had, he had to get down to the lower level again. As he had retraced his steps, he had watched for a more gradual drop to the creek where he might lower himself rather than having to throw himself down the embankment again. Now that the word had been given, he had to move fast.

He sat down and began to scoot on his rear end, letting gravity help him get to the bottom. His ribs and left arm were still hurting; and he thought if he ever had time to stop long enough to check, he would find a lot more on him that hurt. But now wasn't that time.

Once he'd gotten back to the creek, he'd taken care not to get his pants wet again. They had dried enough that Gerald wouldn't notice from as far away as he would be; and he wanted to keep it that way. If he thought this was a ruse, he would surely use his gun.

He worked his way on back west along the edge of the creek and found the spot where he'd landed before. Throwing the gun pieces back toward the general vicinity where they'd been before and placing his backpack in its original position, he lay back down on the rocks. The meat, he thought, and got back up to retrieve the two pieces.

The rocks seemed harder and more-jagged now

than they had before; and as he lay there, he swore this would be the last thing he'd do to catch Gerald. FBI or not. If they asked him to do one more thing for that asshole, he'd just shoot them first and then hunt the guy down and finish him off. He was sick of Gerald, sick of the dogs, sick of Barb, and maybe even sick of Grace.

Gerald drove up to Peterson's place and got out of the car. Pete came to the door as he walked up to the house

"Just thought I'd check back on Bob. It's been long enough now that I'm starting to worry about him. You seen him yet?"

"Nope, not seen him, but I don't think you need to worry yourself about him. He's been known to start tracking those dogs and lose all track of time. Like I said, he must surely be part bloodhound; and once he's got the scent, he usually don't let go."

"Well, I still think maybe I should try to find him again. It's going to be getting dark soon, and I hate to think of him out there alone with those dogs."

"Suit yourself. You just be careful out there."

Gerald waved his hand at Pete and walked back to the car. He was pretty sure he could drive part of the way to the spot; and he didn't want to have to walk through those woods and take a chance on facing the dogs if he didn't have to. As he put the car in gear and headed into the pasture, he noticed Pete in his rearview mirror, running down off the porch and waving his arms at him.

"Screw him," Gerald said and kept on driving.

When he got as far as he could, he slipped on his two guns and added a couple of clips to his

228

pockets.

"I'll be back as soon as I can."

"Well, hurry up so we don't miss our flight. But make sure the bastard's dead."

Bob could smell the cologne, so he did his best not to move. The thought popped into his head that Gerald might just decide to shoot him to be on the safe side; but the more he thought about it, the more he didn't think he'd do it. If he was going to shoot him, he would have done it earlier. No, he wanted it to look like the dogs had gotten him.

He heard the footsteps approach and stop just above him, immediately followed by the sound of the gun being cocked. Had he been wrong about the bastard? It wouldn't be the first time.

It took everything Bob could do not to react; but he consoled himself with the thought that he would probably live through any bullet that didn't go straight through the heart or the brain. But then, Gerald was a pretty good shot. Besides, the FBI agents were on top of things; and if he ended up taking a bullet that didn't hit a vital area, they would have help there in no time. Yeah, right, he thought. Things weren't looking too good the more he thought about it.

Just as he was deciding it was time to take action, he heard the slow release of the hammer and then Gerald's footsteps retreating. As soon as his aroma began to dissipate, Bob opened his eyes and took in a breath. Then he picked up his radio.

"Hey, Redding! What the hell were you thinking anyway? That asshole almost just shot me!"

"I knew he wouldn't. He needed you dead without a bullet in you, because that could have linked

229

him to your death. There wasn't anything to worry about."

"You're a jerk, you know that?"

"We'll catch up with you later, Dr. Bob. We've got to stay on Gerald and Barb, and it looks as though they're headed to the airport now."

"Where's Grace? Is she with them?" Bob asked.

"No. We saw her drive past about five minutes ago, driving like a maniac. We're not going after her right now. We'll keep our sights on Gerald and Barb, and we'll probably pick her up at home later tonight or in the morning. She'd just better hope there are no cops out, though."

Bob clicked off the radio and began pulling himself back up on his feet. It was going to be another long walk back to Peterson's.

He tried to focus on the possibility of the dogs being nearby; but his injuries and exhaustion had taken a toll on him; and the turn of events concerning Barb and Gerald weighed heavy on his mind. Although the situation with the dogs had seemed personal before, this trumped everything. This was *very* personal.

When he finally reached Peterson's house, he stumbled up to the porch and knocked. Pete flung the door open before Bob could hardly blink.

"Dr. Bob! Come in here and sit down. I've been worried to death. That bastard stopped by here and said he was going out to look for ya."

"Yeah, Pete, he did. But I'm still alive, and I guess the FBI are after him and Barb now. I just needed to use your phone to call Mike to pick me up. Do you mind?"

"Hell, no! You just go right in the kitchen there;

230

the phone's on the wall by the table. Can I get ya something to drink?"

"A glass of water would be great," Bob replied as he began to punch Mike's number into the phone. By the time he hung up, Pete had a big glass of ice water sitting on the table for him; and Bob gladly sank into a rickety chair as he gulped it down.

Pete began asking questions, and the two men chatted until Mike showed up less than ten minutes later.

As they drove back toward the ranch, Mike said, "I told Sherry what was going on; and we wanted to go back and see how your dad was doing; but we thought we'd wait until you were back out of the woods. I'm sure he is probably beside himself worrying about you. So tell us what happened. Did Gerald show up again?"

Bob filled them in on what had transpired, and soon they were back at the ranch. Bob had never been so happy to see the place and was eager to get inside and crawl into the tub.

Sherry was the first one out of the truck, and Bob and Mike followed. As the men were starting up the sidewalk, a bloodcurdling scream broke the silence. Bob and Mike reached the bedroom at the same time and found Sherry in Neil's room on the bed, holding Neil in her arms. He was dead.

Mike noticed the bulge of the gun still underneath the covers. What had happened? Had the old man had a heart attack? Or had he been smothered? Or what? This just didn't even seem real.

Bob suddenly turned to leave, and Mike put his hand up to stop him.

"Move."

Mike was worried about Bob. He'd had a rough day; and it had showed; but now with this, he looked like a madman.

"Think about what you're doing."

"I'm thinking. Now move."

"Let's talk to the FBI first."

"You talk to the FBI. I've got other things to do."

Bob started to push around Mike when Sherry blurted out between sobs, "Would you two stop that and get over here and help me?"

She had laid Neil back down and was trying to straighten his clothes and the blankets around him. Mike stepped up to help her. Bob followed; but instead of trying to help them, he sank back down in the chair.

As Bob watched them coddle the old man's body, the tears began to roll down his cheeks. He felt like he was truly at the end of his rope, nothing left to give. When Mike and Sherry finished fussing over Neil, they turned around to see Bob staring out the window. Mike walked over to him and laid his hand on his shoulder.

"Everything's going to be okay, Buddy. We'll take care of this together, and you know me and Sherry will be here for you. Anything you need. . ."

Bob just kept staring out the window, the tears leaving clean streaks in the dirt that covered his face. Mike and Sherry exchanged a worried look.

"Why don't you come on with us?" Mike continued. "There's nothing we can do here, so come to our place and get some rest. Then we'll tackle this whole situation after that. Okay?"

Still, Bob just sat. With a jerk of Mike's head, Sherry came over; and with one on each side of him, they lead him back out to the pickup.

Barb had already packed an overnight bag and stashed it in the trunk before going to the ranch; and now she seemed almost dreamy as she and Gerald headed to the airport. They talked about how easy it had been to get rid of Bob and made plans for the money.

"I'm going to get a nanny for those kids," Barb said. "I'm tired of putting up with them, too. And now with Bob finally gone, I'm sure not going to take care of them myself. And clothes. I need some really snazzy clothes, and maybe I'll even turn this old Riviera in for a new one."

Gerald listened, wishing she'd just shut up. It was hard for him to play along; but with the money just barely out of reach now, he would play along with her for a little while longer.

"Yeah, and I can get that Corvette I've always wanted. What do you think? And after this coke run, I might even be able to pick up some nice real estate at the lake."

The FBI followed a safe distance behind as they listened through their bug to the conversation between Barb and Gerald. They had these two in the bag, and hopefully they'd be able to pick up some names of accomplices.

As they approached Mid Continent International Airport, McGinnis radioed to the men who were ready to board the plane.

Gerald and Barb walked up to the ticket counter, followed by two men in khakis and polo shirts. Fortunately, the terminal was almost empty, and so the boarding and takeoff were completed quickly.

There were two teams waiting at McCarran International in Las Vegas when the plane landed. Team One was waiting in the parking lot of the car rental mall in a nondescript, blue Ford Taurus. They watched as Gerald disappeared into the office and soon returned with a set of keys to a bright-red Mustang. The agents smoothly pulled in behind them without being seen and then radioed to Team Two.

As the Taurus and the Mustang exited the airport property, another car, a maroon minivan, followed. The Mustang headed south on I-15 and veered onto I-215 with the two FBI vehicles following at a distance. After driving about twenty minutes, they had reached the outskirts of the city; and the Mustang turned onto a small street that bordered a park.

It was late; so the few houses that were visible from the street were dark; and there was no other traffic on the street. As they turned onto the street, both FBI vehicles flipped off their lights and slowly crept ahead until they saw the Mustang pull up next to a black Mercedes.

Team Two used an infrared camera to document the event and then quietly followed Gerald and Barb back to the city. Team One turned and followed the Mercedes.

The transaction had been a success, and the bust was in the bag.

Barb and Gerald drove to the strip and played a few games, completely oblivious of the men who followed them. And finally, at two o'clock, they headed back to the airport.

The cocaine had been packed in various forms in order to get through security. Some of it was packed in different sizes, shapes and colors of capsules and pills and put into prescription bottles, vitamin bottles, and bottles labeled as herbal ingredients. There were statues and mugs and other miscellaneous memorabilia that could have been picked up anywhere around the airport; and those, too, were disguises for the powder.

Boarding the plane at this time of the morning was just as easy as it had been coming in late at night. But this time, they split up, Gerald checking in and boarding with Barb about five minutes behind him. And once they were in the air, they both slept like babies.

When they got back to Mike and Sherry's house, Bob immediately headed toward the bathroom. Sherry laid out clean towels and washcloths, and Mike walked in with a bathrobe and a pair of his own underwear.

Finally alone, Bob turned on the shower as hot as he could stand it; and while the room began to steam up, he slowly stripped the dirty clothes off, layer by layer. He stared at himself in the mirror. His torso was resplendent with mostly reds and purples, but his arm looked black. He couldn't tell if it was bruised, or if it was just dirt. He climbed into the shower and winced as the hot water hit him; but soon, his tattered body adjusted; and he began to relax.

Three Toes, Big Dog, Gerald, Barb and Grace began to take over his thoughts. Hadn't all this started with the dogs? Maybe. Maybe not. Maybe it had started the day he met Barb.

Barb and Gerald. Bob couldn't believe he'd

been so blind that he hadn't noticed it sooner. But then, maybe he just hadn't wanted to. And even Grace. She was the last one with his dad; and in his weakened state, she could have easily suffocated him; and he wouldn't have been able to stop her. How could he have been so gullible to think she really was his friend? She was nothing more than just another maggot like Barb and Gerald. As the water washed away the dirt on his body, his heart felt darker and dirtier.

After he'd finished cleaning up and gingerly dried his aching body, Bob put on the clothes he'd been given and walked out into the living room, where Mike and Sherry were waiting for him. A first-aid kit had been set out, and Bob took a chair without question. Sherry began to gently clean up his scrapes and cuts; and for once, she worked in silence. When she had finished, she cinched up his ribs with a large Ace wrap. Bob thought it wasn't sufficient to hold anything in place; but he didn't have the heart to tell her that; nor did he really care. When Sherry had finished, Bob got up and began to pace around the living room like a caged animal. Mike and Sherry sat quietly, pretending to read while he walked.

Neil's death automatically transferred the ranch to him; and with him supposedly dead, too, it would all go directly to Barb. So between the five million dollar insurance policy plus what the ranch and the practice in the city could be sold for, he figured he was worth somewhere around ten million, especially if he died from an accident. Barb had been planning this for months, and she had used Gerald and Grace to help her.

Bob had been so busy going after the dogs, because they were killers; and yet, his own wife was no different. She'd not been any different for many years, and he had chosen to look the other way. Now his father had paid the price for his stupidity. His anger at himself swelled, and his disgust for Barb was of epic proportions. The hatred he felt for Gerald would eat him alive; and he knew it; but he didn't care about that as much as he did the disappointment he felt in Grace. He had never felt like such a stupid and broken man.

Finally, Mike couldn't take the pacing and the brooding anymore and blatantly interrupted his thoughts.

"Bob, what's going on with the kids? Do you know where they are?"

Bob stopped and looked at him through bloodshot eyes, but his gaze seemed far away.

"Whatever you're thinking of doing, you shouldn't forget about them. They're going to need you now more than ever. So if you do something stupid, just know that Sherry and I will have to take care of them; and then think what they'll be like. Hell, they could end up more screwed up than the whole bunch of us put together."

Mike dared to let a tiny smile show on his face, hoping it might break through the darkness inside Bob.

Bob's eyes finally focused on Mike, and then a stunned look came on his face.

"For God's sake, Mike! What in the hell do you want me to do?" Bob yelled at him.

Mike's smile withered away as he sat there stunned that Bob had snapped at him so violently; and Bob just stood and stared at him in disbelief. No one

237

moved or made a sound.

Suddenly, Bob let out a long breath of air, and his shoulders slumped. He made his way over to the couch and sat on the opposite end from Mike. The tears started again; and as Bob rested his elbows on his knees and cradled his head in his hands, Mike reached over and gave him a soft squeeze on the shoulder.

Sherry went to the kitchen, and within a couple of minutes returned with a tray of steaming coffee mugs, a ceramic-cow pitcher of milk, a bowl of sugar and a bottle of whiskey. Bob decided to forego his usual cream and sugar and reached for the whiskey instead.

"I know this isn't any consolation," Mike said, "but justice will prevail, as they say."

"But it won't be my justice. And since I'm the one victim left alive, I should be the one to mete out that justice."

"You're right, Bob. But we're not living in the old west, or I'd tell ya to go for it."

"Yeah. Shame, ain't it?" Bob said.

Bob and Mike had talked often about how they always felt as though they belonged in the "olden days" when men settled things square up. Toe to toe, or gun to gun. But these days, things weren't settled like that. Now they were "civilized".

Sherry was reluctant to bring up the issue of Neil's body, but she knew it had to be done. She suggested to Bob that she call Redding and McGinnis to let them know what had happened; and he merely nodded his head in agreement. She immediately excused herself back to the kitchen, and the men could hear her talking softly on the phone. When she

238

returned, she told them that she had spoken with Redding and that he had assured her they would take care of everything. Law required an autopsy in the case of unknown or suspicious death; and so they would be sending the paperwork over for Bob to sign; and they would take care of the rest of the arrangements as Bob preferred. He also had offered to send a car to pick up Bob in a few hours so he could be there when they arrested Gerald and Barb. Again, Bob merely nodded. There were no words adequate to express his emotions.

After a few more minutes of silence, Bob said, "Do you think a jury will convict me if I kill them?"

"You know the system, Bob. More than likely, they'd perform CPR on him; and you'd end up in a cell with him. And he would probably get out first."

"That's not exactly what I wanted to hear, you know."

"I know. But we both know what the reality of it is."

"Yeah. I know all about reality. But right now, I've got to lie down and rest a little before they come to pick me up."

"Okay. Sherry's got your clothes in the washer, so they'll be clean when you wake up. I'll wake you up in time to get ready."

By the time Mike had finished, Bob had already leaned back against the arm of the couch and had dozed off, hoping that he'd wake up in the morning and this would have all been just a bad dream. But what seemed like a second later, Sherry was shaking him, telling him to wake up. It was four-thirty; and she had his clean clothes in her hands, all folded neatly.

239

It took Bob a while to shake the cobwebs from his head and a little longer to get his stiff joints moving again. He could smell breakfast cooking and suddenly realized he was famished. He'd not eaten anything in almost twenty-four hours. He quickly changed into his clean clothes and then went into the kitchen, where Sherry was putting bacon, eggs, toast and grits on the table.

"You'll need a good breakfast today, so I want you to just eat up everything you can here. And I don't want to hear a thing about how much grease there is. You need some fat to stick to those broken ribs just so they can heal. And besides that, you need all that protein for your energy."

Mike put up his hand to calm Sherry's anxiety, and hopefully quell the jabbering that was already starting up. Bob gave her a little smile to let her know it was all good, and he dug in.

It was almost five when they heard the car pull up. Bob and Mike were finishing their breakfast, so Sherry went to the door to let them in. Mike pulled the small pea shooter that he'd retrieved from under Neil's blanket and handed it to Bob.

"Here," he said quietly. "Put this somewhere it won't be seen, but don't be too trigger happy. Use it only if you have to. And if that happens, make sure you kill them."

Bob quickly took it and stuck it in his boot, finished his coffee, grabbed his hat and headed for the door. As he was ready to walk out, he turned and looked back at Mike.

"Thanks," he said. And then he was gone.

"So where are we going?" Bob asked as the car

240

pulled out of the driveway.

"We're going to the house where we'll be arresting Gerald and Barb," said McGinnis. "And I have to admit that I'm looking forward to seeing their faces when they see you."

Bob didn't know how well equipped he was to deal with all this, but he knew it was something he had to do. Maybe seeing their faces when they saw him would at least be some sort of solace.

They were headed to the south part of Kansas City, where the people who had money, or wanted to look as though they had money, lived. Bob had never driven down this way much; and seeing the mansions all surrounded by acres of manicured lawns was at least interesting. The sun was just coming up, throwing an orange glow on all the multi-paned windows they passed.

Finally, he asked, "Is Barb going to be arrested, too?"

McGinnis looked back over the seat and said, "What do you think?"

It was six o'clock in the morning when they finally pulled into a driveway.

"This is it?"

"No. It's the one next door. We can see the entrance of his driveway from here; but they probably won't be able to see us, especially once they pull up a little ways toward the house."

Bob was suddenly nervous and thankful Mike had given him the gun. They waited quietly in the car, all eyes watching in all directions.

McGinnis said, "I hear you're pretty good at tracking in the woods."

241

"I do all right," Bob said.

After a few more minutes of silence, Redding turned to him and said, "I'm not sure how this is all going to go down, but I'll let you know when it's safe to get out of the car."

Bob nodded, and the silence settled around them again.

From the airport, Gerald and Barb took off for south Kansas City. Thanks to the cocaine, they were wide-eyed in spite of having had no sleep.

Gerald took side jaunts along the way rather than heading straight to the house; and he kept watch in his rearview mirror to make sure no one was following him. The last thing he wanted to do was lead anyone to this guy's house. And it wasn't the police who worried him, either, but the guy he was delivering to. Damion Ferrino was known for his gruesome punishments when he was unhappy; and he was the last person Gerald wanted to piss off. He'd rather be killed than go through the torture that he'd heard about.

Bob marveled at the palatial structure, a light, creamy stucco, red-tiled roof, arched doorways and windows made of leaded glass. The two-story columns were magnificent, probably hand-carved, in spiraled patterns. A circular drive passed under a portico; and the lawn, like all the others within sight, looked like green velvet. Between the driveway and the street was a huge fountain encircled by stone benches; and there was statuary everywhere. Spiraling topiaries stood as sentinels along each side of the property. Bob thought it was a little over the top, but impressive nonetheless.

Within minutes, they saw Gerald turn into the

driveway.

"We'll wait for about five minutes before we move in," Redding said. "That will give them time to get their candy and their money out. Then we'll hit 'em."

Bob felt each minute tick by slowly; but finally, he began to see the SWAT team inching across the lawns and approaching the house. It was time.

The two FBI agents jumped out of the car and headed toward the back of the house. Bob was in awe as he watched the event unfold. It was like a dance, everyone moving in sync to ascend in perfect uniformity.

And then the Presence hit him hard, catching him by surprise. He knew he needed to do something, and he needed to do it quickly. He just didn't know what it was. Then, as he reached for the door handle, he knew.

With a burst of energy, he flew out of the car and ran in the direction of the FBI agents, not aware now of the pain that raced through his body. As he rounded the corner of the house, he saw Redding standing with his gun drawn in front of what he guessed must have been a guest house. He didn't see McGinnis anywhere.

Without thinking, he ran toward Redding, and just as he reached him, jumped and threw himself over the agent, both of them hitting the ground with a thud. A split second later, bullets shattered the windows of the guest house and pock-marked the entire front exterior.

Bob immediately grabbed Redding and began pulling him toward the side of the house farthest from the mansion. He was visibly shaken.

Once they were out of the line of fire, he asked him, "How in the hell did you know?"

"Tell you later. Right know, I've gotta go."

Thomas watched as Bob started running back up toward the rear of the mansion. He reluctantly followed him and caught up with him just as Bob began to pace back and forth across the lawn.

"What the hell are you doing?"

"Gerald came out this way. I'm just trying to figure out which direction he went."

Then he pointed south and started to take off after him. Thomas caught him by the arm and stopped him.

"Where are you going?"

"They're on the other side of that hill right there; and they're moving fast; so let's get them."

"And just how are you so damned sure that's where they are?"

"I can smell him," Bob said as he grabbed the gun from his boot and took off running again.

Redding immediately grabbed his radio and called up McGinnis.

"Jack, Bob and I are heading south from the rear of the house in pursuit of Gerald. Get us backup."

McGinnis immediately motioned for the three closest men to go.

Bob topped the hill with Redding a few paces behind him, but there was no sign of Gerald. Bob noticed a drainage culvert leading into a ravine and pointed. As he took off, Redding radioed back to McGinnis to tell him where they were going and then quickly followed. Bob had already found the tracks

244

leading off into the woods and had started to follow when Redding yelled at him to stop.

"We can't take off through the woods like this. We've got to wait for backup to get here."

"We've got to follow them now. They know where they're going, and we don't," Bob said as he took off running again.

Redding stood there for a few more seconds, not sure of what to do; and just as he started to run after him, the SWAT guys showed up and joined him. It didn't take long for them to understand what was going on and begin fanning out into the woods. Bob motioned for the one closest to him to come back and then showed him the tracks.

"It looks like there are five people we're after. Four men and one woman."

McGinnis came running down the ravine just then, out of breath.

"Okay. Tell me what's going on here."

Redding said, "Ask the tracker."

McGinnis looked at Bob, waiting for an explanation; but before Bob could speak, the SWAT guy spoke up.

"He's right on, Sir. There are tracks here just like he said. Four men and a woman."

McGinnis turned toward Bob and said, "So you want to lead this little escapade?"

Bob replied, "I'm not leading anything. I'm just going after them, and I happen to be the first in line."

As he turned to continue following the tracks, Redding said, "Wait a minute, Bob. Take this with you." He pulled his Glock 9mm from its holster and handed it to him along with three extra clips.

245

Bob stuck the gun in his belt and took off again. He could tell Gerald and the gang were running fast, faster than he was able to; so he would have to keep up a steady pace and move quietly just to catch up to them. They would eventually tire out and need to slow down, and then he would gain his ground.

The tracks were single file, with Barb bringing up the tail. Bob figured they would leave her behind as soon as she couldn't keep up, which was going to be soon, since the most leg work she'd ever done was when she was shopping.

It only took a few hundred more feet when he topped a hill and saw her sitting at the base of a tree trying to catch her breath. He was on top of her before she saw him, and she paled as though she'd seen a ghost. Then Bob noticed the blinking light strapped to her wrist. It was a bomb.

Bob looked back toward Redding, pointed at the blinking light and said, "Here's our little bombshell. Might as well let her sit the rest out." The men began to scatter out around him; and he quickly added, "I have a feeling the reason they've been running in single file is because the woods might be booby-trapped. Maybe all of you should stay behind me instead of off to the sides."

Then he resumed his pace again, with the men cautiously stepping their way back to his trail.

They hadn't gone much further when they heard the blast go off. Bob stopped and turned to the men behind him. "She always was a blast," he said with a straight face. And then he took off again, leaving the men wondering whether to laugh or whether he was a crazy lunatic. At this point, Bob wouldn't have argued against the latter.

Bob slowed down now, wondering if there were any ambushes ahead. McGinnis, who was still huffing and puffing along, was thankful for the slower pace.

About two more minutes passed; and Bob stopped again, his nose in the air. They were still in a fairly heavily wooded area, although he could hear the traffic from the interstate nearby. He sniffed with the determination of a bloodhound, circling the air to find the enemy; and within seconds, he pointed to the one o'clock and eleven o'clock positions and mouthed the words *fifty yards*. The SWAT team went to work. Two began inching to the right, looking before each footfall; and the third guy, along with McGinnis, turned right. Bob and Redding waited thirty seconds and then continued moving straight ahead. Both of them drew their guns as they walked side-by-side.

Suddenly, the silence of the early-morning woods was shattered by the gunfire. Redding hit the ground; but Bob took off running as fast as he could, firing first to his right and then to his left. Redding raised his head just in time to see him hit the ground and roll behind a tree. Then all was quiet again.

Bob edged out from behind the tree and began to crawl toward some heavy brush. As he moved slowly, the SWAT team followed with their guns drawn. About twenty feet into the brush was their first victim, dead from a single bullet through his head.

"Got him," Bob said quietly.

"And one other one who I found in the brush over there," one of the SWAT men whispered back.

"Then that leaves just two more," Bob said as he jumped to his feet and took off.

Redding figured it was safe to get up; and he quickly took off after Bob, while McGinnis, who had to stop to catch his breath again, motioned for the SWAT team to continue on.

There were only two tracks to watch for now, and Bob knew they were only minutes away. His eyes grew sharper as he moved through the heavy woods.

He was looking forward to meeting up with Gerald, and he was determined to kill him when he did. And he would have fun doing it.

His heart was calm and his breath measured as he kept up the pace. The tracks had turned west, and so the south wind was no longer to his advantage. Smelling them now would just be pure luck.

Bob thought Gerald and his fellow partner in crime knew where they were going; but he also figured it had turned into an each-for-his-own situation. That would mean Gerald would likely tire out next and be left behind; and Bob was all but salivating at the thought. He couldn't wait to see him face-to-face.

Suddenly, Bob stopped.

"What?" Redding asked quietly.

"The tracks have changed. Tell everybody not to move."

Redding turned and motioned for them to stay where they were, while Bob looked around to make sure there were no land mines.

He began to backtrack and finally saw what he was looking for. A deep heel mark. Moving on further back, he squatted down and studied the two sets of foot prints, and then looked at Redding.

"How big is this Damion guy? My size, bigger or smaller?"

"Bigger. Probably by about six inches or so. And he's heavier, too."

As he moved back and forth, studying the two sets of prints, he began to notice that the smaller set, Gerald's, was heavier than usual.

"Gerald was carrying something through here. See how his prints are deeper here than here?" he said to the men as he pointed out his findings. "In fact, it looks like he was carrying something in his left hand here and then switched to his right here." He moved on forward a little farther and said, "And here, he handed it over to Damion. See how the prints changed?"

The men just looked at him like he had grown horns. Unaware of their expressions, Bob continued to look at the prints a few more seconds and then stood.

"Let's go."

He figured since Damion was the carrier now, he wouldn't hesitate to leave Gerald behind. And he knew from the hunts at the ranch that Gerald never went anywhere with one gun. He'd be armed to the teeth. Bob started walking and turned to Redding as he did. "I've got a feeling Gerald will be just ahead somewhere waiting for us since Damion's now carrying whatever it was they had."

"Has to be the cocaine," Thomas said.

"I don't think so. That wouldn't be heavy enough. Might be money, but I doubt that, too. Anyway, I think I'd feel a little better wearing a vest now, especially if I'm staying in the lead. Either way, whoever goes first needs to be ready."

Redding stopped walking and started taking off his jacket. As Bob began taking off his own shirt, Redding said, "You can just put it on over your shirt."

"If he sees the vest, he'll go for a head shot."

Turning toward the men behind him, Bob continued. "Now, I'm going in full blast as soon as I know where he is, which hopefully will be a few seconds before he sees me and starts shooting. But once you know the general direction of where he is, shoot like hell."

Then Bob took off, eyes alternating from the tracks to the woods in front of him. He wished the wind was in his favor now, but he'd have to do the best he could without it.

Just when he started to think he'd been wrong in his calculations, something hit him hard in the chest, causing him to fall backward into the dirt. Suddenly, he felt as though he had more broken ribs. The men opened fire as he rolled behind a tree and tried to catch his breath. That one hurt really bad.

He sat up and looked around the tree. Two of the SWAT guys were down, wounded but not dead. Then the gunfire stopped, leaving an eerie silence.

"Damn it, Bob! I thought I killed you yesterday."

"Wrong again, asshole."

"Ah. No need for name calling now. You're gonna be dead soon, so you better play nice."

Bob needed him to keep talking just so everyone could know where he was.

"You still think you're that good, huh?"

"That's what I like about you, Bob. Your self-confidence. But you know, it's your lack of respect for your enemy that will be your downfall, you stupid fool."

"Now, now. Play nice. Remember?"

250

"I have been playing nice. With your wife."

Bob had managed to locate the voice and peered through the limbs and bushes to see Gerald crouched down. He let a single bullet fly. It hit Gerald in the right shoulder, knocking him to the ground and out of sight.

"Damn, Bob! If that's the best you can do, I can see why you haven't gotten those dogs yet."

"Stick something else out, and I'll shoot that, too," Bob yelled to him. Then, so the other men could hear as well, he said, "Hey, Redding! Have your men stand off. This one's mine."

Gerald didn't say anything.

"What's wrong?" Bob finally said. "You dead already, or are you just hiding back there?"

"Not a chance," Gerald replied as he got back into position.

"Why don't you give it up and come on out, Gerald? It's over, and I promise I won't kill you."

"Well, the way I see it, I either die here taking you down or Damion kills me later. Either way, I'm a dead man; so I think I'll stick it out here and enjoy the fact that I'm going to take you with me when I go." Gerald fired, clipping the tree next to Bob; and he could feel his ear stinging from the bark that flew toward him.

"What's wrong, Bob?" Gerald said in a mocking voice. "You dead or just hiding?" Gerald let out a hysterical laugh.

"No. Like I said, you're not that good."

Gerald had ducked back down behind the brush; and Bob took advantage of the opportunity to quietly slip to his left, where he took cover behind another tree. He could see Gerald a little better from here; and he quickly took aim and fired, hitting him in his left leg. Gerald yelled and tried to turn for a wild shot in his direction; but the next shot took his left forearm; and then he was down for good.

Bob ran to where he lay writhing in pain and kicked the guns away from him. If he'd been an animal, he would have shot him just to put him out of his misery. But this man was worse than any animal, and he didn't merit that much consideration.

Bob held the gun steady at his head until Thomas came running up to them.

"Here's your chance, Bob."

But instead of shooting him, he pulled up his gun and knelt beside him. He checked for more weapons, and then said, "What is Damion carrying?"

"Bite me!" Gerald said.

Bob's anger instantly peaked, and he reached over to stick his thumb in the hole in Gerald's leg.

"Try again," he said.

Gerald cried out in agony and then replied, "Missile."

Bob took his thumb from Gerald's leg and said, "What's it for?"

"I don't know," Gerald said in a whiny voice.

Bob stuck his thumb back in the bullet hole, and Gerald cried out again.

"I don't know! I really don't know!"

Bob pulled his thumb from the wound and looked up at Redding.

"He doesn't know. If he did, he'd be squealing like a pig right now."

The SWAT team closed in around the men.

252

Bob turned to Redding and said, "I'm going to leave Damion up to you and your men. I got what I came here for."

The thumping sounds of a helicopter invaded their thoughts. It was more SWAT, and they were flying low overhead. But just as they saw it, they heard a loud, whistling sound; and then it erupted into a ball of fire, sending pieces flying through the air as everyone on the ground scrambled for cover. A second chopper followed close behind and headed in the direction of the missile launch.

When the debris had stopped falling, and the second chopper was out of sight, Bob walked back over to Gerald and said, "Was there just one?"

Gerald nodded his head. Just one.

"I'm gonna head back to the house, if you don't mind. And if I don't see anybody on their way back here, I'll be sure they know."

As Bob made his way back through the woods, he kept hoping Gerald would bleed to death before anybody got around to helping him. He stopped abruptly when he came across Barb's body parts; and after he thought about it for a moment, he walked on without saying his prayer for the dead.

As he cleared the woods, there were medics heading in the direction he'd just come from; and it wasn't long until everyone was being taken care of. Bob trudged back to the car and finally let his weary body relax.

A few minutes later, Redding joined him. As he slid in behind the steering wheel he said, "You okay?"

"Aside from tired and sore and pissed as hell, I'm okay."

"What are you going to tell your boys?"

After a few moments pause, Bob said, "I don't know yet. Maybe something nice will come to mind before I have to tell them anything."

He'd always been a stickler for the truth, but this time, maybe he would bend it a little for his kids' sake. They didn't need to know their mother was a drug smuggler and a murderer.

"What's the status on Grace?" he asked

"She was to be picked up this morning at their house."

"What about Dad? When will the autopsy be done?"

"I'm not sure. We put a rush on it, but we've not received word back on it yet. It could be anytime, but I'd say late today or early tomorrow at the latest. And when you're up to it, we need to know where you want the body to go as soon as possible."

Bob's thoughts were scattered, and he didn't know what to think of first. After another minute of mulling things over, he said, "I need to find out where the kids are and get them picked up as soon as possible. Think you can help me out with that?"

Redding pulled a piece of paper with three addresses on it from his pocket and handed it to Bob.

"That's where they are. We separated them and had some of our people taking care of them; so you can rest knowing they're fine. And here," he said as he held out the keys to the car. "Take the car, go pick them up, and we'll touch base as soon as possible."

"Thanks," Bob said.

As the FBI agent started to get out of the car, he looked back at Bob and asked, "By the way, do you ever hire out as a tracker?"

"Nah. I don't think I'd be any good at it."

Redding chuckled as he walked away.

As Bob pulled out of the drive and headed back toward home, his thoughts turned to Grace. What was she going to think when she found out about Gerald? He had a hard time believing she was a part of any of this, but he wondered if he should trust his instincts. After all, she was thin, something that he knew was often seen in druggies; and he'd known her for such a short time. Maybe he was just being gullible again. Hell, he'd known Barb forever, and he never would have thought she was capable of the things she had done.

CHAPTER 14

Once he had gathered up the boys, he headed back out toward the ranch. He had no desire to go back to the house he'd shared with Barb; and Mike and Sherry would be a good help with the kids.

The boys were excited to see their dad, and even more excited when they learned they were going to the country. Bob did his best to listen to their stories about their friends and school; and then, when they began asking questions about the dogs, he decided it was time to tell them. Besides, he had an out. He had to drive, so the boys wouldn't be able to tell he was lying. He couldn't look them in the eye and say what he was about to say.

"Boys, I need to tell you something really important right now. Okay?"

Sensing the gravity of the moment, they all grew quiet.

"There was a man, Gerald, who was a friend of your mom's. He was the one I took out hunting with me, remember? Well, it turned out he was really good at tricking everybody into thinking he was a good friend; but he wasn't. While we were out hunting yesterday, he pushed me over a cliff; and I got hurt pretty bad."

Bob watched them in his rearview mirror and saw the scared and confused looks on their faces.

"But your mom, she found out what Gerald had tried to do; and so she went to talk to him, to tell him what a bad thing he had done. And, boys, I hate to have to tell you this, but Gerald hurt your mother."

257

The boys were still silent, and Bob wondered if he could actually say the words that were next.

"She died. She was hurt badly enough that she died."

After a few more seconds of silence, Christopher said, "We're not going to see her ever again?"

"No, Christopher. We won't see her ever again. But she'll always be with us, watching us from Heaven."

All three of them began to cry, but Bob couldn't stop to look at them. He knew he couldn't try to comfort them, or he would break down, too.

"It's okay, guys. I know this is really sad, but there's something else I need to tell you. Something happened to Grandpa; and we're not sure what it was yet; but he died, too."

Matt became angry and started to kick the seat in front of him.

"No, Dad! You're lying!" he shouted.

"Yeah, Dad!" Christopher chimed in.

Bob drove on until the two older boys had settled down; and then he said, "I'm sad, too, but we'll be okay. We've still got each other, and we'll all be fine. You'll see."

The rest of the trip to the ranch was punctuated with crying spells and questions.

"Did Gerald die? He *should* have died!"

"Maybe Mom's not really dead."

"Why are we going to the ranch if Grandpa isn't there?"

When they pulled into the driveway, the boys were reluctant to go inside.

258

"It's okay. Grandpa would want us to be here right now. You know how much he loved you and always wanted you out here."

After a little cajoling, he got the boys inside the house, where they huddled together in the middle of the great room for a few minutes and then began to scatter. David found a corner of the couch to curl up in, and Christopher turned on the television. Matt wandered into his grandfather's bedroom, and Bob followed him.

The bed had been stripped to the mattress, and everything was neat as a pin. Sherry must have been over and cleaned up.

Leaving Matt sitting on the edge of the bed, Bob went into the other room and called Mike. Once he'd brought him up to date on all the events, he told him the story that he'd told the boys and asked him to keep to that story.

"I don't know, Bob. That could come back to bite you in the ass."

"I know. And you, of all people, know I don't like lying. But I can't tell them everything right now. When they're older, I can break it to them a little at a time. And if they want to hate me then, so be it. But this is my decision for now."

After they'd finished their conversation, Bob picked up his backpack and pulled his broken 8 mm Mauser out of it. Just looking at it made him furious.

He set about busying himself with some superglue and soon had stuck the old master back together. He was pleased as he looked at his handiwork. It almost didn't even look as though it had broken. It broke clean, and it went back together clean.

Too bad his ribs couldn't be fixed that fast.

Bob peeked back in the bedroom, and Matt had curled up on the bare bed. Checking on the other two boys, he saw that David had fallen asleep; and Christopher was also starting to nod off in front of *Sponge Bob Square Pants*.

He sat back down at the table and put his head in his hands, trying to figure out where to go from here. Funeral arrangements had to be made for his dad; and then there would be the services for Barb, which he would only attend for the sake of his boys. And the dogs were still out there. He would have to call Cindy to get his stand-in back in the office for the week; and by then, he should be able to get back to a normal schedule at work.

For the week, though, he and the boys would stay here at the ranch. It would be easier for them to cope with everything if they were here, where there were lots of things to keep their hands and minds occupied. And Mike and Sherry would take care of them when he had to be in the woods.

As though he had conjured her, Sherry knocked at the door, jarring him out of his thoughts, and then walked in a few seconds later, carrying several teetering bowls of food. Once she'd set them on the kitchen counter, Bob walked up to her and put his arms around her. He laid his head down on her wide shoulder, and the sobs finally began to escape.

"Thank you," was all he could say.

Sherry held him tight. "I'm so sorry about everything, Bob. I assume they caught Gerald and Barb? I just can't believe it. But you know we'll be here for anything you need. Mike is taking care of things out in the barn right now."

Bob pulled back and whispered to her, "Barb's dead, and Gerald's almost that way."

The shock of the news left Sherry speechless for a change; and then she put her arms back around Bob and hugged him tighter.

"Dad?"

Bob looked around to see Matt standing in the doorway.

"Hey, Matt!" Bob said as he wiped the tears from his cheeks. "Look! Sherry brought some food! You hungry?"

Matt shrugged his shoulders.

"Come on over here and sit down. You need to eat something. We guys have to keep our strength up, you know."

As Matt climbed into a chair at the table, Christopher walked over and sat down next to him, while Sherry took over getting their places set and the food dished out for them.

"I'm going out to see what Mike's up to, and then I'll be back. I could probably use some of that food, too."

When Bob got to the barn, Mike stopped working on the stall he'd been cleaning and looked at him expectantly.

"Well? What happened today?"

"Barb blew up. Literally. Got blown up by a bomb."

"Oh, hell, Bob! Are you serious?"

"Yes. And I'm not so sure the world isn't a better place now. She was evil, Mike. Pure evil. She is the last thing in the world those boys need. Or anybody else, for that matter."

"Holy shit! What about Gerald?"

"I shot him."

Mike looked at Bob with dread on his face.

"It was legal. I think. He was trying to get away; and our two friendly FBI agents were after him, along with a whole shit load of SWAT guys. So I took off after him; and when he started shooting at me, I just shot back. Unfortunately, he was still alive when I left there, but we can keep hoping."

"And Grace?"

"I don't know yet. They were picking her up this morning; but I don't know how much she was involved or what they did with her."

Mike shook his head as he went back to cleaning the stall. Bob grabbed a shovel and began working with him. There was a part of him that felt only relief. No more fighting with Barb, no more put-downs or whining and bitching, because he didn't make enough money. No more fights between her and his dad, and no more denying the boys all the wonderful experiences they had been missing out on at the ranch. But at the same time, there was anger, too. Anger that he had allowed his wife to get away with so much for so long, and anger that he'd been so gullible that he'd walked right into the trap she and Gerald had set for him. And he was even angry at the damned dogs and at himself for not stopping them sooner.

Suddenly, he felt exhausted and wondered how he could possibly muster the energy, mentally or physically, to confront all the rest of the things that were still left to do.

When they were almost finished with the stalls,

the boys came out to see what they were doing. The silence was broken by a little voice.

David said, "Dad, can I help?"

Matt and Christopher were standing behind him.

Bob gave them forks and shovels and told them to start loading the manure spreader. Bob watched them for a couple of minutes; and then, Sherry called from the house to tell Bob he had a phone call.

"Hell!" he mumbled under his breath as he dragged himself back inside.

"Hello?"

"Hi!"

The voice sounded tiny; and with the racket in the background, Bob couldn't figure out who it was.

"Who is this?"

"It's Grace."

Bob's heart stopped.

She hurriedly pushed on. "Please don't hang up. They told me about your dad, and I know they think I had something to do with it. But I wanted to tell you that I didn't. He was fine when I left. They said they were doing an autopsy, so you'll see that I'm telling the truth when you get the results."

Assuming it was true, this was the first good news Bob had heard in a long time; and more than anything, he wanted to believe it was true.

"Okay. Where are you?"

"They put me in jail, Bob. Quite a new experience for me. But, I'm fine. They're treating me okay. Anyway, I just wanted to let you know that I'm so sorry about everything. . ."

Her voice cracked; and Bob thought he could

263

hear her crying; but he wasn't sure with the noise surrounding her.

She finally went on. "I loved your dad, and I would never have done anything to hurt him. I had no reason to hurt him; and even if I did, that's just not the way I work."

He could easily tell that she was crying now as her voice wavered, and she sniffled between every other word.

"Why don't I call a friend of mine? He's a lawyer and might be able to help you get out of there."

"No, I'll be all right. Really. You don't need to go to any trouble. Like I said, once the autopsy report comes back, they'll let me go."

Her voice was soft; and Bob hesitated, not knowing what to say next. Then the phone clicked off.

He hung up the phone slowly, sad they'd not had more time to talk. She had touched his heart like no other; and the more he thought about it, the more he really did believe she was innocent. And it was killing him to stand there and do nothing while she sat there in jail.

As though the sound of her voice gave him inspiration, Bob suddenly knew what to do. It was time for him to step up to the plate and start taking care of the problems at hand. It was time to begin building a new life, and now was the time to do it.

He gathered up his weapons and the old camera from his dad's bedroom closet, and then he headed out the door. He stopped off at the barn and told Mike he was going out to get some pictures of what was left of the calves to send to the insurance company. The three boys immediately started begging to go along. He wasn't sure it was a good idea; but after thinking about it for a few seconds, he decided a little excitement might be a good thing to get the boys' minds off their mother. He could take the truck; and he would just go for the pictures and leave the dogs for tomorrow when he was a little more rested.

"Sure," he finally said, and the boys began to jump up and down. Bob was glad to see their excitement and felt as though this was just the beginning of a new life for them, too.

As they drove to the south place, the boys started talking about the dogs and how mean they were. Like Gerald. Bob was amazed at the resiliency and the clarity of the kids; but he was sad that they had to learn so many difficult lessons at such early ages.

He wondered for the hundredth time if there had been anything he could have done to bring about a different end result; but then he was right back to debating his grandfather's idea of "the Plan" and his father's approach of free choice. He thought maybe he should make up his own philosophy and to hell with theirs.

They pulled up to the south place and parked; and the boys started scrambling out of the truck, while Bob strapped his magnum on his hip and grabbed his rifle and the camera. With the boys following, Bob headed to the first drop-off that would take them to the second tier where the calves lay; but halfway there, Bob spotted Three Toes and the gang also headed toward the calves.

He quickly turned to the boys and held his finger to his mouth. They stopped in their tracks, and their eyes became as big as dinner plates. Now what?

he thought as he looked at the boys and wondered what the hell to do. How do I handle this potentially ugly situation?

"Screw 'the Plan', Grandpa. I'm making the decisions now," he said under his breath.

He thought it through a few more seconds. He knew if he sent the boys back to the truck, he couldn't be sure they'd stay there, especially if they were to see him in danger. After all, they'd just lost their mother and grandfather; and they weren't likely going to want to lose their dad now. If he took them along, though, they were open game for the dogs. Finally, he decided taking them with him was the lesser of the two evils; and he prayed the Presence would protect them, regardless of what happened to him.

After the dogs passed out of sight, Bob turned back to the kids and whispered, "Follow me. Stay right behind me, and don't make a sound."

They started walking down the hill; and, instantly, the sounds of the boys' feet breaking sticks and rustling leaves brought Bob to a halt. Turning back around, he squatted down in front of them and explained how they needed to step exactly in his footsteps to keep from making so much noise. They all nodded their understanding; and they continued on toward the creek somewhat quieter. Bob hoped the wind might rustle the trees and brush enough that the dogs wouldn't hear them. He walked as fast as he could; but with the boys little legs trying to keep up, it wasn't as fast as he'd liked. He knew the safest thing to do with the boys would be to find a tree they could climb somewhere near the area where the dead calves were. But the second level, where the calves were, was pretty much void of trees; and putting them in a tree here on the upper level would put him farther from them, and maybe even out of eyesight. Might as well have left them at the truck for all the good this is going to do, he thought.

As they moved on ahead a little farther, he decided if at all possible, he'd take the dogs on now and just get it over with. If they continued to elude him, though, he'd thank his lucky stars that the boys had stayed safe; and he'd just stick with his earlier plan to take care of them tomorrow.

Bob saw the pack ahead of him again as they weaved through a small patch of brush. Simultaneously, he felt the Presence.

"Just take care of my boys," he said in a low voice.

Fifty feet to the left was a tree that looked like the kids could climb easily enough. There were a few branches low enough they could reach and lots more above those that they could climb and rest on comfortably. He took David by the hand and motioned for the others to follow.

When they'd reached the tree, Bob knelt down in front of them and said, "If anything goes wrong, you guys climb this tree as fast as you can. You hear me?"

The boys' eyes grew even wider as they realized they were about to witness the bad dogs in action; and David started to cry. All bravado was gone from them now. Instead, the fresh loss of their mother only served to enlighten them to the possibility of death striking anywhere.

Bob wiped the tears from David's eyes and then looked at Matt. "This is where you have to be a big man now. If something happens to me, you help your brothers get up in this tree and keep them there until Mike shows up. Okay?"

Matt nodded in agreement as his eyes glistened from the yet spilled tears. Then Bob smiled at them and whispered that he loved them.

It was time. At least the wind was on his side; and there was enough brush at the edge of the ridge of the second tier that he thought he might be able get close enough to take them out.

The pack had moved to within a hundred yards from him; and their noises and smells grew stronger as he quietly crept ahead. Finding cover behind a scruffy hedge, he surveyed the situation.

The dogs seemed unaware that they were being stalked. One of them was on top of one of the calves, and Bob aimed, prayed and pulled the trigger. The dog flinched and started running away, while another one ran in from the left. It was about a hundred-and-twenty-five yards away when Bob fired again, taking this one to the ground. Behind the dog that now lay dead was another. Without missing stride, it barreled on toward Bob; and he fired a third time, taking this one down, too. Then he saw Three Toes and another dog to his right. They were headed straight for the boys. Big Dog and an accomplice were coming in from the far left, and they were headed for Bob.

He swung around, pointed the gun toward Three Toes and pulled the trigger, then swung to his partner and fired again. Both dogs were down.

Big Dog and his cohort were about fifty feet away when Bob began to fire at them. The smaller dog immediately tucked tail and ran, but Big Dog didn't stop. Bob dropped the rifle and drew his pistol and began fanning bullets toward the dog; and he knew the chances of missing the mongrel were slim to none with all the bullets he'd fired. But the massive dog kept coming straight for him. He fired his last shot just as the dog leapt toward him. The dog's head caught Bob just above the knees, knocking him over.

As Bob rolled away and jumped back up to his feet, taking aim at the dog again, but then realized it wasn't moving. Big Dog was dead.

As he caught his breath, Bob heard whines and yelps coming from two of the dogs that he had shot. He picked up his rifle and reloaded it as he walked toward the one closest to him. He took aim and fired, and then moved to the next, where he repeated the action.

As the silence began to settle back down around him, Bob looked around at all the dead bodies strewn around. But there were still two not dead. The first one he'd fired at had run away, but he was fairly sure he'd hit him. And then Big Dog's partner had tucked tail and ran. And besides those two, there had been one other one with the pack that he hadn't seen at all today. Two on the lam, one of them wounded. One AWOL. And five dead. Not bad, he thought. With Three Toes down now, the other strays would likely wander off on their own.

Bob started to head back to the boys when he suddenly heard the whines of a third dog. It was Three Toes. He ran toward the dog with his rifle aimed, half expecting it to still get up and go after the boys. But when he reached it, he saw that Three Toes was dying. Bob saw sadness and pain in the dog's eyes, and he knelt down beside him.

"Shoot him, Dad!" Christopher yelled.

Without looking at the boys, Bob sat down and gently pulled the dog into his lap.

"Shoot him, Dad!" David yelled, mimicking his brother.

He began the prayer of death as his tears dropped onto the dogs face. Bob stroked it lightly between its ears, and he prayed that Three Toes would soon be happy on the other side. "I'll be there with you someday, and we'll be friends then. Okay?" Bob whispered to the dog. And then, Three Toes closed his eyes and died.

The stress had been too much; and now that it was over, Bob began to shake uncontrollably as his anguish became audible. The boys ran and gathered around him and Three Toes as they joined in the lamenting. The kids cried for their mother and their grandfather, and for their dad, too. Bob just cried for everyone.

The roar of a tractor in the distance was heard, and Bob could tell by the sound of the motor that it was Mike. The boys and Bob stood and waited for him to arrive. When the tractor topped the hill, Mike was coming toward them full speed ahead and was loaded down with guns and ammunition.

When Mike saw the carcasses strewn around and Bob and the boys standing calmly, he slowed the motor down and drove on up to them.

"Any of that blood yours?" he asked.

"Not this time."

"Well, I heard you shooting down here, so I thought I'd come and help you out."

"You're late," Bob said as he nodded toward the bodies scattered around.

"Did you get the whole pack?"

"No, there are three left," Bob said as he looked around. "But I think I clipped one of them, and another one just ran away when I started firing. There may be one more roaming around out there, but I'm not sure about that one."

"Is that the gun that got busted up yesterday?" Mike asked.

"Sure is. I glued the gun stock back together; and it looked pretty stable; but the second I pulled the trigger, I knew something wasn't quite right."

They both walked over to Big Dog, and Mike squatted down to look him over.

"Damn, Bob! You hit this dog at least twice in the body and three times in the head! But look at this! Two of the head shots didn't even penetrate the skull!"

The analyzing was cut short when they heard a yell from Matt, who had slipped away unnoticed. He was just past some bushes on the next tier down; and both men took off running to where he was standing over the wounded dog.

"Dad, I followed the blood trail just like you talked about, and guess what? I found him!"

Christopher and David were right behind the men, and now David piped up. "Are we going to bury them, Dad?"

"No, we won't bury them. We'll leave them for Mother Nature to take care of."

Bob leaned over the dog and said his prayer; and Christopher looked at Mike and whispered, "What's he doing?"

271

"He's saying a prayer so he'll be friends with 'em when he crosses over to the other side."

"Can you teach us the prayer?" Matt asked.

"I don't think so. I think you have to make up your own."

Bob finished and stood up. "Let's go home," he said.

The ride back on the tractor was crowded with the boys, while Bob followed slowly behind in the truck. He watched them laugh and kid each other and was thankful they had a few minutes where they could forget all the ugliness that had surrounded them the past few hours. They were amazingly resilient; but even the strongest had their breaking point; and he made a promise to himself that he would do his best to help them take every opportunity for laughter that they could find.

CHAPTER 15

The boys ran ahead into the house to tell Sherry the whole story. Bob and Mike sauntered in behind them to find Sherry enraptured as she listened to their tales. This was what she had always wanted, a house full of energetic boys. As she listened, she looked up at the men and smiled radiantly. Bob wondered if this was destiny, that she had been put in their lives for this moment. Or maybe they were put in her life so that she could someday have the children she had always longed for.

Mike and Bob returned to the barn to finish up the chores; and before long, Christopher ran out to let them know dinner was ready. The boy had seemingly forgotten about the tragedies for a while; but Bob knew tough times were still ahead for all of them.

He draped his arm around Christopher's shoulders as the three headed back toward the house.

Christopher looked up at Mike and asked, "Is it all right if we call you Uncle Mike instead of Mr. Curtis?"

"Sure it is. That is, if it's okay with your dad."

Before Bob could respond, Sherry stepped out of the door and waved for Bob to come faster.

"Phone call!" she yelled out to him. "I think it's Grace!"

His heart skipped a beat again, and he began to trot toward the house.

"Grace? Is that you?"

"Yes, it's me. I've only got a second, though, so please just listen. I told you before that I didn't kill

273

your dad. But there's something else I have to tell you, too. I…I love you, Bob. I have loved you all my life, even before I knew you. I just didn't know what you looked like or what your name was or where you lived."

There was a short silence on the phone line; and then Grace finished with, "That's it. That's what I wanted to say."

"Is Redding there?"

"Redding? I just told you that I love you, and you ask for Redding?"

"Shut up for a minute, will you? If he's there, I'd like to talk to him right now."

Without another word, he heard her hand the phone to someone; and after a couple of clicks as the call was transferred, he came on the line.

"Redding here."

"Yeah, this is Bob. Hey, listen. I need to know where Grace is."

"I'll have to clear this with the higher-ups before I can tell you, Bob. You know how it goes."

"Then clear it and call me back. Tell them I won't take no for an answer. And remember, I can track you down if you don't tell me."

Redding laughed and told him to stay on the phone. In less than a minute, he returned and said, "I have it cleared and even got permission for you to come and see her if you want. But you need to keep in mind the autopsy isn't done yet; and there's still a chance that she's going to have had something to do with it."

"Just tell me where she is."

"She's at the Federal Building downtown."

274

"Thanks!"

Bob slammed down the phone and turned to see everyone staring at him.

As he picked up his keys, Sherry asked, "Are you really going to go there right now?"

"Yep," he said, and he headed for the door.

Mike yelled at him just as he was pulling the door shut behind him.

"You probably should leave that boot gun here, or they're gonna think you're gonna steal something."

"I am."

Then he turned to the boys and said, "I'll be back really soon. No more problems, okay?"

They all just nodded at him, not sure what was happening now. Bob knew he was off on yet another journey, but this one was a journey of the heart.

He arrived at the Federal Building in record time and began banging on the heavy glass doors when he found them locked. A guard finally showed up and let him in, then began frisking him. Just as he was getting close to the gun, Redding walked out of the elevator and toward them.

"Bob! I thought you were out at the ranch when we talked just a few minutes ago!"

"I was. But listen. I have to thank you for showing up when you did. The next thing on this guy's list was to do a cavity search; and I was just going to have to go back outside and wait for a civilized person to come down and let me in."

Redding chuckled as he waved the guard away.

"I can't believe you got here so soon. And it's a Sunday night, Bob. What did you think your chances of getting in were going to be?"

"I figured I'd have to raise a ruckus and might get thrown in jail, too, but I had to try."

"I suppose you want to see Grace?"

"Yes, I do. Can you do that for me?"

"Come on. But if anyone asks, you're her lawyer." Bob followed Redding as they got into the elevator and dropped down to the bottom floor. Then they walked through a maze of corridors until they reached what Bob thought might have been a foot-thick lead door. Using an encoded plastic card, Thomas got them in and then pointed in the direction Bob was to go.

"Take your time. Call me on that phone there when you're ready to go. Just dial three."

Grace couldn't see who was coming in and obviously wasn't expecting him. When he rounded the corner, and she saw him, her eyes lit up the room. She jumped up and ran toward him, and he met her with arms wide open.

"I love you, too, Grace," he said. "I just didn't want to say it over the phone. I wanted you to see my face when I said it so you'd know I was telling you the truth."

She kissed him, and they were both finally home in each other's heart and arms.

Thomas walked into the room.

"Sorry to break things up here, you two."

"Thanks a hell of a lot," Bob said as he and Grace turned loose of each other. "What's so damned important that you couldn't give us more than thirty seconds together before barging in on us?"

Thomas smiled at them and said, "I just wanted to tell you that the ME's report just came over the fax.

276

It seems your dad died of a blood clot, likely caused by one of the wounds. So, Grace, it looks like you're a free woman now."

Grace looked at Bob and said, "Yes, I am."

Bob said, "No, you're not," and embraced her again.

As the two walked hand-in-hand to the old Suburban, Bob knew that "the Plan" and "Free Will" were both valid truths. Together, they worked like pieces of a puzzle that fit tightly together. Each piece was important; each piece was needed. He knew he had been presented with a set of circumstances that could have led him in many different directions; but by choosing to follow what he thought was right along the way, it seemed "the Plan" had ultimately blessed him.

EPILOGUE

Join us for a day in the country
And share in our happiness
As we celebrate our marriage
With family and friends.

Saturday, October 15, 2007
Two o'clock in the afternoon

Shoes optional